ICON

ALSO BY

GENEVIEVE VALENTINE

× × × × × ×

PERSONA

THE GIRLS AT THE KINGFISHER CLUB

THE PERSONA SEQUENCE

ICON

GENEVIEVE VALENTINE

SAGA PRESS

LONDON SYDNEY **NEW YORK** TORONTO NEW DELHI

SAGA PRESS
AN IMPRINT OF SIMON & SCHUSTER, INC.

1230 AVENUE OF THE AMERICAS, NEW YORK, NEW YORK 10020

Text copyright © 2016 by Genevieve Valentine
Jacket photograph copyright © 2016 by Getty Images/Eduardo Barrera

SAGA PRESS is a trademark of Simon & Schuster, Inc.

For information about special discounts for bulk purchases, please contact Simon & Schuster Special Sales at 1-866-506-1949 or business@simonandschuster.com.

The Simon & Schuster Speakers Bureau can bring authors to your live event. For more information or to book an event, contact the Simon & Schuster Speakers Bureau at 1-866-248-3049 or visit our website at www.simonspeakers.com.

The text for this book is set in Vendetta.

Manufactured in the United States of America

First edition

10 9 8 7 6 5 4 3 2 1

Library of Congress Cataloging-in-Publication Data
Valentine, Genevieve.
Icon / Genevieve Valentine.—First edition.
p. ; cm.
Sequel to: Persona.
ISBN 978-1-4814-2515-5 (hardcover) — ISBN 978-1-4814-2517-9 (eBook)
I. Title.
PS3622.A436I29 2016   813'.6—dc23   2015027931

ICON

SUYANA SAPAKI PERSONAL ITINERARY

[Classified]

6:00 a.m.—Breakfast
6:30 a.m.—Exercise/body sculpting [trainer confirmed]
7:30 a.m.—UARC local news briefing [Suyana, Magnus]
8:00 a.m.—Faithful Friends volunteer arrives with dog to walk, walk dog [cameras expected]
10:00 a.m.—Breakfast Event: Brighter Tomorrow [keynote speaker, approved speech attached—MS] [cameras expected]
10:45 a.m.—Private car to chambers [confirmed]
11:00 a.m.—Roll call in chambers [cameras scheduled]
11:30 a.m.—Endorse Amendment 14 [approved speech attached—MS] [cameras scheduled]
12:00 p.m.—Vote [UARC voting yes—MS] [cameras scheduled]
~~12:30 p.m.—Beauty team~~ Global news briefing—SS [compromise: have it during.—MS]
1:35 p.m.—Private car to Piccolo [confirmed]
2:00 p.m.—Lunch with Grace [Face, UK] [cameras expected]
3:30 p.m.—Private car to apartment [confirmed]
4:00 p.m.—Stylist arrives
6:00 p.m.—Ethan arrives, private car to Lincoln Center red-carpet premiere of *Longitude* [cameras scheduled]
6:30 p.m.—Give press interviews with Ethan on red carpet
7:00 p.m.—Film screening
~~7:30 p.m.~~ 8:30 p.m.—Leave film screening in Ethan's private car
~~8:00 p.m.~~ 9:00 p.m.—Dinner at the Bridge View [cameras scheduled]
10:30 p.m.—Walk to cocktail event at the River Terrace Club [cameras expected]
12:30 a.m.—Private car to apartment [confirmed]
1:00 a.m.—End of day

1

Suyana wore sleeveless gowns so people could see where she'd been shot.

On red carpets, she cheated her shoulder so the scar—a gleaming planet, the skin around it spidered in raised threads—was visible. She never wore necklaces, so the scar was the first thing your eye went to; it was the thing you recognized her by.

Daniel couldn't swear to it, but he thought maybe once or twice someone had even brushed the scar with makeup that sparkled, just to draw attention. He didn't want to think it was something Suyana would allow, but he'd never had the courage to ask. Easier to hope.

The red carpet was crowded. People had lined up since the early morning, and Daniel had been sitting third row back since four o'clock, holding a small handwritten sign that read GRACE 4EVER. Grace never looked into the stands except when the *Weekly* suggested she wave, and the *Weekly* had set up shop practically at the theater door, so his sign in a sea of them rendered him invisible.

He should be standing outside Suyana's New York apartment so he could catch what happened in the moments before something was scheduled to happen. That was how he'd met her; that was what he'd been best at, for a year. But on a night like this, Faces were careful, and Li Zhao wanted her snaps where the pictures would be pretty, and so he was parked where it was easiest to get good pictures of dresses and handlers puppeteering from the sidelines.

Grace walked by without a glance—she wore pale blue draped low in back like a singer in a movie, and was deliberately alone. The UK Face could afford to stay single, and Daniel suspected she liked reminding people. Her handler, Colin, hovered out of camera range like a ring bearer at the wrong wedding.

Daniel was surprised anyone had allowed their Faces at the premiere of a biopic about the founders of the IA, but if their handlers and home countries didn't mind critics drawing eyebrow-raising comparisons between what the founders had wanted and what they had now, Daniel supposed there was no reason not to trot them out for an evening of glitter where the little people could get a look.

Martine was in white, a beaded dress so heavy he could hear it slapping her legs with every step. She'd have bruises.

He was really close to the front, he realized—maybe too close, maybe the angle wasn't worth the risk of being seen— but he never thought about those things until it was too late, or until he saw Martine.

One year in, he still went for the closest shot he could get. Bo warned him against it—people at the edges of the frame could be important, he should keep farther from the crowd and care less about expressions—but expressions sold copies, and Daniel didn't need anyone looking at anything that happened at the edges with Suyana. Bo was welcome to record eight hours of group shots from twenty paces back (or to pretend that was what he did; Daniel had seen what Bo was like when he knew he had Margot all to himself). Daniel kept as close as he could to his subject and trusted Suyana not to break formation.

Daniel's shots still ended up on the evening news, can-dids of Grace and Martine conspiring during a vote, or Suyana smiling and smiling at Ethan above the newscast's title bar IS THIS LOVE FOREVER?, and that was all that was required of him.

On Martine's walk along the crowded carpet, she spared a single look at the seething knot in the press pit, where half a dozen arms were reaching to get her attention, an anemone of mics. She never even slowed down. Her handler, Ansfrida, who was waiting in the background holding a cape for Martine like she was actually a Valkyrie and not just playing one, closed her eyes with a sigh so long-suffering Daniel could feel it a hundred feet away.

Daniel kept Ansfrida out of the frame (it seemed mean to capture this moment too clearly) and caught a decent shot of Martine glaring at the peasants over her shoulder.

In the last year, Daniel had watched Martine breeze by a terrifying amount of press for someone with name recognition as high as hers was. She was on at least four magazine covers a year, and though she didn't conduct any political business whatsoever (Hannah was bored out of her mind on that beat; they were cutting her when everyone went to Paris for the session), any exclusive candids of Martine paid Bonnaire's rent for two months. They were easier to come by than Daniel would have expected—apparently Martine's official photographers didn't work regular shifts, and it was open season for Hannah if Martine went out for coffee.

He wondered if Suyana would ever reach that level of recognition, the magical threshold where you became an ecosystem. He suspected she was too new. The next Face of the

United Amazonian Rainforest Confederation might be able to coast, but Suyana would always be scrabbling.

Suyana and Ethan showed up as soon as the door closed on Martine (of course—peak crowd, peak desperation from the stands, peak press attention). Suyana's hand curled under Ethan's forearm, and she gave him a wide smile that aimed, just for a second, into the crowd.

She might have been looking for Daniel. It might just have been kissing ass for the cameras. Daniel had given up trying to decide the difference.

Her hair was always arranged, these days; braids and buns and ponytails threaded with a single thin strand of gold beads. She pulled it back so nothing covered the scar.

"Elegant," *Closer* had proclaimed her new image, and talked about how Suyana had grown up since the Disappearance; being kidnapped had been good for her wardrobe.

(One of the anchors on *Tonight in the Spotlight* had joked that she'd been lucky, because a black shirt and pants were the chicest, most practical thing to get kidnapped in. Daniel was in a hole in the wall halfway through an order of dumplings when the show aired. He'd stood up and left cash on the counter, not interested in whatever fashion advice was coming.

For the next three months, whenever Suyana had to look

casual but serious at informal events, she wore black pants and a black shirt rolled to the elbows, the collar artfully low to show off her earrings.

Daniel had filmed it all—his job was to watch her, whatever she did, for the rest of her tenure or the rest of her life—but occasionally during those months he had glanced over her shoulder or at the ceiling or the exit, just to have somewhere else for his eyes to go.)

She was in black tonight, too—sleeveless and with a collar that rose at the back of her neck and made her look slightly like an evil queen. Daniel assumed the silhouette was trendy. There was no way Magnus would have let her out of the house in clothes that suggested she was capable of plotting something.

Magnus was haunting the far end of the red carpet with the rest of the handlers, his fists in the pockets of his suit like he was trying desperately not to reach over and fix something Suyana was doing wrong.

Impossible, these days. Suyana was a polished stone, and nothing got close enough to scratch her any more.

The first of the interviews was in full swing—it might actually be *Tonight in the Spotlight*, son of a bitch—and it had probably been a question about their upcoming anniversary, because Suyana was curling her fingers against Ethan's arm, glancing up at him through her lashes as she said something fond and placid that had the reporter grinning.

Ethan laughed and tapped Suyana's left ring finger as he answered, his words lost as the crowd shrieked and applauded at the idea of the United States and the UARC making it official right in front of them. Suyana grinned, holding up her hand palm-in and narrowing her eyes at him like a reminder of a ring he'd long promised, and the clapping in the stands escalated to screams and stomping.

Daniel tuned it out, tried to decide if her loaner earrings were smoky topaz or champagne diamond. Did the UARC think she rated diamonds already? No way they were diamonds. Had Ethan given them to her?

As Ethan laughed and the reporter leaned into the frame for the sign-off, Suyana tapped her thumb and forefinger lightly together twice as she dropped her hand, like she was nervous.

Between one microphone and the next, Ethan leaned down and whispered in Suyana's ear. She squeezed his arm just a little, glanced up just a little, too small for the news cameras to clock it.

Smoky topaz earrings, he decided. She'd want topaz. They were closer to the color of her scar.

He followed Ethan and Suyana's progression slowly, turning his head to keep them in sight without holding too still (it was easy to hold still, after a while, but it creeped people out).

His phone buzzed. Bo, checking in.

He waited three minutes before he handed his sign to the woman next to him and slid through the stands and out. Bo was near the rope and stanchions that guided the gawkers off the sidewalk and safely away from the drop-off lane, where black sedans were still spitting out the occasional C-level Face amid the actors.

Daniel didn't look over. Not his beat, not his problem.

"Where's yours? I didn't see her."

Bo shook his head, unflappable but unhappy. "She went in through the caterers' entrance—two others with her, waiting for IDs now, but it's too late to follow. No idea why she's trying to play it under the radar, it's not like she can change the movie by staying invisible. Got the shots, though."

For all the good it would do. Li Zhao never seemed to find a buyer for Margot's shots, which seemed strange for the head of the Central Committee. Either Li Zhao was creating scarcity to drive up prices—which Daniel had never dared suggest to Bo, who tended to be very stolid about work and wasn't ready for the idea that Li Zhao was playing the market—or she was waiting for an international scandal to sell the lot. In the meantime, Bo spied on the most powerful diplomat in the world for no return on investment.

"When are you off duty?"

"Now. Our man in Catering clocked Margot inside, and Reg takes over in ten minutes. You?"

"Same," said Daniel. "Magdalena should already be inside when Suyana finally snaps and murders Ethan. You want dinner?"

"Sure." Bo barely frowned; Bo was hard to rattle.

They set off together down Broadway, Daniel using the only-slightly-embarrassing gait he'd adopted to keep up with Bo's mountainous strides. But Bo wasn't in a hurry, so it was easy enough.

Daniel wasn't in a hurry either. Suyana had given the signal. She couldn't meet her Chordata contact until two a.m.; Daniel had hours to spare.

2

Every time Suyana kissed him, she saw lights.

Not romantically. God forbid. Flashbulbs.

(At an official luncheon Kipa had asked, "What's it like to kiss Ethan?" She'd cut that line of inquiry short. From Grace it might have been a tactical question, but Kipa had sounded too hopeful. Suyana didn't want Kipa ever doing what she was doing now.)

There were the national photographers—the UARC government had assigned her a few as her profile improved, and they'd started agitating for candid shots of her daily life as part of some future biography, but Ethan had dozens and had always had dozens and they recorded *everything*.

He went swimming and three cameras were going; he went out to a movie and they made him walk up to the marquee four times until they caught him in the right light. He barely looked at them; he moved through and around them like you would a pack of hunting dogs you kept in the house. He was a fool not to realize what he was handing over, but she didn't have much room to talk about what sorts of privacy people were willing to give up.

There was the international press, who lined up outside the fund-raisers they attended and the hotels they stayed in and his apartment in New York, to see if they could get a quick word from the couple on the events of the day.

(*Global* magazine had asked them about the news that Hae Soo-jin was being forcibly recalled in favor of a new Korean Face, and she'd been so surprised she'd forgotten her official stance of being too calm to care about anything, and said she'd miss her. She'd had to spend three nights of polite, awkward clubbing with Bin Mee-yon before the Korean press stopped being angry at her for possibly suggesting Hae Soo-jin was the best Korea could do. Bin Mee-yon had reacted as pretty much anyone would; she hadn't spoken to Suyana since.)

And then, everybody else. Tourists in Paris caught them at the Louvre and cooed about the way they'd dressed— him in black and a trench coat, her in a dress of burnished gold—as if it was an accident they looked like a matched set impossibly at home among moody Impressionist studies and gilded frames.

Closer had paid a record amount for a candid for their next cover. In the shot, they were standing in front of one of the crowd-scene oils with their heads bent in conversation, pretending not to see the cluster of tourists behind them taking pictures. The photographer had caught their images in the screen of every phone, two characters as posed as any in the painting. *Closer* put THE ART OF LOVE as the headline, neon-pink graffiti across the painting that loomed behind them. It had already been parodied on four late-night talk shows.

It was one of Daniel's best shots ever. It must have stung something awful not to be able to take credit.

(She'd seen Daniel, in the instant Ethan was leaning in, and had tilted her head to make the most of her jawline—the longest arch she could manage, leading right to Ethan's half-closed eyes, his cologne heavy in her nostrils and voices echoing as everyone taking photos decided how sweet they were.)

The story inside *Closer* was cobbled-together press-release fluff about how the relationship had coaxed him down from his playboy years and steadied her at a time when she needed it most.

Magnus had fed them the quote about how she was steadier now, complete with the reminder that she'd lost her first handler and Ethan had come along just when she needed a strong man the most. Magnus was practically every "Staffers close to the couple say." He made up enough stories for ten men.

Twenty minutes in, Suyana decided *Longitude* was actually an impressive movie.

It didn't get everything right—that would take ten years and be postwar bureaucracy interrupted with periodic wretchedness—but it made her care about the formation of the IA, which was more than the actual IA often managed. Plus, Margot had left an hour in, when the Founding Fifteen discussed how to appoint the chair of the Central Committee, and the actress playing Priyanka Lal had her big scene warning everyone against lifelong appointments.

"That way lies the seed of deepest corruption," she said as the music struck a minor chord and the actress's eyes filled with tears of righteous anger, and Suyana had been painfully careful not to look around to see how the room was taking it. Margot was behind her three rows and over her left shoulder, and it would be impossibly obvious to turn. But Margot had made the mistake of wearing two bracelets, and when she got up three minutes later and left, Suyana heard her just fine.

It was mostly a romance, of course; Priyanka and Brynolf's breakup had affected the personal-relationship bylaws of the IA more than international policies ever had.

(It was one of the reasons Faces were discouraged from marrying; Brynolf might have forgiven Priyanka for voting in his stead, but the bylaws hadn't.) But the director had clearly wanted verisimilitude in politics, such as it was, unfolding in a movie-ready Assembly Hall twice as grand as the real thing; the Assembly hadn't let them film, and the studio had clearly balked at reconstructing an awkward, drafty room with inexplicable bubbles in the carpet.

But for all that, it was engaging: it even had a Peruvian and a Brazilian Face—not important enough to have names, but their countries were subtitled in a very serious font as they were recruited to the Second-Wave Seventy in montage.

"You all right?" whispered Ethan.

She hated him. It still astonished her how much she could, out of nowhere.

She held still a breath longer, grateful for the dark. (It subsided—she forced it to, she wasn't good enough to wholly despise him and still sleep with him—but when it rose it buried everything.)

"Of course," she said after a pause she knew was too long. She smoothed her hand where she'd been picking at a loose thread on her loaner dress; the scented shimmer Oona had spread on her arms had left a spot on the black, a comet on a star map. Horrible tell. Hakan would have been mortified. "You try sitting through a movie in a dress this tight."

He huffed a laugh; he glanced at her, then away like he hadn't meant to. A moment later he took her hand.

She let him. She spread her fingers slowly, let them sink between his fingers as his breath caught, let the tips of her fingernails just barely scrape the underside of his palm as he curled his fingers around her, brushing the last of the sparkles off.

She'd stepped on her anger, and all was well, and the end of all this was too far away to start counting the minutes now.

The theater lights came up slowly enough that Suyana could gauge the mood of the room without getting caught actually looking around. India and Finland and the rest of the Founding Fifteen looked pleased with themselves. Exceptions: Ethan, who straightened the hem of his jacket twice in a row as he stood, and Grace, who was already sidling toward the exit next to Martine.

(THE INTERNATIONAL ASSEMBLY REMAINS THE MOST POWERFUL DIPLOMATIC ASSOCIATION IN THE WORLD. IT INCLUDES 227 COUNTRIES AND HOLDS AN INTERNATIONAL STANDING ARMY, the closing title read. Suyana wasn't sure if that was praise or disappointment. Grace seemed to have decided.)

"I'm starving," Suyana said. "Do we know the menu at Bridge View?"

"Salad of microgreens and spiced nuts," Ethan recited. "Then sea bass for me, with slices of sweet potato, I swear to God just because Harold doesn't trust me with any food that could roll off the plate. For you, eggplant medallions with potato puree. Fruit sorbet. Champagne."

There was something about the dip in his delivery right around "puree" that made her look him in the eye. "You want to skip it and get pizza?"

He considered it for three seconds, looked at his wristband for another three. Tallying messages, maybe. Maybe calculating the logistics of redirecting the cameras waiting outside the restaurant.

"Yeah," he said, mostly to the wristband. The gesture looked strangely serious, even though he was smiling. "Let's ditch and get pizza. We can still make cocktails, right?"

"Oh, the UARC has two cameras scheduled at cocktails. Magnus would shoot me if I wasn't there."

His head snapped up. "That's not funny."

He was wrong. His vigilance about the *S* word was one of the few things about him that didn't feel grown in a lab.

"We'll be back by then," she promised, trying not to grin so close on the heels of the shooting joke.

He tugged on his jacket (third time, she set her teeth against something without knowing what) and took her arm. "An hour for pizza, then. There's a place not too far from Bridge View."

As they passed, she caught Magnus's eye and shook her head once in answer to his raised eyebrows. He slid his hands in his pockets, watched them go.

"How are your heels?" Ethan asked at the door.

"I'm not walking, if that's the question. Did you want me to describe them?"

He flushed, just at the tips of his ears, when you caught him out. "Nope, that's the question. I already know how they look."

He was so predictable it worried her. Black pumps, some stockings, long hair, a little lip gloss. That was it. He never even joked about the contract when he was flirting with her.

("If he does...invoke the terms in an inappropriate way, let me know and I'll speak to his handlers about it. It's bad form," Magnus had told her, not meeting her eyes, just before her first overnight date with Ethan.

Grace told her, "If he shouts the clause number when he comes, run for it.")

It stung to slide into the backseat of the car. Of course she could walk there; she didn't wear any shoes she couldn't run for her life in. But it was no good reminding anyone you were a fighter. She sat back and let the fifteen blocks slide by, carefully not thinking of anything at all.

She goaded him into getting a mushroom pizza ("The whole thing?" "Harold can't see you. You afraid of looking hungry?" "…We'll take the whole thing"), and as they ate he told her about a high school visit he'd made where they gave up on lunchtime crowd control as people lined up for his appearance and just threw a school-wide pizza party before he got there.

"It was my first leftover pizza! It was delicious. Maybe I was just really hungry—I'd been at a photo shoot all day—but it was like, stuck to the cardboard a little and the cheese had kind of dried up, and I swear, it was the most delicious thing I've ever eaten. It was cool to sort of connect with them that way."

"Were they watching you eat?" Louis XVI had done that—eaten in front of the court, ten courses to prove he could, and let the courtiers dive for the scraps.

He cracked up around a mouthful of pizza. "God, no, that would be so weird! I had a meet and greet with the Model Assembly team. They'd made regionals or something because of their debate on the water crisis. They were really into it. It really made me think about the water crisis, actually. Those were smart kids."

Suyana had grown up in a water crisis. Crops had failed two years in a row, and that was all it took for riots to start. The government had sent out the military, here and there. By the time the land-rights groups were marching, it was too late.

"I was fifteen the first time I saw a body of water I couldn't walk across," she said.

It was a strange thing to tell him. Too honest; she hadn't thought about it before she admitted it. But when she had her pleasant smile back on and looked up, he was watching her steadily, unblinking, looking for a moment sharper and more present than she thought of him.

"Sorry," she said. "I stepped on your story."

"No, you didn't." He wiped his fingers. "I know so little about you. Whenever you tell me something, I try to pay attention."

"Oh."

While she was trying to think of a way to deflect him without sounding dismissive, he leaned forward, tracing the ridge of her knuckles where they met the back of her hand.

"I remember the mountain range you showed me the night we met," he said, with a pretty uncertain smile for a guy who had gotten her on a silver platter a few weeks later. "Where you grew up."

Where she was born, maybe. She'd grown up in the aisles of the IA, severed from home and watching the games people played to pretend they had power, but she wasn't here to ruin the mood. "I hoped you'd notice me."

"I figured."

She glanced up from his finger, which was resting on the

knuckle of her index finger like he was claiming it for Spain. He was grinning.

"If you say that's because all the girls want you to notice them, I will pelt you with mushrooms until your ego is small enough that we can walk out of here."

His grin melted into a laugh so big they drew a few stares. Her fingertips suddenly felt sensitive against the table, some horrible fondness creeping up on her as she looked at the line of his throat. (This surprised her too, always; it surprised her as much as her anger.)

"We should go," she said.

The car was several blocks north—New York didn't care how famous you were, you had to park like everybody else—and they made it a block and a half before the first round of flashbulbs.

Ethan tucked her under his arm—she gently pushed away the half of his jacket he was trying to wrap around her like he was the Phantom of the Opera—and they picked up the pace. She counted four photographers, all offering advice in English. They could be hers, speaking English for Ethan's sake, but it was unlikely. Magnus would never want pictures of her walking out of a pizza place. Ethan could slum it sometimes if he wanted; she had to prove her sophistication, every time.

"I told him not to call cameras," Ethan muttered. He

never got angry (angry was bad for business) but he sounded like he really had wanted a night alone.

God forbid.

"Better make the most of it," she said quietly, and when he looked down at her, he had on the smile he only wore when other people could see, and she met it with the smile she'd grown just to match. He pressed a kiss to her temple as they walked, and she tucked her head an inch into the crook of his shoulder, where she could feel the heat from his body through the fabric, and it would make a better angle for the cameras.

3

The ID came through halfway into burgers and fries, and it was enough that Bo raised his eyebrows.

"If she's talking to more killers for hire, I nominate the night team," Daniel said.

Bo glanced up at him, back at the phone.

"Shit. No. You're kidding. No."

"No," Bo agreed, setting it down before Daniel could decide whether to smack it out of his hand. "We got some audio off her conversations during the party. Whatever the US and Norway are working on right now is turning into the poster child for international cooperation. The boss wants to increase surveillance on Martine and Ethan in case Margot starts courting them under the table."

"What does Margot have on Martine?"

"Whatever she needs, I guess."

They sat hunched over the little table, silently deciding the same thing: if Margot wanted you on her side, you were going to end up there, and how much of your life she ruined first was sort of up to you.

If Martine was smart, she'd be more selectively social and make her weaknesses disappear until she was wherever Margot wanted her to be. And if Ethan was smart, he'd know that any offer from Margot was going to include a clause that left Suyana in the dirt.

Daniel checked his watch.

He got rid of Bo with nearly an hour to spare, because Bo would accept your first invitation but never your second, so after burgers it was going to be good-bye no matter how hard Daniel tried to make it look like he wanted company.

"The bar's supposed to be decent, and the river's really lovely at night," Daniel tried, with passable enthusiasm, but Bo had only said, "I know. I'm all right, thanks. Enjoy it."

"Someday I'm going to do something you've never done and you'll die of surprise," Daniel muttered.

"You've done a lot of things I haven't done," said Bo, looking at him sidelong.

Daniel exhaled carefully. "Just—go home, Bo. Good night."

The crowd was thin this late, but it took him a few seconds to pinpoint Bo. Skill was skill. A guy who could vanish like that kept you up nights.

Daniel hit the bar anyway and nursed a beer for a while. Technically he was off duty and his feed would be archived unless he alerted them to a story, but Kate might be awake in Paris. When Kate was watching, he did exactly what he said he was going to do.

After the beer, he walked around with something that could map like aimlessness, a loose spiral that would bring him one block north of Suyana's apartment building.

The neighborhood was halfway to trendy and still had the occasional snarl of taxis at the bigger intersections. Daniel bet Magnus just loved working around tourist glut. But he knew Suyana had insisted on something a little farther away from IA's residential territory, and Daniel suspected that in the wake of Suyana's good publicity, Magnus could find no reason to deny her.

He suspected Magnus could find no reason to deny Suyana much of anything; in public, so close it was hard to keep him out of the shot, Magnus watched Suyana like the gunshots would start any second. Understandable for a guy who'd lost his Face in broad daylight. Daniel was a little surprised Suyana hadn't traded him in, but she must have reasons. Who knew these days.

There had been a time she'd have told him what was going on, or he could have looked at her and known. But these days she looked like nothing; like a lantern, thin and ready to burn. Maybe Magnus could love her that way, made of nothing but paper. Some people don't notice those things.

The car pulled around the front of the hotel five minutes before time, and the half-dozen official photographers started their flashbulbs as Ethan helped Suyana out of the car. The two of them walked slowly enough not to ruin the shot, and waited until the lobby—better light, warm wood, mirrors, the Deco mosaic behind them—before she kissed Ethan good night, sliding her left hand around his neck to pull him closer. He tightened both arms around her and bent her slightly backward; her scar curving around his shoulder gleamed like a missing tile.

They separated soft and slow, as she looked up at him with hooded eyes. A year ago Suyana wouldn't so much end a kiss as break it, like she was surprised to realize what she was doing, and Ethan would be left closing his mouth around air and trying to get his dignity back before anyone could line up a shot of it. They'd worked it out since. Daniel never really thought about it. It did what they needed it to do.

As Ethan walked back to the car, the photographers

walked out with him (shift was over), so they missed the shot in the lobby mirror of Suyana turning away from them, her face dropping back into a mask that looked like a stranger as she punched the button for the elevator.

Daniel didn't miss it. He held perfectly still, to make sure he got it all.

He moved on before the elevator came; she wasn't going to get in, and that shouldn't be on camera.

"All right," he said to no one, "guess I'm signing off." He made a show of looking at his watch, and then pulled up the hood of his jacket, just far enough over the camera to cast a shadow over any images it picked up.

Suyana came out the back door of the building, prompt to the minute.

(She'd explained it the first time they'd met in New York, not long after Suyana had been officially returned to the fold. There was a storage unit in the basement under someone else's name, paid in cash, where she kept her things and changed when she was planning to disappear. If she ever died, she told him, the police should break into the storage unit for 5D, and Daniel should have half a dozen snaps nearby so nothing could get swept under the rug.)

She was wearing jeans and a thin coat with a high collar. Her scarf obscured the edge of her jaw that made her recognizable, and nobody so much as glanced at her as she headed west.

Daniel crept up to a block behind her after about a quarter mile, just enough for her to sense that he was behind her and the coast was clear. He trailed her west and south, until the city gave way in a single breath to the piers and the park and the flat black water.

He had the strangest impression, just for a second, that she was going to keep walking right into the river and vanish. His mouth went dry; he clenched his fists like he was going to run, but never moved.

She watched the water for a little while, like this had been her reason all along, to come to the edge of a river and stare at nothing until dawn. Her shoulders were rigid—Faces had postures like statues—and he didn't dare get closer. The breeze worried the edge of her scarf where it covered her ears.

When she turned again and headed down the line of the park, he didn't have the heart to follow very far. He found a bench under a light that would flood out whatever the shadows couldn't hide, and close enough to a busker that the audio feed would be laced with terrible electric guitar covers of sixties hits, and waited.

When she sat down next to him, he could just catch the last of her perfume.

"Lovely terrain," she said quietly. The all's-well; it was his turn to reply with something about the light for all's-well, or something about the temperature if it wasn't safe.

"I think the Beatles have us covered," he said. "You can speak up."

Her hesitation was brief—diplomats knew how to rally after rudeness. "Are you all right?"

"Of course."

He waited for her to ask him what was wrong. In his peripheral vision she was a smear of color, the burgundy scarf and her black hair. Something silver was still caught in it—she'd gotten sloppy taking the bun out. Her breathing was too steady and too calm; she was working at it. Chordata must have had bad news for her.

He'd have felt better if she was breathing heavy. If she'd cracked and told him what was wrong. He'd like her more if she felt like a person at all, and not some memory he sat beside for old times' sake, in a cloud of someone else's perfume. He hadn't met with her in three months. He hadn't looked her in the eye in nearly a year. She could send a stranger to this bench, and he didn't know how long he might be fooled.

That wasn't fair, he made himself think a second later. But she could look at him in a way he couldn't look at her; the fairness came a second too late.

She settled her shoulders, started to stand.

"Your boyfriend's going to be under more surveillance," he said. "Margot's following up on America's environmental research partnership with Norway."

She stayed perched at the edge of the bench, her hand braced behind her. She was in his field of view, nearly—he glanced over and watched her shoulders collapsing. An inch, no more; even with two bullet wounds, in a cramped room in a cramped quarter of Paris where she thought she was going to die, they'd never dropped farther than that.

Some of her hair had come loose from the scarf. His neck ached from sitting so still.

"They're building a facility back home," she said.

It was so quiet Daniel barely heard it over the singer, who'd moved on to something high-pitched that required him to slap the guitar every so often to keep the time.

Of course. That was what her Chordata meeting had been about. They'd want it gone, and she'd need to help them if it was going to work. She had the path to the Americans.

Finally he managed, "You going to see it?"

Bad question—the answer wouldn't tell him whether she was just taking an anniversary trip with the boyfriend or actually planning to do something about it. He was still amateur at this. He didn't know how to talk around things that mattered.

"I think he'll want me to take him," she said. (Vague, deliberately—he guessed Magnus for the first one and Ethan for the second.)

Then she looked over. He couldn't see her expression,

just the shift of her hair giving way to a crescent of her skin, one dark eye. "I don't know if I want to."

That answered the question he'd asked, and one he hadn't.

"Well, send postcards, come back soon." He saw one dark eye, the shadow along the curve of her nose, the corner of her mouth.

"If I don't come back, it's not because I decided to retire. Don't believe that, from anyone."

Oh, shit. He hadn't even thought—he'd seen her slide a knife right through someone. He took it for granted she'd live through the tough years.

The buzz of traffic was beginning to drill right into his ear. "You'll come back," he said. It sounded deeper than he meant it. He cleared his throat. "When do you leave?"

"As soon as I can convince him it was his idea." She stood. "Any idea who . . . anyone I should be looking for once I'm abroad?"

For a second he could see her in the streetlight that carved circles under her eyes and sucked away the living depth of her until she was two-dimensional. He wished he hadn't looked. It was being thirsty and swallowing air. How could she go back to her country with some lie? What did it matter? What could she do about it except bring more weight on herself? Don't go, he thought. You're someone who can never go home.

"The boss would never tell me. But you'll be fine. You're a good liar, and you can tell when the cameras are rolling. You'll see whoever it is."

He felt like she was holding her breath, like he'd wounded her, and the flash of guilt was hard to hang on to. He needed some of his own back. If she hated being called a liar, she was in the wrong line of work.

Without knowing why, he asked, "How long did it take you to clock me tonight?"

The shadows sliced across her face as she looked past him and above him, east. "I knew where you were standing as soon as I opened the door. Take care."

There were footsteps on grass, then gravel, then pavement, then gone. Daniel had a moment of vertigo, as if there was so much behind him that he must be tipping forward, sliding somehow. He gripped the bench.

The world ahead of him, where he knew there was a river and a far bank and roads for hundreds of miles, was nothing but black. It all dropped off suddenly at the edge of the lamplight; he had been staring at it so long he'd forgotten how close anything was.

4

Suyana opened the door of her apartment forty-one minutes after Ethan dropped her off in the lobby, wearing the same dress he'd dropped her off in, her hair undone and her shoes in her hand.

Magnus was at the dining table, his shirtsleeves rolled up and his tie draped over the doorknob of his bedroom, work laid out around him in careful white tiles. He still worked on paper; he claimed it was for accountability, but she suspected he enjoyed the old-fashioned shuffle of accomplishments. Judging by the stack at his right hand, he'd started getting nervous about her maybe an hour ago, when the last fifty pages started to go askew and had yet to be corrected.

He glanced up when she came in, went back to reading. "I hope all that dishabille happened after the photographers were finished, or we've wasted an evening's wages on Oona alongside the little dinner detour that cost us six hundred for the empty table. Did you stop for ice cream and fall?"

For a moment she considered dropping the shoes just for the sound they made, but she knew how much they cost. She watched him breathe in, carefully out. IA trained; you couldn't get him to breathe heavy if you ran him a mile.

"Would you like to hear how Ethan and I spend our time between official functions and this door?"

Ten seconds went by. He never looked up, never turned the page. It was the luckiest thing in the world that he had this weakness, and whatever it was (jealousy, disgust, some shred of privacy), he'd never check the lobby cameras to confirm her story. He'd consider it low.

"Was the pizza your idea?"

"He likes a spontaneous woman. Makes him feel like I really believe it."

"It disturbed our plans for the evening."

"Ethan had me under his arm looking surprised and protective, in a situation that was actually candid. You can't plan anything that effective."

Magnus looked up, as if the "you" had been a singular

accusation rather than a tactical given. "Suyana, I'm sure you think this is sufficient, but this isn't just a relationship between you and the public. It's a relationship between our office and Ethan's office, and whatever you think you'll gain from cute stunts, you'll lose if his office begins to think of you as unpredictable."

"Only if they can convince Ethan to leave me behind. What are our numbers?"

He glanced at his watch, like that was where the answer was, and said with unimaginable coolness, "Seventy-two percent approval, last I looked."

"Then I suppose whatever we do after the photographers are finished is good for business, isn't it?"

Eight seconds.

"The trainer's due in at six thirty," he said. "Better get some sleep."

"You too. You lie better when you're rested. That page is blank."

If he looked up again, she didn't see it. She slid the lock on her bedroom door, set her shoes in the closet, and stepped under the shower until the makeup and the hair cream and the body lotion and the scented shimmer and the perfume and the remnants of Ethan's cologne caught on her temples were gone, and she smelled like nothing at all.

× × × × × × ×

To get Ethan to Peru, Suyana would have to talk to Martine. To talk to Martine, you talked to Grace.

The Paris sessions made the most of curled-plaster moldings and rich wood that always made their votes look vaguely like a royal affair; something exciting and carefully considered under the domed fresco of the morning sky, and everyone who raised their hands to vote was pointing to the coming dawn. The New York branch office was supposed to exist as a courtesy to the Faces when they traveled to the States to conduct business, but the building was a Plan B in case they got locked within American borders, and everyone knew it—including the designers, who had constructed the sort of high-ceilinged, antiseptic affair that would look good in the background of photographs of grim decisions being made.

She waited for Grace in the lobby of Grace's office. The hallway outside was as anonymous as the hallway in Suyana's wing—in a Plan B you had to make sure no one knew where to reach the people who mattered—but the offices were so different that Suyana had laughed when she walked in, and was glad only the receptionist saw.

Suyana's suite had two small offices that branched off a windowless room just big enough for a table and four chairs, facing each other and waiting for guests that never came. As Suyana's star had risen over the year, Magnus had requisitioned some funds from back home. Now the chairs all matched, and the empty wall was filled with an enormous photograph of the rainforest. Magnus hadn't asked for her opinion, so she refused to tell him she liked it, but having that deep green arching under the blue sky made it easier to breathe when the door was closed.

Grace had a lobby big enough for a receptionist and two couches. It looked out into a glass-walled meeting room with a view of the courtyard, and a hallway that disappeared into a number of rooms Suyana was afraid to imagine. Somewhere there were sounds of a kitchen.

Colin opened the door and stepped inside, and a moment later Grace blew in—an outfit of chiffon and leather that looked so uncomfortable there must have been a photo shoot—saw her, and said, "Don't give me that look, please."

"Suyana, lovely to see you as always," said Colin, in a way that sounded both welcoming to Suyana and scolding to Grace.

"Thank you, Colin."

Grace stopped short of rolling her eyes, but she zipped up the leather jacket over the low neckline of the sundress with a violence that made the receptionist flinch.

"Your charge is unprofessionally hungry, and forgot she'd promised to take Suyana to lunch. We'll stick to the neighborhood," she said, as Colin frowned and scrolled furiously through his tablet. "No cars necessary. We'll be back in an hour."

"I really only need a minute," Suyana said softly to Grace as they headed out. This wasn't on the schedule—she'd miss her global briefing with Magnus, which was one of the few things he was good for, and she'd be in front of cameras unscheduled twice in twenty-four hours, which would grate on him even though it was only Grace.

Grace said, "Then the price is lunch. I'm famished. They wouldn't let me eat after lunch yesterday so my stomach would be flat in this hideous dress during high winds."

"You should date Ethan," Suyana said, rolling up the cuffs of her shirt the way Oona had taught her and scooping her hair over one shoulder to make a backdrop for her face. "Last year magazines called me overweight. Now that he's seeing me, I'm a bombshell. When we go out, we're supposed to order dessert."

"Tempting," Grace said as her bodyguard opened the front door ahead of them and Grace plastered her hands to her thighs as the breeze picked up and photographers on the sidewalk started photos, "but it's Ethan. I'll pass. You're doing so well, I'd hate to interrupt a winning streak."

Suyana scraped her teeth across her lips to bring color into them, and followed.

× × × × × × ×

They had the kati roll place to themselves, given that only two people could stand inside it anyway, and Grace's bodyguard was outside, preventing photographers and patrons alike. (Suyana had tipped twice the cost of her food to make up for the trouble, and still had to try not to glance outside at the line.)

Grace was trying hard to maintain a diplomatic face stretched too tight across curiosity. "And you want Ethan to take you."

"Yes. It should be his idea. That has to be the press take-away."

"Why can't it seem like something you wanted?" she asked; it was demanding more than incredulous.

Suyana looked at her. "I'll be conducting some personal business."

Grace's expression settled. "Mmm. Well, I can't tell you how much I appreciate the vote of confidence in my ability to get Martine to do anything. However, the Paris session starts in five weeks. If I suggested to Martine that she take a trip to the homeland and burn out a week of freedom by touring research facilities for Margot's pet project, she'd knock me into the street."

Suyana couldn't bite back a smile. "Maybe you could convince her that touring facilities in Norway with Margot would get her in good standing the next time there's a shuffle in the Central Committee."

"And would distract Margot from whatever godforsaken thing you're planning to subject yourself to," Grace pointed out, pulling napkins out of the holder as the cashier passed her a brown paper bag. "You don't plan by halves, I'll give you that."

"Can't afford to." Suyana took her bag and thanked the cashier as Grace tapped the glass door with a fingernail to let Adam know they were coming out.

(From where he was standing, third in line, Daniel looked slowly from Grace to Suyana, as if he'd been daydreaming and was only now noticing the place was shutting them out.)

"You know, it's terribly odd, but because of some dismal legislators who have nothing to do with me, the United Kingdom's trade relationship with the United States has been a little rocky recently," Grace said, not looking at Suyana.

Suyana's stomach sank. America and the UK weren't on good terms? Why hadn't Ethan told her? How could this lunch be spun out by the British press? Why would Grace want to go outside with her if she knew it would put Suyana over a barrel?

That was exactly why, Suyana realized a second later. This lunch was in broad daylight on a busy street so that Suyana would be caught in the middle of whatever the press tension was and have to help Grace in order to get out clean.

She was angry for a second, but only at her lack of research. Grace was asking for a very small favor on a very large debt; she was happy to pay.

"What a shame," Suyana said, falling into step with Grace for the walk back to the International Diplomatic Corps offices. (Paris had decided fifty years ago that only they housed the actual Assembly, and the States would have to make do with whatever title they could manage for the administrative setup they'd already built.) Grace's legs were so much longer that Suyana struggled not to give up and switch to double time, but double time looked bad in photos. She pushed through.

"Isn't it? When you're back from your rainforest honeymoon, I could use some quality time for something charming and selfless."

"We'll walk dogs for charity," Suyana suggested. "The three of us."

Grace sighed and assumed a carefully pleasant expression, since one or two cameras were still pacing them close enough to catch it. "How wholesome."

"Did you want to make conversation with him at dinner all night?"

"God, no," Grace said, as they scaled the stairs and ducked inside. "You win."

As they parted—or rather, as Grace slid effortlessly

through the bustling admins and Suyana watched her and felt like a boulder—Suyana nearly asked again about Martine. She needed to be sure Grace would follow through.

But you only got to demand terms when you were the person in charge. And if she couldn't trust Grace (and she should; only old habit kept her doubtful), it was just because Suyana was a gourd too cracked to hold water, and that was the last thing Grace needed to see.

"Dog walking in Paris," she said instead.

"I'll try and become a dog person by then," Grace called over her shoulder, just before she turned the corner and the hallway lost all its life.

"The committee meeting's in twenty minutes," Magnus said as she came into the office, "which gives you enough time to tell me what you and Grace talked about."

"Boy trouble." Suyana dropped the paper bag on the table. "This is for you."

Magnus raised his eyebrows for a second before he could get his face under control—he must be worn down; he wasn't usually this stressed until a week into chambers. "Thank you. And for yourself?"

"I have a photo shoot in a week."

He passed it back. "Your figure is being celebrated. Weight loss invites speculation."

For a moment Suyana could only look at the bag he held

in two fingers. He glanced at her, then decidedly away, until she reached out and took it back.

"I can skip the committee meeting," Suyana said. "I'd prefer a news update."

"An agenda item we've actually planned for. How novel," Magnus said, but he was already reaching for a folder at the far edge of his desk, and Suyana sat at the cramped table and armed herself against surprise.

Most of the time you volunteered on a committee was justifying the time and money being spent on you. Suyana had been asked to be on the Cultural Heritage Committee after she returned from the Incident (which was the way everyone inside the IA talked about it, except Kipa, who always called it "your captivity" in a way that sounded both patently false and the kind of solemn that comes with a saint).

Since Suyana's first year in the IA, she'd tried to work just hard enough that no one resented her presence, and not hard enough to raise eyebrows. She'd attended the Taste of a Hundred Lands fund-raiser, speaking briefly about mazamorra corn pudding to a group of people who were paying four hundred dollars a plate to listen to her be pleasant. She'd helped draft a plan for a Cultural Grievance Committee to which marginalized groups could appeal without having to first declare themselves at war with their government. "A move toward mediation, rather than confrontation," she'd written, because if there was one thing politicians liked hearing, it was the idea of a middle ground.

Murat Eren had been the draftee to present it to the Assembly for ratification (Suyana wanted nothing to do with any of that). He had dark eyes and a sweetly sly expression that blesses one diplomat in a thousand; the Assembly was scheduled to vote in Paris a month from now. Suyana was very nearly proud.

The trick to the rest of it was lying low when you had to. When France and Sweden nominated themselves as the Cultural Heritage delegates to the International Exchange Conference, Suyana arranged a "Ten Great Things About Being a Girlfriend" interview with *Elite* the afternoon of the vote. France and Sweden were Big Nine; she couldn't quite bring herself to vote for them, but you didn't vote against them. She and Magnus had worked out ten things that were mildly infuriating to them both; Magnus tapped his stylus too fast against the desk whenever he said things like, "The way he smiles when you wear the necklace he bought you."

But she didn't want to think about necklaces any more than Magnus did, when the time came. She'd had one once, it hadn't gone well, and there was no point reminding anyone. She'd made the number three thing "The way he's so proud of my accomplishments" instead.

For a second the interviewer paused, and Suyana wondered if she'd blown it. Then the woman grinned and said, "Oh God, that's so sexy. I love a sensitive guy, I always guessed that about him," and waxed for a while about the merits of a supportive boyfriend. When the interview came out, they'd run a sidebar of Ethan's casual outfits and explained how each one proved his sensitive side.

In the morning, after the trainer and breakfast, Oona dropped in to make sure Suyana's eyes looked as awake as possible—eyedrops, white liner inside the lids, shimmer under the brows, and past that Suyana lost track and just held still with her eyes closed.

"Inside date or outside?" Oona asked, Suyana's chin in one hand and her brush pushing against Suyana's eye socket with the other. Suyana sometimes felt guilty that she thought of Oona mostly as a blur of orange and gold from behind closed eyes.

"Outside."

"Ugh, God knows why, midday light is so punishing." Something was rubbed into her cheeks, presumably to help prevent the sun from punishing her, and Suyana shrugged carefully and said, "Ethan likes an outdoors girl."

"He should like what you like. You had your pick of boys when you came back from the crazy thing. He's on the cover of three magazines this month and he's not on any of them alone, I'll tell you that much."

"I'll make him window-shop," Suyana said. "Buy me some sapphires."

Oona shook her head. "Emeralds. It'll remind people of the rainforest."

"Right, of course," said Suyana, and opened her mouth for the gloss.

Ethan was already laughing as she opened the door, either at her face as she braced herself or because it would look good for the cameras if he was happy to see her. And he did seem happy; he always did, his white teeth and white skin and hair that curled but never too much. There were wrinkles just at the edges of his eyes that made Suyana wonder, in her stupider moments, if he really was pleased to see her, sometimes.

He kissed her lightly hello (she could feel his teeth behind his smile), slid his hand down her arm until he could catch at her fingers in the way he only did when he was content with himself. Two cameras on the curb were already jostling for the best position.

"Hello. You look like you've been out here making plans."

His grin got wider, and he said, "Well, have you heard about Martine?"

5

The New York office of Bonnaire Fine Tailoring was a town-house in a neighborhood choked with baby carriages and tasteful wrought iron. Only a plaque outside suggested it was a place of business. (Attorneys; apparently Li Zhao had worried people might actually try to bring business to a tailor.) Daniel avoided it except when the boss called him in, because it gave him the creeps.

"The only knock we ever got on that door was when the plants died and someone asked Bo to put in nice ones for the sake of the neighborhood," Kate said. She was in the basement of the Paris office, and the light made her smile sepulchral. "We put up the plaque after that, but somehow the number of people was never a problem. They just thought the help was coming and going."

"Charming," Daniel said, and Kate waggled her eyebrows in something that almost felt collegial, from Kate.

Then she glanced down at something on her screen. "Okay, she's ready," she said, and a moment later she blinked out and Li Zhao appeared. It was three in the morning there, but her black suit was crisp, her red lipstick tattooed with her usual precision. Only pride kept him from sitting up straighter—that was why she wore all that armor, and he didn't want to admit how effective it was at establishing a pecking order. He did as he was told these days, but he had his limits.

"Hello, Daniel," Li Zhao said. "You won't be going to the UARC with the happy couple. Was there anything else?"

He'd expected to be arguing about his request, just not instantly. "She trusts me," he said. "In a strange place—"

"The Amazonian Rainforest Confederation is her home."

Not anymore, and Li Zhao must have known it, but that wasn't something Daniel wanted to say—not about Suyana, not now. "I don't like how this feels," he said instead. "It's too fast, and Margot's mirroring their trip, which feels like trouble. I suspect you don't think much of the whole thing either, because there's no other reason to keep me out of the assignment when we follow them from Paris to New York every year anyway."

"You'll stick out more in Peru than in Paris."

"Bullshit. And I can disappear into a crowd."

"But not to her," Li Zhao said. She leaned forward, and the light from her desk lamp highlighted the brackets on either side of her mouth. "I like to flatter myself that you'll stay where I've told you to stay, but you should understand this anyway: you're the last thing she's going to need where she's going. A home tour is hard enough without holding on to the hope that you have friends. Nicodema is covering the story, and you can follow the photos online like everyone else."

It's not just some empty hope, he thought, why the hell do you think I'm begging to go with her? But neither the venom nor the earnestness in it would do him any good against Li Zhao.

Instead he said, "So what, I stay here and wrestle Pietro for the honor of scouting C-listers while I wait?"

"You shouldn't sound like you're above that," Li Zhao said, and his stomach knotted even though it barely counted as an insult. "But no. I have another assignment for you."

"Oh, lovely." If Li Zhao thought she was going to distract him just by shifting his assignment, she was free to try.

"You're assigned to Martine. You and Bo will be going to Norway to track their visit. He'll keep you posted on travel plans. Be ready to move."

Somewhere beneath this nauseating reminder that Li

Zhao knew exactly what she was doing, Daniel thought about the last time he'd looked Martine in the eye—the moment after she'd learned what he was, and slapped the panic button strapped to her wrist to call her hired gun.

"Well, uh, as far as I know, Li Zhao, Martine wants to kill me."

She'd leaned back from the desk already, checking out of the conversation—she never discussed, and if you thought she was, she was just giving you your orders in a way you could take—and the last thing he heard before the line went dead was, "Good thing you're so good at disappearing in a crowd."

Two days after the trips had been announced, Suyana went out for a night of clubbing with Martine to celebrate the venture, and they brought Grace, who Daniel figured had been asked by the UARC or Norway to keep the other two from eating each other alive.

Not that you'd know it from the way they stood on the curb outside Martine's apartment building in front of the photographers, waiting for a private car that was strategically five minutes late. Grace was telling a story, Suyana was smiling at appropriate moments, and Martine barked a laugh once around her fake cigarette. All three wore the black slim pants and heels that signaled wanting to be dressed up but not wanting to look as if it was an effort. Grace and Martine wore sparkling tops; Suyana wore a white silk tank, and her scar gleamed under the awning lights. Grace's and Martine's bodyguards stood at a respectful distance, hands identically folded, looking like accessories.

(The first time he met with Suyana, back when her face still softened when she saw him and his hand shook as he covered his camera, just from seeing her, he'd asked how she managed to avoid getting a bodyguard. Even Magnus must have been willing to set aside funds for one after what she'd been through. She said, "It's important that people see I'm not afraid," in the timbre that she used in chambers, and he'd smiled to imagine her reciting it obediently to Magnus, and when the cloud had crossed her face and she'd glanced over his shoulder to make sure no one was coming, he'd told himself it didn't matter. That was a year ago.)

From where Daniel stood—not quite directly across the street, grabbing an espresso from a window walk-up, a tablet in hand like everyone in line behind him—he could see the group of teenage girls who'd gathered just close enough to them to be making bets about which one would go over and beg for a photo.

Before they could, Grace called over, "Hello, girls, you all right?" and lifted her palm in a wave.

"Oh," said the one who'd been closest to the front, "no,

sorry, we're—*stop*," she hissed at a friend behind her trying to take a photo, "we just wanted to say how cool we think you are."

"All of us?" Martine asked, glancing once at Suyana, and it fell just short enough of offhand that Daniel raised an eyebrow. Even the teenager blinked. Suyana leaned forward an inch and glanced down the street at the car that wasn't coming.

It struck him that she might actually be nervous; the last time a car had been late she'd nearly died. Was it hard to stand on the curb if she felt like a target? If he asked her, would she tell him? Did she even know herself?

"Uh. Yeah, no, I mean, all of you are so amazing! We've seen you in *Closer*, and it's just so cool to meet you!"

"That's very kind," said Grace, and shifted her clutch under one arm with the ease of an old pro as she beckoned over the national photographers. "You girls want a photo?"

The farthest girl squealed, and as the leader of the group turned around to shoot her a murderous glare and hissed, "Oh my God, Claire," Suyana and Grace smiled fleetingly back and forth. Suyana's smile died when it reached Martine. Grace's turned into something older and long-suffering, and Martine raised an eyebrow and exhaled through tight lips.

Two weeks in Norway following Martine around, trying not to be seen or get shot. He should tell Suyana, after she was back. Someone should get a laugh out of what he was about to go through.

She'd need one. The Americans had been slow—Ethan might be happy to crawl up her nose for the cameras no matter who was taking pictures, but this UARC press setup was the first sign the American office actually saw her as an asset. He didn't like it. The long wait for a gesture of goodwill might have made Chordata nervous, and while Suyana might be able to talk them out of killing someone (him, killing *him*, he should be grateful for the favor), he worried what they'd do if they thought this was their only shot to make headlines with Suyana.

Suyana was between two of the teen girls at the far edge of the picture. Grace was in the center, and Martine had half-heartedly dropped her cigarette from her mouth just in time to give the photographers (holding the girls' cameras) the world's sweetest smile. Grace was smiling in earnest—it was her idea, of course she was, easy to be polite about your own ideas—and Suyana was smiling well enough to fool anyone who wasn't Daniel. But Martine wasn't fooling anyone, it just *was*—for ten seconds, those girls were the best thing that had ever happened to Martine.

When the girls were gone, Martine shot Grace a look. "For the love of God, what's next? Picking up trash for charity? Planting trees for Coalition Day?"

"Antismoking campaign, maybe," Suyana said as the car pulled up. "Terrible habit. Looks so desperate."

Suyana sank out of sight in the car, and just before Grace got in, she shot a warning look inside at Suyana, and a satisfied one over her shoulder at Martine, who got in without any sign she'd heard.

The last thing Daniel saw as the car pulled away was a cloud of water-vapor smoke that brushed against the back window and blotted everything out.

6

Just before the private plane landed, Ethan's stylists (Brad for hair, Chris for makeup, Andrea for clothes) pulled him aside to put finishing touches on his outfit.

"If you weren't so oily, we wouldn't have to do this," said Chris with rapidly thinning patience as they moved him into the bedroom, and Ethan made such an abashed face at Suyana that she couldn't help but smile.

"Your secret's safe with me," she said, and he stuck his tongue out just before the door closed.

At the front of the plane, the two American handlers assigned to the tour—Stevens and Howard—were reviewing the itinerary with Magnus.

"Can we cut short the photo op outside town on Tuesday?" asked Howard, already scratching a line through something.

"The photo op with her *mother*?" Magnus let the derision sit for a second. "Howard, if you'd like to make it look like Ethan doesn't care to meet Suyana's mother during her triumphant homecoming, be our guest, but Suyana will be using the full time allotted, so Ethan will be traveling to the next location by himself."

It was the hardest line Magnus had ever taken with the Americans. Suyana put one hand on the armrest as if expecting turbulence.

Howard sighed. "Jesus, Magnus, just a suggestion."

"And it was as sterling as all your others," Magnus assured him. "Now, Stevens, you mentioned press issues regarding the actual site tour?"

"Yes—as this is a US-Norway project, I'm afraid your photographers are being requested to stay off site."

"Of course," said Magnus, back to form. If he glanced up at Suyana before he went back to the schedule, that was to be expected; if he was looking at her like he hoped she'd heard him, that was a problem she could avoid for a little while longer.

"Oona," Suyana said absently, but Oona was twisting her curly red hair into a messy bun, that thousand-yard stare already going.

"Oh, if he's not shiny, you won't be shiny, and you don't

need three people to get rid of it either."

The plane was landing by the time Oona was done with powder and lip gloss and shimmer under the brows ("Always shimmer," Suyana murmured, as she dipped her finger in the pot and brushed it across her scar). Oona banged her way into the bedroom in back to sort through the designer loans for a jacket that Suyana could carry over one shoulder for five minutes of photos.

Magnus took a seat next to Suyana. "The cameras are already waiting on the tarmac," he said, and Suyana couldn't tell if it was meant to be reassuring.

"I appreciate you preserving my time with my mother," she answered instead. Her lips were glossy, and her hair had just been combed so it looked windswept, and Ethan wasn't here; there would never be a better moment for him to take pleasure in her being grateful.

He looked at her too long before he dropped his eyes to his tablet. "Well, I'm certainly pleased you'll get to see her, but largely that was to handle Howard."

"I know. But still."

"Behold," called Ethan as he opened the door, "the matte-est man in town!"

Magnus nearly rolled his eyes before he could stop himself. Suyana ignored it and looked at Ethan over her shoulder. "Is that the jacket you're wearing?"

"Yeah." Ethan smoothed the front of the oxblood leather. "It's kind of cool, right? I get so sick of blazers. It's nice that we can just be casual on this trip. Be ourselves."

"Oh, absolutely."

Ethan sat on her other side; Magnus had vanished, but she supposed his disapproval must have lingered. "I'm really looking forward to just playing it by ear a little on this trip," he said. "That pizza date was the most fun I've had in a long time."

"Well, I'm looking forward to seeing the country with you," she said, curling up in the seat to face him and trying to tamp down the embers of dread in her stomach. "There's so much I don't even remember. I've barely been home. It will be amazing to see the country together."

"Sure! Totally! But I'm just saying, I think we're over-scheduled on some really dumb stuff. Like, the government people I get, we have to meet them, but this research site tour is booked for four hours, and I will honestly be asleep by then."

She pointed a finger at him. "You better not fall asleep when you meet my mom," she said, as teasing as she could, some character in a movie who had a mother she saw all the time, who understood how her mother might bore the new boyfriend, and he laughed and closed his hand around her fingers. He kissed the heel of her hand; she flushed, felt ill.

"Sweetheart, your mom is going to love me," he promised, and she was still smiling at him, just the way she'd been taught, when the plane landed.

He stood up as soon as they slowed, smoothing his jacket. She slid on her heels and tried to breathe.

He couldn't cancel the site visit—why else was she here, allowed to go home for the first time since Hakan? Why else was this outpost getting built except under the auspices of their relationship? Why had she made sure that Ethan led the whole affair of coming here, except as a cover, so no one could make a connection between these two visits any deeper than proximity?

The airplane door was open, and Ethan was being ushered out the door by his team, and she was following by rote, but her throat was so tight that as she passed Magnus— lurking at the back of the crowd as if he was above it all— she stepped close, reached out, gripped his hand.

He was so startled he gripped it back, and she looked at him and remembered the way he'd leaned against Hakan's desk and looked her over like she was somebody's runner-up, remembered the press of her arm against his throat a year ago, when she'd thought for half a breath about what it would be like to kill him. He'd promised her his loyalty. She'd worked hard to accept it without needing it; he was a railing she didn't dare lean on. But before she was past him, she whispered, "Don't let him leave me behind."

Magnus's eyebrows tilted up just at the inner corners. "I won't," he said, low, and so earnest it was good to hear it, and she wondered if she must have meant it, a little, that it was such a comfort to have his answer.

She dropped his hand and took the steps down to the tarmac to meet Ethan, settled into the arm that was already reaching out to pull her closer, and smiled and smiled and smiled.

The tour:

Two days in São Paolo, two days in Rio de Janeiro. "Should have been three, but didn't seem like the best press," Magnus said the first time he showed her the calendar. Suyana didn't blame them; she was Peruvian, and the UARC could only ever have one Face—the Central Committee's sidelong punishment for allying without IA approval.

("When someone actually manages to shoot me, make sure my replacement's Brazilian," she'd said. After a beat, he'd said, "They all are.")

Two days in Lima. Eating at restaurants that had verandas or windows, taking pictures with tourists, visiting museums, attending an evening of the UARC Film Festival that was a last-minute addition. Suyana ended up in matte gold sequins that fell to mid-calf, and a black leather belt of Ethan's that Oona knotted to look carefree. On the red carpet,

Suyana and Ethan got more screams than the movie stars. "Home court advantage," Ethan murmured, like it was news.

In Ipanema, she and Ethan went shopping at prearranged locally owned stores and bought local swimsuits to wear to the local beach, improving some invisible retail clout over foreign bathing suits. Suyana wore a long-sleeved cover-up that came to her knees, even in the water, because to wear just the bathing suit would invite speculation about her figure.

"Modesty implies self-awareness," Magnus said just before they got out of the car at the first glittering swim boutique. "You should enforce that impression as much as possible."

What he meant was, Don't look so grateful to Ethan; people can see you.

On their way in, Ethan shot a grin at the photographers and waited until the doors closed behind them. Then he said, "Don't let Magnus or anybody shame you out of anything. You're amazing. If you want to just buy a two-piece, I would support that. I really would."

She couldn't help laughing. "Yeah, you're a saint," she said, and he didn't deny a thing, but they had twenty minutes to kill in the store before moving on and her things were already waiting with the cashier Oona had called a week ago, so she picked up four things off the first rack she came to, and then took Ethan's hand and led him to the dressing rooms without a word. He wasn't hard to please. He liked the smallest things, she'd barely had to learn how to keep him happy, whatever she tried seemed to work—but she made sure not to always wait for an overnight visit. Let him press her up against the wall of a dressing room, let him wrap his hand around her fingertips and slip away with her at a party. Everyone liked feeling like they were hard to resist; even a contract relationship should build on possibilities. It was a game he was good at—he never pushed, and he was good in bed. Generous. He was easy to want to please.

On the beach she wore the black cover-up but only loosely fastened, so when she walked the camera got a glimpse of her thick thighs, her soft stomach. The national press seemed slightly stumped, but tourists loved it, and they got looks all the way down the beach. Ethan grinned down at her, and she smiled and glanced around and cataloged faces.

They toured the Government Palace in Lima with the president, nodding solemnly at the portraiture and admiring the architectural detail, and spent an afternoon shaking hands with ministers and chairmen at a luncheon in the Peace Room as Ethan vacillated between a consummate statesman and a shy boyfriend meeting an extended family, depending on his audience. Across the room, with another set of strangers, she nodded solemnly and smiled politely and admired him for his ease. That alone seemed noteworthy. A warning of something.

Between passed hors d'oeuvres and being seated, Suyana pulled aside the administrator of the Amazon Forestry and Conservation Initiative to ask him about the new research station, in Spanish.

"It sounds very ambitious," she said, as pristinely neutral as she'd ever managed. Hakan would have been proud.

"It certainly is," the administrator agreed, far less neutral, "and I'm looking forward to all their preliminary reports and explanations about erosion prevention actually justifying their plans for expansion, as soon as their head office conde-scends to give it to us."

Suyana had a dozen questions before he was done talking, but she couldn't voice them—she wasn't supposed to even know what to ask. So she smiled and said, "Well, I can't wait to see the forest again, it's been so long," and let him murmur some polite nothing and wander away and think of her as an empty doll they dressed up and sent to Paris twice a year.

Outside, where the national press and the tourists were waiting, Suyana made eye contact anywhere she could—good photo etiquette—as she looked at face after face, noting whoever seemed less intent on their camera than on her.

The press couldn't get enough of the visit, which, assas-sins or not, felt like the return of the prodigal daughter. Magnus's press service sent him a preview scan of *Global's* weekly Hot or Not list, in which Suyana was walking beside Ethan down the beach, cover-up flying.

BOMBSHELL IT, they'd slapped across the photo, under HOT. *Show just enough—then leave him wanting more—with a hot suit and a barely-there cover-up.*

The boutique sold out of the suit and cover-up in fifteen minutes, Magnus told her on the way home from a dinner appointment. They were already taking orders for next year.

"I'm so glad," she said, and ticked off three places on the shopping map that were Quechua-owned. "The PR's paying off," she told Magnus as she pushed it back toward him. "Hakan always said a little Quechua pride would be good for me."

Magnus glanced up but said nothing, which was a mercy. The three shops appeared in her itinerary, one after the other.

"I hope you're getting something for yourself out of this trip," he said. "The PR is necessary, but I know you don't often make it home."

"We should go dolphin watching on the river," she said after a while.

There wasn't time to book a private boat, but by the time the tiny plane had taken them from Lima inland, the security team had frisked the tour group and had the police do a sweep for weapons, so they had the all clear, and the tourists were nice enough to come up and ask for pictures instead of pretending to take pictures of the water in their direction.

As a trio of American backpackers were bonding with Ethan about a shared homesickness for burgers and fries, Suyana handled a line of young women and teenage girls who held maps or crumpled receipts for her to sign, talking about how lovely the river was and making jokes about how she needed high heels just to be able to see Ethan.

One of the girls stepped up and offered a map of inland Peru, and said, "For Sotalia."

Suyana kept her eyes on the paper until she was done writing the name, and then she glanced up only as would be expected. "Is this your first time seeing the dolphins?" she asked, as she circled a coffee shop that had a view of the staff entrance of their hotel in Iquitos (Sotalia had dark eyes, hair that she'd put in a ponytail to make her look younger than she was). "That sounds lovely, what a nice trip," Suyana said in response to whatever Sotalia had told her, as she wrote *Enjoy your three days in beautiful Lima! Best wishes*, and, "It's so nice to meet you," Suyana said as she handed the map back, and Sotalia glanced it at and nodded once before she clutched it to her chest and thanked Suyana and shuffled away to take photos of the water.

Three days. Time enough for a visit to the site, and then

a meeting with Sotalia at the hotel, to tell them whatever had to be done.

Suyana took photos alongside everyone. The dolphins eventually found the boat, and everyone cooed and laughed and took pictures as the dolphins quacked up at them, but Suyana aimed her camera at the wide, shimmering line of the river, at the canopy of trees, at so many shades of green her eyes hurt.

The last time she'd had someone teach her something that wasn't IA business had been so long ago she was still learning statecraft from Hakan. (They'd passed the apartment he'd rented, on the drive from one place to another. Only she knew he'd ever lived there.)

On one of her final lessons—someone was packing up her apartment during the session and sending her clothes to Paris, it was so close to the end—the science tutor taught her about the eye as a fossil record. The human eye, she said, sees so many shades of green because humans had evolved from prey animals and needed to be able to distinguish safe places; people were born knowing they'd be hunted, and had to take advantage.

7

The first stop on any ecological tour of Norway, it turned out, was Bergen, where Martine and Margot walked around the historic pier for the benefit of the press, security guards nowhere in sight, looking like a side-by-side time-lapse photo of Norwegian nobility.

This far from the Central Committee, Margot ditched the suits for nice trousers and sweaters that probably cost what Daniel made in a month. Martine wore scarves so voluminous they'd have swallowed the bottom half of her head except that her stylists folded down the front so her purple lipstick always showed. Neither of them bothered smiling, though cameras lined the streets every time they left the hotel. They were doing Norway a favor just by showing up.

"You must be loving this," Daniel said from behind a map of Bergen. "The two meanest women in the world come home to celebrate."

Over the comm in his ear, Bo said, "It's a nice town. Busier than I expected. So far no trouble keeping them in sight."

"You're the world's most boring person," Daniel said, "and when I find out how you ever got into killing people for a living, I'm going to die of shock," and muted the connection for the next five minutes just so he didn't have to hear whatever Bo was yelling at him.

After Martine and Margot had spent the requisite amount of time gracing local boutiques, they got into a single car to go to dinner, and Daniel went back to the room he and Bo were sharing undercover as a couple so he could crash before the late shift.

The trade-off happened just shy of midnight, as Daniel took up his post at the outdoor café opposite the glass-walled bar where Margot and Martine were deep in conversation.

"What are they plotting, do we know?"

From inside the bar, Bo glanced casually at his phone, wrote back, *Sounds like Martine's in line for Central Committee thanks to this*, and took a sip of wine that Daniel resented him for having. Bo was going to trail Margot home soon and get in bed and sleep the sleep of the just, and Daniel was going to be stuck out in the chilly night for however long it took Martine to finish her mandatory clubbing and go to bed.

It took three espressos on his end, and he lost track of how much wine on Martine's, before anything happened. When Margot seemed satisfied and left, Bo did his magic trick of disappearing in plain sight, and Daniel was left following Martine and her hired muscle wherever she was headed next.

He fell in line behind her and let the tide carry him. He'd pinpointed the six most exclusive clubs in Bergen, but it was dangerous to try to overthink your target. Daniel just haunted them down the streets, between the couples on dates and the groups of young people, until they reached Sessrúmnir. It had been third on his list by rank of probability; he needed to work harder.

That was the problem of stepping in on someone else's beat cold—you had to start up the hill all over again. He could tell without thinking when Suyana had wound up too tight under the cameras and was planning to slide out the kitchen door and meet with Chordata just to pretend she still had a reason to keep going. That pattern he had nailed down to the day.

At the door, Martine whispered something to her hired

man, and after some hesitation he nodded and went inside. As soon as she was alone, she yanked her fake cigarette out of her jeans, shook it awake, and sucked in a pull so deep he heard her breath from down the block. The lights outside the club were blue, and she looked like an ice statue with her chin tilted up toward the dark.

Still staring at the sky, she held a hand and crooked a finger toward him.

Goddammit. He thought about vanishing, but there was no point, once you'd been made. At least if Martine had him murdered, Li Zhao would have to admit he'd been right about Martine having bad blood.

He approached slowly, not wanting to put himself between Martine and the bodyguard inside, but she waited until he was within arm's reach without looking over, and even then she exhaled another lungful of vapor before she said, "A little far afield for a taxi dancer, isn't it?"

"I go where the dancing is."

She pulled a face. "Jesus, that's terrible. I was debating whether to disappear you, but you might have just made up my mind."

"Can it wait two weeks?" he asked, when the air had come back to his lungs. "I'm expecting news from someone."

She frowned. Then she said, "So why aren't you with her?"

It had somehow never occurred to him that Suyana must have explained him away enough to avoid disaster. It should have—there was obviously a reason Martine hadn't gone to the national press with an exposé on snaps sneaking into the Faces' inner sanctums, and her goodwill toward the press wasn't it—but he couldn't picture Suyana and Martine having a civil conversation for long enough. Good for them, he thought vaguely, above the drum of his pulse.

He said, "Couldn't resist a chance to see you in your element, I guess."

Martine shot him a look that made him feel like the false ashes from her cigarette—that hatred that came right before someone admitted something, and before he could think, he brushed his hair down over the camera to obscure her.

It took Martine all of two seconds to figure everything out, and she lit up as soon as she realized it, positively delighted in her disdain. "Wait. What the fuck do you all think I'm going to be doing up here that's more important than the show she's putting on down there?"

He needed to run—he needed to get out of here before she got bored with him or before he told her anything he couldn't justify—but he couldn't afford to make her angry, and he was too stung to lie. "Nothing, apparently. You smile and pretend you can stand Margot, and I watch you and worry about somebody else."

She tapped the cigarette off; it became a shivering ember between her fingers, an aftereffect of her grin. "Oh, friend, that Amazon's going to eat you alive."

Daniel had no argument to make. He'd been doing the math on that for a year.

"Tomorrow we're taking separate cars to Dovrefjell," she said, so casually it sounded at first like she was making travel plans with him. "There's a photo op outside. Then Margot tours the site, and I go right to the Kongsvold Hotel and drink myself stupid overnight. Then I go to Oslo and party for a week and pretend I care about ecology for an hour or two a day during meetings. My laziness about it all will get me a place in the Central Committee, once Spain gets off his ass and retires as press liaison. Who knows from there?"

She slid the cigarette back into her pocket, kept two fingers on the tip like it was a homing beacon. "And I don't care about anything she's asked me to do. I'd agree to worse things than ignorance. But if she wants me out of the way for that site visit, and I'm the one she *trusts*, then I don't know what that means for the other site."

When she turned to look at him, her irises vanished into the wash of blue light above her. She looked blank-eyed and distant and helpless as a ghost. He wished he'd left the camera clear; he was missing a beautiful shot.

"I'm going to be here for a few hours," she said. "You can try to follow me if you want, but you won't get in. This place has standards. Have a good night watching for me and worrying."

The door closed behind her. If the bodyguard came out to clean up, Daniel didn't stick around to see it.

8

Oona dressed her in white and blue for the visit.

"You should look like the evening sky coming down to bless whatever cement block they're taking you to," she said as she plaited Suyana's hair into a single complicated knot at the back of her neck.

"It's an ecological research facility."

"God, we'd better get you some jewelry, then. And a jacket."

From the dining table of the suite, Magnus smiled down at his paperwork.

She ended up in a navy-blue silk jumpsuit that looked like a sleeveless mockery of a scientist's smock, and a white linen jacket that only made it worse, and Magnus looked her over skeptically as they waited in the lobby.

"It's the best of bad options," she said. "I wanted the work boots and jeans, but she begged me to look like I cared." She tried a smile. "I'll end up in a cocktail dress if she keeps going."

Magnus looked as though he wasn't sure it could be worse, but he just smoothed his own lapel and said, "It will do. We'll leave the jacket in the car. It will be more . . . subtle."

She nearly laughed before she caught it, and Magnus glanced at her, surprised, just as the car pulled up and Ethan and Stevens got out.

"Morning, Samuelsson," said Stevens, mostly to his tablet. "Morning, Suyana. Ethan, be back here by four, please. You have the dinner scheduled."

"Roger that," said Ethan, scooping Suyana gently by the elbow, and she must have made a face she couldn't help, because he said, "Don't worry, it's fine. I'll get you back in one piece."

Suyana's stomach lurched, and without thinking she leaned back to make herself heavier. "But Magnus—" she began, and looked behind her, where Magnus was beginning to move in her direction, though Stevens was stepping in front of him and saying something about security clearance that didn't come through.

"I'm not going either," Stevens pointed out in the tone

handlers used when they knew they were talking about people they'd outlive.

"This is unacceptable," Magnus was saying as Ethan helped her into the car, as it pulled away from the curb, and when she looked out the window as they turned the corner. Magnus was staring after her, one fist held tight to his side and his phone already to his ear.

Too late, she thought, the queasy feeling settling and sliding into something else that felt far away. She calculated, briefly, the chances the Americans had arranged for something to happen to her on-site, and was comforted by the low number. She was less comforted by the chances that Margot had arranged for something to happen, but she concentrated on how unlikely it was that Margot would get rid of a perfectly biddable American Face in the bargain—because for Margot to keep clear of a disaster, they'd both of them have to go.

"Is this your first time visiting one of these?" she asked, her voice so calm it must belong to someone else.

"Yeah, in person, but Margot and I did a bunch of funny-looking photo ops they're going to roll out in the news once these facilities are all established and there are results to publicize. Some of them went out with the first round of press announcements like we were actually working there. They're so embarrassing. In one of them they made me look into a microscope and make a really serious face, as if anyone would believe anything I had to say about microscopic anything."

"I saw that first picture. You looked very believable."

"Why do you ask?" His smile had fallen off; his eyes were narrowed. "Are you not interested in this?"

She wished there were cameras. She wished there were a dozen. Why weren't there any cameras?

"Oh, no, I'm very interested. This is for the benefit of the country I represent to my utmost duty," she repeated, as if it was something Magnus had told her. As if it bored her.

His smile came back. "It won't take long, I promise. We have the president's dinner to get to, and I promised Stevens I wouldn't be late."

That improved her chances, then; you didn't kill people on the way to presidential dinners unless you wanted a bigger storm than this was worth. It was just smart planning on Margot's part, to keep her off balance; Margot knew Suyana liked witnesses, and Suyana shuddered from the chill of being known. Magnus wouldn't get there; they'd never let him reach her when he could still do any good, he'd still be in full diplomatic fury with Stevens by the time they came back—and by then she'd already have been separated from whatever they didn't want her to see.

× × × × × × ×

Columbina was tall, so tall that Suyana had wondered about the logistics of having her for a contact (how could they keep quiet if Suyana had to strain to hear her?), but she soon saw the game. Columbina had olive skin and sharp green eyes and dark hair cut into a bob that swung against her jaw as she moved, and when they went out together, no one gave Suyana a second glance.

She'd given up Zenaida after the shooting; it wasn't safe to go back to old comforts. But they had been invisible together because Zenaida acted like her mother. Columbina made her invisible just by showing up.

("I see," Suyana had said, when Columbina introduced herself, and Columbina had laughed and steered her into the crowd at the flea market. Suyana had developed a taste for flea markets that bored Magnus, just around the time Columbina appeared.)

"Everyone's suspicious of the whole venture," Columbina had confided that first day, setting down a pair of opera glasses. "They say it's for the environment, but that's what they always say. Someone on the inside says it's the thin end of a corporate wedge. Even if it isn't mining, we want to ... discourage it."

"We already discouraged corporate interests," Suyana had said. There was a basket of baby dolls at her feet, their eyes staring hopefully up at her, and she stepped aside before she kicked it.

"We might have to do it again."

"That doesn't seem wise."

"Maybe not, but if we let in one problem, where will it stop? They can't grow roots there."

"I barely survived the last time," Suyana said, trying to sound wry and light, and failing just at the end.

(Zenaida would have bought her a little animal from the brass collection, some figure that had nothing to do with her work—a deer, a dog, a polar bear—and given it to her as a keepsake, and told her quietly, "No one can force you to agree.")

Columbina nodded slowly. "I understand," she said. "But we'd like you to make the opportunity, if you can. We want more information. That's all."

Two strikes in five years, on a country that had been under scrutiny too long for a year of magazine spreads to make people forget. All it would do was make her a scandal instead of a victim. Chordata made sure incidents were happening everywhere; the world was a wide place, and little discontents were always brewing—oil pipelines broke down in the Arctic, waste dumpers found their barrels lined up on the lawns of their estates. But two hits as obvious as this, the second so soon after the first and in the same place, would become points in a pattern.

And if she said no, they might act anyway. The last strike

had been clean, no human injury and no spreading fires, because she had looked out for all of it and they had known how to plan.

If they acted and she hadn't seen the place first, she'd never know if they had been right about needing to remove it. She was struggling to find a conscience these days, and before she trusted anyone, she was going to have to see it in the flesh.

She'd survived Chordata last year, but not because Chordata's terms were kind. She had survived because Onca had seen *her* in the flesh, and in that cramped apartment in Paris, the moment Onca had her orders and a gun in her hand, Suyana had made her believe.

(She didn't know if Onca was still alive; she was something else Suyana could never go back to.)

It had been easier to be young, and to not care if Zenaida was directing her where she needed to be led, and to assume Chordata was clear-thinking and honorable. Easier to be young, when a woman had lowered her camera and pointed at the forest and told her she could save it all. Suyana hadn't believed it even then, but it was something to fight for, and that had been enough.

"Let me know when we need to move," she'd said. "I'll work on Ethan. We'll get over there. Then I'll meet whoever I need to meet. No other promises."

Columbina grinned. "After your premiere, then. We'll talk about Sotalia. See you soon."

After she was gone, Suyana stood a long time just at the edge of the stalls under the shade of a tree, where no one could tell what she was looking at. Daniel was across the street. He had looked very carefully at Suyana all the time Columbina was leaving, like he was trying to make sure Columbina wouldn't register to anyone checking the feed. Some girl had excused herself to walk past Daniel's mark, and that was all.

When Magnus came to pick her up, she'd been sitting on a bench, looking at the dot of green the park made among the towers of cement.

"Didn't you buy anything?" Magnus asked as he opened the door for her, an edge in his voice.

She didn't look for Daniel then; if he was worrying for her, it wouldn't do her any good.

"Nothing's worth it," she said.

She left the white jacket in the car. Her earrings—silver, purchased in Lima—brushed her shoulders, and as they walked from the car up the dirt path to the facility, her heels sank a little into the ground with every step.

It was ridiculous, but it worked enough as cover; grumbling about the soil gave her the chance to lean close to Ethan's side for a moment, so he couldn't see her looking around like there was some better path, so she could mark where the perimeter cameras were and see where the brush was deepest around them.

The canopy rose up behind the squat, bulging facility like it was trying to wave her over; the tops of the trees were swaying slightly from monkeys or the wind, and there were so many insects on the trunks that out of the corner of your eye it looked like the forest was breathing.

It was just as she'd remembered it, a long time ago.

"How'd they get this place so deep into the jungle?" Ethan wondered, frowning at the pile of lumber beside the facility (made of the interlocking-pod system ecologists usually used on uneven terrain, lumps of unrisen bread dough three stories high).

"The lumber roads were probably already here," she said. "Or the path for the gas pipeline."

Ethan glanced at her sidelong, just keenly enough to worry her, and she bristled and shrugged and said, "What? Magnus tells me the news!" as if she was offended and not terrified, and he cracked a smile a second too late.

Their guides were waiting just inside the doors. He was a politician, you could tell from a hundred feet, and she was an administrator in the genetics division who looked like she hated them being there and was afraid of saying something she shouldn't. The photographer, who had a site pass but no national badge, took four or five pictures that wouldn't come close to print quality and then vanished into the open hatch between two pods.

As they went inside, Suyana messaged Magnus: *Are you trying to get here?*

Both of the guides were very helpful and very enthusiastic, and talked at great length about their plans for seed preservation, and steered Suyana and Ethan away from any of the pods where people were working and any meeting room that had a whiteboard in it. Windows opened onto the forest everywhere you looked. In three directions it felt like the green had walked up and pressed its face against the glass, the plants were so crowded. In the fourth, the mud flat sat outside the window like an accusation.

"So, uh, you guys piggyback this location off the pipeline?" Ethan asked, peering out. He winked at Suyana when their guides glanced at each other.

"The pipeline was fifty years ago," said the man, and the woman said, "It wouldn't be safe to build near the pipeline, actually. Since it was installed, we've been playing a losing game with the soil."

Magnus: *I'm sorry. I can't.*

Suyana's throat was thick. "Oh?"

"The erosion caused the loss of so much trees and brush cover that the birds had to move on, so the seeds aren't traveling the way they used to," the woman explained, as the politician got silently redder. "This year the Yanesha Reserve has reported markedly low levels of deer. The monkeys are leaving."

Suyana already knew. The scraped-bare land had been a line of rotting flesh you could see from the plane.

Ethan frowned. "And so you're researching how to fix the erosion?"

"Unfortunately, the damage is just too far gone to reverse quickly, even if the budget for such a large-scale fix was possible. At this point we're researching how to encourage corporate activism to raise the money to grow and replant ground cover, until we can reintroduce seed growth more naturally."

It was rehearsed, a return to the prescribed track from that moment of accidental information, and Suyana tried not to curl her lip at the idea of corporate activism. It might work—growing seeds in a greenhouse that would take up acres, trying to replant in stages what had been lost. Of course, it would be sponsored by an American company— the UARC couldn't afford to sustain a several-year project on that scale. They'd be asking the Americans to take point. They'd be handing it over.

That was the whole point of the venture, then: make the UARC grateful for a solution they couldn't afford to a problem caused by someone else.

She wasn't a fool—whatever was happening in the labs they couldn't see meant that pharmaceutical companies and nutrition conglomerates would descend on whatever this group found, looking for patents the government would have to fight across international lines and exerting pressure to own it all, in exchange for keeping it alive.

But that might not happen until after the plants had taken hold. It might be the reason there were enough plants in the first place; cultivation and domestication on something that might be wasteland otherwise. The UARC was getting better trade deals now that she was dating Ethan; they might be able to buy back some of the land rights before the corporations could close their fists around it all. And until then, what was to be done that was better than trying to hold on to the dirt? Should she give the word to let the place burn, and let the ground eat its fill of the trees?

(Once she thought, Did Margot know there would be mitigating factors? Did she let me see this just to find out what I would do?)

"Miss Sapaki, would you like to see some of our seed practices?" the woman was asking, and Suyana watched the politician draw Ethan aside to meet with some people in one of the forbidden meeting rooms, full of the people she needed to know and never would.

ICON

"Sure," said Suyana finally. She felt heavy everywhere. "I'd
love to see the seeds."

I'm just the girlfriend, Suyana reminded herself as she
nodded over little envelopes and tiny seedlings being grown
under hot lamps. I'm the local celebrity, and the girlfriend of
the powerful man. I'm not a threat. No one will remember
me except as a pair of earrings and high heels covered in mud.
I'm a host, and I'm a shell in order to be safe, and anything I
need to know I'm going to have to take.

She took it in the small talk she made with the biolo-
gists, joking about the chaos of her office back home amid
their tidy rows in different bins, noting which species went
into which bin (some went into a smaller box, selected for
review by whoever was coming later to sort through them
and decide which to patent). She chatted with one of the
preservationists about their favorite animals, and Suyana
pretended to be fascinated by the photos of birds the preser-
vationist had taken.

Suyana mimed her heels sinking into the dirt until everyone was laughing, and reapplied her gloss using the selfie
camera on her phone; behind her, across the room, were lists
of species grouped on a whiteboard that they hadn't bothered
to cover, because it wouldn't mean anything to her.

And it wouldn't. To her.

If she gave it over to Chordata—how was it an if, but

the deer were vanishing and sometimes help was help—
someone would know whether you could grow those plants
on the open seam of mud, or if this was merely another
logging venture with someone else's blessing.

It would wait; the danger was farther away. Still, she
stayed close enough to a door or a window that no one
could get to her without her having a way out, and by the
time they took the stairs back down to where Ethan was
shaking hands with the people who mattered, Suyana was
counting forward and backward from five with every breath
to make sure they were long enough and steady enough not
to draw attention.

She walked outside a little ahead of him, shook hands a
little faster than he did, and the moment she was clear of the
crowd she opened the call, said, "Keep that video," and hung
up on Magnus, before anyone else was close enough to hear.

In the car on the way back to the hotel, Suyana watched the
road—there was so much mud, it would be so easy to slip—
until Ethan rested his hand on her leg. Then she remembered
herself and laid her fingers in the spaces between his fingers,
rolled her head along the seat back to face him.

"I'm glad you were here," she said, and meant it. She'd
embraced him outside the facility just before they got in the
car, her head tucked against his chest; the blanket of green

had stung her eyes for a second, and she hadn't wanted anyone to see.

He looked at their hands. "What did you see when they pulled me aside? Was it more fun than what I saw?"

"I don't know. How fun do you find seed packets?" He smiled, and she gambled and said, "They were setting aside a lot of potential patent seeds for that one guy, though."

"It's not one guy, it's just the name of the company," he said.

Anger flared heavy and wretched just behind her ears when she realized he wasn't going to tell her whatever he'd been told, and her empty palm itched.

But she let embarrassment wash over her face and said, "Don't tell Magnus. I have to give him a full report for the budget, and he'll be so mad that I wasn't paying attention to something."

"I won't."

"You promise?"

"Of course," he said, some lie worrying at him that he couldn't quite conceal. It seemed new, or newly sharpened, and Suyana watched it and wondered what the hell she was going to do to save herself if he really was an enemy. When he leaned in toward her, she met him smiling for the kiss and thought of knives.

× × × × × × ×

Magnus was waiting up when she came back to the suite, carrying her earrings in one hand and her shoes in the other, and he watched her and held perfectly still.

In the elevator lobby outside Ethan's suite, she'd glanced at the street and seen two men in suits hovering near the back door of the hotel. When she'd looked up at the head of the stairs, Stevens was at the turn that went back to Ethan's suite, watching her get in and descend. No telling what they suspected—maybe nothing, maybe this was just heightened security after an off-camera site visit—but all the way to her room, she was being watched.

(She wished she knew what her new snap looked like; she could use them now.)

Suyana stood beside the dining table, so close that Magnus had to tilt his head up to meet her eye. She felt like a mountaintop, far away and useless.

"What did Margot tell you about the research post, when you called her and asked why they'd kept you out?"

She so rarely asked him a direct question that when he answered, it sounded like she'd surprised the truth out of him.

"Her office told me it was underwritten by the International Assembly Ecology Committee, and until it was established in all the countries where it had gotten approval, it wasn't open to press. Ethan got in as a favor, because of the work the US has been doing, and it was not my place to dictate the terms of the visit."

"But someone took our picture. Who approved Ethan and me?"

He shook his head, that controlled back-and-forth that suggested a lifetime of practice at not feeling anything too much. "The committee votes are private. It was a yes vote. I don't know who was involved."

Then he looked right at her and said, "What frightened you?"

"I thought about how easy it would be to kill me while I was out there. No press, no handlers. I remember how easy it is to disappear."

Magnus flinched for a second before he could get it under control. "I'm sorry. I had no idea of their plans, I called—"

"He left me behind."

She had the satisfaction of seeing him blanch. "Suyana, what happened?"

"Nothing. All clear."

"Suyana." He'd gone even paler, but he hadn't blinked, and his fingertips were curling along the page he had marked. "You messaged me. You asked me to save video of nothing. Something's happened. Just—be honest with me."

Her shoes were heavier in her right hand than her

earrings were in her left; she felt like she needed her hands, but she couldn't let anything fall.

It would be easy. It would be so horribly easy to tell him. Grace was far away and could never know what was at stake, and there was no Daniel here, who so often knew where she was going and met her because she could never meet him.

She needed allies. She could lay Ethan down in bed and leave him stupid and heartless, but there would be no fooling Margot, and Margot moved faster—Suyana's enemies had gotten here first.

Nothing in the world made more sense now than stepping close to Magnus and kissing him and letting him burn away his guilt with her until he was of use. Suyana couldn't win this alone. She wouldn't survive.

But Magnus had never been honest with her. Everything he gave had been in trade or by accident, in moments of weakness. He said a lot of true things—he was her handler, his life was a clipboard of true things to tell her—but now, standing in front of him and longing to keep a hand free for the fight, she couldn't tell him what she needed him to know.

"I'm being followed," she said instead. "Tell the Americans they can either drop the security insults or get better at hiding it. Up to them."

He frowned. "Why would they follow you?"

"It's been an eventful day for everyone, I guess."

She was moving quickly; she'd already reached her door when he asked, "And the footage?"

She looked at him over her shoulder.

"If you can give it to me with no questions asked, then I want it. Destroy it otherwise."

When she slid into bed, she checked her tablet and found nothing.

She was still staring at it, blank-minded, two hours later, when the video arrived.

9

Dovrefjell was a nature preserve eight hours northeast of Bergen, a patchwork of color studded with animals that looked inflated with heavy winter coats. It all felt to Daniel like a meadow in a storybook, if the trees had been replaced by rocks and everyone in it wanted to kill him.

"Reminds me of the moors," Bo said as they got their bags from the backseat of the cars. "Margot visited Independent Scotland personally to escort their first Face to the IA session."

"How generous of her."

"She was mad at the UK. It was a lesson about how she'd reward the fracture of power."

"And you went with her?"

"No. Li Zhao didn't want any record of me there. She hired it out local."

"So you just looked at the footage when it came in? Did Dev let you? Must have been." Dev operated under the assumption that sometimes it was best to let snaps see what they were curious about so they could shut up; he had a lower threshold for cruelty than Kate.

"Don't remember." Bo hoisted his bag effortlessly over one shoulder as he turned, and Daniel ducked without thinking about it. He had Avoiding Bo down to a science.

"If Margot likes countries that make independent decisions, you'd think she'd like the UARC a little more."

After a second, Bo said, "You'd think."

They checked in under the hyphenated fake names that had been arranged for them—"Happy anniversary," said the clerk, and Daniel said, "Hopefully by the end of the trip it will be," which got him a beleaguered glance from Bo—and set up shop in the room.

"I thought I was the one who was going to explain we were on bad terms," Bo said. "Why am I suddenly the problem?"

Daniel stood at the window, where he could see through the sheer curtain across the yard to Martine, pacing in the shadow of the main building with a glass of wine in one hand and her cigarette in the other.

"Don't worry," he said, as she flung some imaginary ashes to the ground. "I'm definitely still the problem."

He hadn't even made it around the corner from Sessrúmnir before he'd opened the channel to Bonnaire.

As soon as the comm picked up he was talking, so fast he worried it wasn't even English, "Dev, Dev, tell me you heard what she said. We have to move."

"Oh," said Kate, "you wish it was Dev."

His stomach lurched. He rallied. "Fine. Did you hear it? Is the boss there?"

"I did. She's on her way in. Daniel, there's nothing you can do."

"You can put me through to Nicodema before Li Zhao gets there. I just need two minutes."

Kate exhaled, a static burst of disappointment. "Daniel, if you're not sharing an assignment, you're not in touch. End of story."

"Suyana could be in serious trouble."

"She could be," said Kate, and Daniel picked up the pace, tried not to be more infuriated with her for agreeing than he would have been if she'd dismissed it. "But it's not likely. Margot wouldn't endanger her relationship with the States by trying anything that could affect Ethan."

"She's already tried!"

It was too loud—a few people stopped to look. He shook his map and muttered something in Korean so people would be reluctant to help, and kept walking until he was around the corner and safe from prying eyes.

By the time he could focus again, Kate was talking to Li Zhao (she must live close by, then, and Daniel filed that away alongside the fact that she felt too safe in Paris to ever leave), and Bo was looped into the comm. Daniel could hear him packing over the line, the shuffle of fabric and the chirp of zippers.

"Don't touch my stuff, Bo. Li Zhao, what are we going to do about Suyana?"

"Nicodema has had no problems so far. If she senses anything wrong around Suyana, she'll report, and we can respond."

"How? By selling the photos of her corpse to the *Times*?"

"Daniel, we have no imperative here. We're press. We observe events, not influence them."

There was a moment of silence as Bo stopped packing. Daniel heard it for the admission of guilt it was.

"Can you just tell Nicodema to look out?" Daniel managed at last. "We can at least warn Nicodema, right? She'll need to be careful."

"The only careless recruit I employ is you, Daniel. Good night."

The click clawed down his skull; he walked the rest of the way in silence.

Bo was sitting on the end of the bed, his packed bag waiting politely on the floor.

"Kate's already told Nicodema about the danger, off the record, so she's prepared," Bo had said, above the slam of drawers as Daniel threw clothes into his bag. "We take care of our own when we can. That's all we can do."

Daniel looked at Bo until Bo looked away.

After a little while, Daniel said, "Did they say whether our itinerary changed, since we won't get within a mile of the site?"

Bo hesitated, and for a second Daniel wondered if Li Zhao had actually decided to test Bo by asking him to disappear in the Arctic scrub long enough to get pictures.

But Bo just said, "We're going straight to Dovrefjell. Li Zhao says that if you're going to announce yourself to all your targets, you might as well get whatever you can out of them while they still think it's charming."

Daniel had thought about Martine's drained face against the gray wall of the club, her features cast in blue and in darkness, and wondered what part of her shaking hands had suggested she was charmed.

"You're driving," he'd said, and zipped up the bag so fast he snagged his finger. It didn't stop bleeding until they were five kilometers out of town, and there was nothing ahead of them but the land.

x x x x x x x

The morning was a tourist outing, as Martine made up for being disinvited from the research lab by hiring a car to take her to the park monument, so she could get pictures standing in between the two towers of rock, which looked as if they'd split open neatly in the center to make room for a sacrifice.

"Quick," she said to the photographer, "before they slam back together and put me out of my misery."

Bo and Daniel stood behind a map and pointed this way and that way, their dummy backpacks pivoting around them like turtle shells. They pretended for half an hour that they were moments away from starting a meaningful hike before they gave up and realized the monument was as far as she was going.

By late afternoon, even that pretense of business was over; Bo was standing sentinel at the north window and Daniel was standing sentinel at the east. Daniel managed to wait through two hours of nothing before he started scrolling through the news feeds.

It was a slow news day out the window. Even Bo had started sneaking looks at the menu for the restaurant downstairs. "Order champagne for the table when we go," Daniel said as he scanned headlines. "The clerk's probably worried about our marriage."

It took him four minutes to find the flood of pictures

of Suyana and Ethan shopping and dining and going to the theater. Those he scrolled through without much looking. He was numb to them, mostly, unless he was taking them himself. Without any investment in the angles or the light or not losing them in traffic, the pictures became one endless blur of the pair of them walking blandly arm in arm like they were glued.

There had been times last year when Daniel had combed through pictures that never made it to the papers, looking for signs. (Dev let him spy on the feed every so often, with a mildly pitying, "Sure, man, I guess it's yours," and a twenty-minute disappearance to get coffee.) He'd watched for moments when Ethan turned calculating, moments where Suyana was looking for exits. He still looked for them. That was his job.

But Suyana had gotten better at acting since he'd first seen her dealing with Magnus outside a little Paris hotel, because that mask never dropped anymore. And Ethan was either a better actor even than Suyana had become, or he was a dope who really loved her and didn't realize the score. Daniel couldn't tell which one he preferred. After a while of being unable to decide, he'd just spared himself and stopped looking.

It was nearly an hour into the search when he saw the picture of them outside the Ecological Coalition research facility—a small picture, in some small-time Brazilian eco-journal reprinting an article from an IA newsletter with a new headline that seemed more excited about Ethan than their own Face and didn't mention a word about where they were—and he lifted his finger off the tablet like it burned.

"Shit. Bo."

Bo leaned over the chair and looked at Ethan and Suyana standing on the front porch of the research facility— or Daniel assumed it was, given that everyone else was cropped out and the building had no identifying markers except a wash of green through the windows on the far side of the lobby.

Ethan wasn't quite making eye contact with the camera, which was practically a hostage indicator coming from a guy who knew his angles as well as Ethan did, and Suyana's hand was curled so tight around his forearm that her fingertips were haloed on his skin in bloodless white.

Her face was calm. Her face looked like it had when she was talking Chordata into letting her go out on a mission that was actually a double cross, when she had lost blood and sleep and didn't expect to come back.

The photo was four hours old.

"When did she get back from there?" Daniel asked, and his voice sounded stupidly tinny—of course she was fine, nothing could have happened if they'd put the picture up. If

Margot was trying to get rid of her, then Suyana's last photo would be her doing something frivolous, not standing like a martyr amid the quiet green forests of home. That was just bad press.

But Bo was already moving for the computer, and Daniel asked hopelessly, "And where the hell is Margot?"

"Doesn't matter. It's not like she has to establish an alibi if anything's happened—Norway's her alibi. Don't get distracted."

Daniel looked out the window. Martine wasn't outside. He needed to know what the hell was going on—what were the chances Margot would make a play for Suyana on her home turf? Enough; enough to worry him. If she died at home, it was the UARC's problem. They'd call up her spare as soon as the medics confirmed Suyana was really dead, and Magnus could bring the new kid right back to New York in time to get outfitted and fly to Paris to be introduced at session. Goddammit, where was Martine?

"I'll be right back," he said. "Send me whatever you find."

"Where are you going?"

"I need a drink."

Bo didn't look up and didn't stop him. Some excuses only needed to be good enough for the cameras.

Martine was staying with Margot in one of the smaller buildings—they'd probably bought out the whole thing; they liked their privacy. She sat on the front steps, her forearms resting on her folded-up knees, looking younger than Daniel would have imagined.

There was nothing he could do. He was under surveillance even if she wasn't. He stood where he was and watched her stare out at the road, glancing at her watch every five minutes. Then every two.

Margot's late, Daniel thought, and the hair on his neck stood up. He messaged Bo, *Is she all right?*

Margot arrived before the answer. Daniel knew she was coming a full minute before her car came into view on the path, because Martine lit up the cigarette and wreathed herself in as much vapor as she could manage before Margot's car crested the far hill.

Suyana wouldn't let herself be seen as a threat, Daniel decided. Not until she'd told Chordata whatever they needed to know.

Margot back at hotel. Is Suyana all right?

He stepped around the corner of the main building, so he could see only a sliver of the stairs down the way. Margot said something to Martine on the way up the stairs, and Martine made a great show of waving the vapor away from the steps as she stood and headed across the yard toward the bar.

He watched Margot moving back and forth behind the

sheer curtains of her room for three minutes before he confirmed to Bo, *She's packing. Back to NY early? Can we confirm?*

Bo's message came back with a buzz that sank right through Daniel's hand.

Message received. Kate looking for alterations on tickets. Li Zhao changing our itinerary. Nicodema has visual on Suyana, all clear. Advise if Suyana will return to NY early?

Once he was sure he was well out of sight (he'd had enough conversations with Martine, no point pushing his luck), he wrote Bo back: *Don't know—can't tell mental state until I see footage/talk to Nicodema.*

If Margot wasn't actually packing to head back to New York—if she was just sick of looking at Martine and planning to drown her sorrows back in Bergen—he'd be in trouble for jumping to conclusions, but he wasn't above using the benefit of the doubt to his advantage. He needed to see Suyana, and he didn't care what he told people in the meantime.

Strange to think about being the authority on Suyana. It happened, he knew; Kate sometimes called Bo to ask if Margot would be more likely to go to a state dinner or meet with the Committee on a pressing vote. Bo was a big game hunter, and it was his job to know. But Daniel had never forgotten the way Bo looked at Margot when she stood in a cramped little museum in Paris, being no one in particular. Was that how Daniel looked at Suyana, when no one was watching?

As soon as his phone rang, Daniel picked up and said, "Nice to meet you, Nicodema," because of course it was—he'd had leverage. When he said, as if tallying numbers, "How much is she looking over her shoulder compared to yesterday?" and Nicodema answered, "I thought she'd made me and was going to tell her handler, that's how much," Daniel guessed she had less than a day left until the meeting with Chordata. She'd stop casually looking around after that, since then it wouldn't matter who was watching.

He tried not to let it tire him, how much he knew about her. That was the advantage Daniel brought to the position.

So he told Nicodema, "She got like that in Paris, too, when she was trying to meet friends under Magnus's nose and he was making it difficult for her to go off itinerary. He's such an asshole—well, you probably know," and Nicodema grunted. "She'll probably sneak away in the next day or two, and once she's got a little rebellion in, the nerves should stop. If she's still nervous two days from now, then something's wrong and you should get backup and run for the airport. Otherwise just keep your distance, and watch out for Magnus."

"What about Ethan?"

He'd assumed Ethan had his own snap—he was A-list, and Daniel just figured Li Zhao had made plans for coverage and not told anyone else. (Hiring freelancers for an assignment this big would be weird, but Daniel couldn't fault Li Zhao for avoiding whatever grief he'd give anyone she hired in-house.) But Nicodema was covering them both, and he wasn't going to waste a gift.

"Oh. Well, if it comes down to choosing, follow him. She's not going to do anything to risk that contract, but he's better off. He might have something going on the side. If he does, we should know."

Lying directly was so much more productive than being relayed through techs. No wonder Li Zhao forbade it.

Somewhere behind him, Martine was drowning her guilt and waiting for the morning, when Ansfrida would pick her up and they'd drive away from the mountains and the scrub and the facility Martine hadn't been allowed to even see.

She wasn't used to being denied admission. She must be furious. If he approached her now, when she was half-drunk and angry, she might tell him anything. But Martine wasn't his problem, and he didn't dare look away from Margot. It had surprised Bo that she was changing her plans. Nothing about Margot should have been able to surprise Bo. Something big had changed. Whatever she was going to do, she'd decided, and there was no point waiting around.

10

At the door to her mother's building, Ethan took her hand (it was clammy, she was ashamed of herself, there was no reason to be nervous, it was her own mother).

"You know," he said, glancing up at the tower of glass, "I think I need to swing by someplace and get a cup of coffee first. Can I bring you anything? It might be cold by the time I walk back, fair warning."

Magnus had barely been able to talk the American cameras out of coming to take photos of the three of them having a family reunion; it was still definitely meant to be a visit for them both. Suyana had been given no time alone with her mother, officially.

He was hiding something—he was running his thumb absently across the side of her finger, he only did that when he was in the middle of a lie—but she couldn't guess what it was, and she was too grateful to ask.

She turned into his chest and had wrapped her free arm around him before she could think better of it, and it must have been different from most of their embraces, because he hesitated a moment like she'd startled him before he hugged her back.

"Go on," he said into her hair after a moment. "She's been waiting a long time to see you."

Fondness choked her, anger choked her, relief choked her. "Enjoy your coffee," she said, sounding to her own ears like she was already miles away, and she watched him until he disappeared from sight.

She stood a moment longer, steeling herself, until she caught a glimpse of the woman—early thirties, sturdy-looking, careful red lipstick, clothes deliberately nondescript—who hovered between steps a moment before she moved to follow Ethan, turning slowly so as not to jostle the camera.

Her mother answered the door with the smile she always wore for the UARC photographers on their annual visit to her apartment to record an evening-news Happy Birthday to her daughter—fixed, polite, beatific. Her graying hair was pulled back in a braid, and she wore some clothes that Magnus must have sent ahead new, because she was tugging on the hem of her blouse even as she started her greeting in English.

When she saw that Suyana was alone, her expression dropped into the smile Suyana remembered, smaller and closer to real.

"Daughter," she said in Quechua, and Suyana was surprised she remembered the word; it fell through her, clattering against her ribs.

Suyana hugged her (she was as tall as her mother, when had that happened?), said, "I hope you're well" in Spanish, and then, before her mother could answer her, "Do people visit you? Your friends?"

Are you lonely, she couldn't ask. Are you sick? Do you miss me? Don't say you miss me, it couldn't be true. I'm not even the daughter you said good-bye to a decade ago. You're my mother, can't you tell?

Her mother nodded yes, stepped out of the hug like she was shy, and gestured vaguely into the living room. It was large and light, and Magnus must have continued to bribe whoever Hakan had originally bribed to get her this apartment, because the paint was fresh and the furniture was new. Her mother looked rested and healthy, and that was good. It made Suyana less guilty.

"Come sit," her mother said after a silence awkwardly

long. "I made lunch. I thought your boyfriend would be here—is this too much food? Is he not coming?"

She meant, Did I do something? Suyana's throat was tight. "No, he's coming. He'll be here soon. Sit down and tell me everything."

Her mother was well fed. Her mother had joined a church committee to organize a school for children in the slums outside town. Her mother had gone to the Heritage Festival during the summer. She was thinking of going to see Machu Picchu with three of the women from her church.

"I've always wanted to see it," her mother said, and Suyana thought about the postcards in the town square when she was too young to understand anything at all, except the anger that sometimes pooled in her fingertips when she thought about her mother.

"It will be beautiful," she said, made her smile wider than it needed to be. "I'll get you a new camera to take with you."

Her mother demurred—Suyana did enough, it was already too much—but her mouth turned up at one edge. Suyana nodded, falsely solemn, said that maybe she would just look, just to see if there was a camera on sale somewhere.

The bell rang.

"That's Ethan," Suyana said, standing as her mother stood, but her mother put a hand on her shoulder so firmly that she sat back down. From this angle, her mother's eyes were as sharp as she remembered.

"Is he the reason you're unhappy?"

Suyana couldn't breathe. She couldn't feel the tips of her fingers. Her spine was going to fall to pieces. She was ten years old, and all her skill at lying escaped her.

"No," she said.

And it must have been true, or true enough, because after a moment her mother nodded, and went to open the door.

Later, in bed, she said, "Thank you."

"You're welcome," Ethan said, in the lecherous drawl he only used when he was teasing, and she flicked him on the shoulder so hard he yelped through his laughter.

She'd tried to think of it as an operation, at the beginning. To go through the motions she'd seen in movies (and in the other sort of movies) and play at it all. It had been pure, clinically productive in its strangeness—she felt remote and sharp during sex, noting responses and trying to decide how to set a pattern that could sustain itself for however long this contract needed to go on.

But the day had come when he moved his hands somewhere and breathed something into her skin and it all felt better, felt *more*, and now the line between Necessary and her own weakness was a lot less clean.

It was still useful, she told herself often. Lying all the time means you have no room for error. If you both believe something enough, then your mark will start making excuses if they catch you in a mistake. ("Strange girl," Ethan said sometimes, early on, when she'd broken the lovebird act with a direct question or a stony face. Then he'd shake his head fondly, lean in to kiss her temple, and go to bed beside her. He'd never had a troubled night's sleep, not once in a year.)

"I mean it," she said. "It was good to see my mother. Thank you."

He blinked over at her, trying to smother a yawn. "Did she like me?"

"Everyone likes you, Ethan. Go to sleep."

He snorted. "So she hated me."

Suyana rested her hand across Ethan's eyes. He laughed quietly, just his shoulders shaking against the mattress for a second, before he closed his eyes. His eyelashes brushed the palm of her hand.

Her mother actually hadn't said a word about Ethan, who had been careful to go downstairs early and call the car too, to give them a few more minutes together. Her mother had just taken her by the shoulders and looked at her a long time. She didn't say she was saving up, but it had been five years, and might be five more, so far as her mother knew.

Suyana had let her mother look; she knew more about her chances of coming home again.

At the outdoor folk music concert someone arranged for their last night in Lima, Suyana and Ethan stood at the front of the crowd like it was a pleasant festival they'd just stumbled upon and they were enjoying it too much to even see the cameras.

It was a night full of acting. The two men behind them pretended not to be UARC police, and the crowd pretended Suyana and Ethan were just like them, that no one had been searched on their way in to make sure they weren't carrying any political paraphernalia.

The Americans rented a conference suite in the nearest hotel as a staging area. Oona had made sure to take up as much space on the table as Ethan's team, even though she'd only brought two outfits. When Magnus raised an eyebrow at the light packing, Oona had said, "Well, *some* people are able to make a decision early and know what will look good," and then had pointedly finished slapping Suyana's belt buckle shut. It was as big as Suyana's hand, and it locked in place with a sound like a prison door.

Magnus had watched Suyana in the mirror, glancing past her every so often to where Ethan's team was sweeping his face with powder, carefully smudging black pencil at the edges of his eyes.

(Whenever his team did that, Ethan scraped his knuckles there before following her to bed, like he hoped she'd think he was a different person in bed than he was when he smiled for the cameras. If she was sure there was a difference between the two, she might have found it revealing. If she cared about him, she might have found it affecting. She liked him better with it on.)

She caught Ethan's gaze in the mirror and smiled when he smiled. But it was the flat one he gave when he wanted to end a conversation, and when Ethan couldn't see her any more, she'd looked Magnus in the eye until he looked away.

Then Suyana had lifted Oona's pass card from the back of the chair and tucked it inside the belt, and on the way out of the hotel and through the handful of autograph-seekers, she had passed it to the woman wearing a Dolphin Watch sweatshirt who handed her the map she'd autographed for Sotalia and said, "Sign it for Maria, please."

Suyana waited nearly two hours, swaying in time with the crowd, not really hearing any of the music (trying especially hard not to hear the one or two songs that reminded her of home). When everyone seemed lulled but not yet bored, she ducked out of the festivities, waving Ethan and Oona to stay.

Even then, a bodyguard followed her straight through the lobby and down the hall until she cleared her throat and asked if he'd particularly mind standing outside the conference suite while she handled her personal affairs. As soon as he guessed her meaning, he hemmed and stammered in that way men often did when women talked about bodily functions, and took up a very studious position in front of the outer door.

Sotalia was waiting in the conference room bathroom, well out of sight of the main door, sitting on the counter and swinging her legs idly. She wore a maid's uniform, and there was a cleaning trolley beside her.

"Just in case," she said when Suyana looked her over, and turned on the water in the sink. Sotalia was young. Suyana didn't quite know what to make of someone so young being the contact for an operation as dangerous as this, but Columbina had seemed sure of her. Her dark hair was shot through with red in the sickly light from the bathroom, like the plumage of a bird.

(The last contact Suyana had met on home soil had vanished—prison or dead, Zenaida never told her. He had been expendable; contacts always were. Suyana was the constant they risked it for. If she came back again, and there was more work that needed doing, it wouldn't be Sotalia. Sotalia would be long gone.)

"I couldn't get much," Suyana said, and rolled out the length of paper towel, sketching the rise of the hills in concentric circles.

After a few marks for the trees, Sotalia said, "Is it really that close to the forest? They must be serious about pretending they care."

"It looks that way," Suyana said, her stomach pulling tight, suddenly, from doubt. "The mud flat faces the entrance approach, but they keep most of the seeds right above the entry pod."

Sotalia looked at her, skeptical. "So what? We should be careful not to set the charges there when we burn the building down?"

Suyana took a breath, straightened up. Not that she had much full height to draw up to, but she was taller than Sotalia. "You shouldn't set charges anywhere yet. I talked with one of the administrators, and I think we should wait until they've gotten the first planting in, to hold back the erosion. The erosion is a bigger threat than the red tape right now. I want this to be a reconnaissance mission."

"I beg your pardon?"

"They're getting sponsors to buy enough plants to slow down the erosion. If they mean it, then the planting needs to happen first. And if they do it in good faith, then maybe they're serious about conservation. I think you need to wait and see."

Sotalia folded her arms. "Yes, of course, I had forgotten

the meeting where we decided to believe everything we were told by the people in charge."

"I'm not saying trust them. I'm saying wait. It's at least structured for conservation—it's messy and we have to be careful before we let them get away with patents or anything permanent, but—"

"And I remember how the mining outpost was supposed to create jobs that would make it worth all the trees they were tearing down."

"They aren't some American mining company," Suyana hissed.

"It's outsiders trying to make money off the forest! There's no difference between one outpost and another!"

Too young for this, Suyana thought. Reckless. Her hands were beginning to shake. She pressed them harder against the counter. "Maybe no one's told you my connection to the last group of outsiders."

"Oh," said Sotalia, with weight. Her dark eyes glittered. "No, don't worry, Lachesis. I know who you are."

Acid rose in her throat. The last man who did what you're doing is gone, she wanted to say. The last time I did this, I was sure it needed to be done (I'm still sure, surer than I am of this, surer than I am of anything now). The last time this happened, I lost the only man I trusted in the world. Don't ever say my name like you don't think I earned it.

What she said was, "Then you can be damn sure I know the difference."

Without looking away, she slid the paper under her hand sideways, right under the water. It ran over her fingers, ice cold, and it would take care of the ink.

"I have specifics," she said. "I have the names of the plants they're hoping to patent—that has to be stopped, and I would think that's something Chordata would be interested in. I know the facility layout, and their timeline, and their potential. And you won't be getting any of it until I can be sure you know the difference, too."

On her way out, she scooped her tablet off the table, just in case Sotalia got any ideas about procuring information the hard way.

Tell me I'm not a coward, she thought to Hakan as she met her bodyguard and walked through the lobby with a marble floor that cost more than some towns made in a year. Tell me I'm not doing this just to spare my mother; tell me I'm right to believe that letting someone pay to assuage their guilt in exchange for good press isn't just some lesser devil. Tell me there's still a believer left somewhere, and not just a shell that looks like me.

The singer onstage was finishing a lesser Yma Sumac song when she got back. Suyana slid back into place, nudged tight alongside Ethan by the crowd, and caught the final key-change chorus in time to applaud the soprano. The soprano's nerves looked like they had returned the instant the singing stopped, and she nearly tripped trying to bow and smile at the same time.

"Poor thing," said Suyana. "Why would she be so nervous when she can sing like that?"

"Because she knew what was coming," said Ethan, his voice falling out of hearing just at the last, and Suyana didn't understand why until she'd processed that he was kneeling, that he was holding a ring, that the singer was still onstage behind the mic and waiting to say something. To sing something. Everyone was waiting.

Ethan was looking at her, a smile tugging at the corners of his mouth, but amid the hundred flashbulbs that had gone off, she could see the crow's feet that tensed around his eyes when he was nervous and thought he was in the wrong.

He'd gone for coffee, he said when she was alone with her mother. He'd been strange since they got back from the research facility. She'd known Margot must have called him, and had assumed the worst.

Turned out Margot could still outdo her.

"Suyana Sapaki, will you marry me?" he asked, and the crowd went wild (her answer didn't matter, she didn't have an answer, she had a given), and she looked over at Magnus's ghostly face and out at the sea of people behind them and down at Ethan, whose hand was beginning to tremble. She looked at the smooth column of his neck and thought, That's where the knife would go, if I carried one—I could use my knife and run for it, and you wouldn't know any different.

She said, "Of course I will."

11

Daniel spent three days shadowing Martine through New York.

"We're still deciding who to assign as her new regular," Li Zhao had told him, and he thought of Hannah, taking pictures of Martine filing her nails in Assembly sessions and heading out clubbing for years, removed as soon as things got interesting.

Not that Martine was interesting. That was the point.

None of the Big Nine had much public personality—when you were Big Nine, you didn't need one—but Martine's was the only one that felt cultivated. There had always been a sense of deliberation in how inert she was, even back when he was first doing research for Hae Soo-jin's press pit. Not that he blamed her. The IA was unstable. Martine was trying to be a block of marble amid electric wires.

But Daniel watched her wrap her huge scarf around her neck—she vanished above it, glossy lips and a pretty face and nothing else—and thought about Suyana telling him she had to go home but had no way to get there. Then she'd gone out with Grace and Martine for a single night, and suddenly the path had opened.

Martine got coffee, and went to museums and absorbed culture like she was supposed to, and spent most of her time alone. Ansfrida hardly ever went with her. It took him two days to realize that was the normal run of things, and not some strange negligence on Ansfrida's part. His first guess was that Martine had someone on the side, but Martine never used the solitude to contact anyone. She'd had one lunch with Kipa, but only New Zealand's cameras were there—they were the ones getting the favor—and it was just tacos from a truck a few blocks south of the IA offices.

After that, Martine took Kipa to a matinee (some action movie where Martine spoke to Kipa every time the shooting started and Daniel couldn't catch a word) and then dropped Kipa back at the offices like dry cleaning. Martine didn't so much as step onto the sidewalk in front of the IA, and she spent the rest of the day walking up Madison and down Fifth, pretending to shop and not buying a thing.

He sent a marker to Bonnaire, flagging her hesitation at the IA border for review. Was she wanted in another country, and couldn't leave United States soil? (Wasn't hard to imagine her wearing out her welcome somewhere.) Was everything all right, and this empty fishbowl of a calendar just what it meant to be powerful in a place that asked nothing else of you except to do as you were told?

He didn't buy it. Martine was lying low. He just didn't know what for.

"What did Li Zhao think of it? Am I looking for a pattern with Martine? What's her plan?"

Kate *ooh, mm-hmm*'ed like a nagging aunt. "Daniel, Li Zhao fainted from the excitement of it all, just as soon as she heard."

Dev snickered. "Li Zhao hasn't—" he started, then paused before he said, "We don't know if there's a pattern yet."

Daniel imagined Kate waving Dev silent, wondered what exactly *Li Zhao hadn't*, what plans he was excluded from.

Martine conducted no business at all for two days, meeting other people only after the sun was down and she was wearing sequins like chain mail. Then, with the cameras on, she grinned and gnawed her cigarette and pulled back her hair so tight it scraped her skull. She'd go out in a knot of the Big Nine, and when they reached whatever ridiculously dim club it was, she'd leave them all in the VIP section and dance in the center of the crowd, eyes closed, where nobody could reach her.

By the third night, he'd started sending emergency messages to Bo. Whatever this was, he wasn't going to sit through it alone.

This is the weirdest beat. I'm tailing a cloud

Hold until further notice.

Has Margot moved on anything? Feels like Martine's waiting for something

Negative, follow and hold.

Has the boss gotten someone for this job yet?

Negative.

Have we heard from Suyana? Did Nicodema say anything?

Negative.

She's going to another club, Bo. Request cover

Cover unnecessary, follow and hold.

Cover urgently requested, I can't stay up until 3 a.m. again tailing her

I'll cover at 1:30. Give me coordinates.

At Hypatia. May be forced to engage mark if cover not available by 1 a.m.

Negative, follow and hold.

Confirmed, visual contact maintained, I'm waving

Not sure if you're joking, given your track record.

Fuck you

She says hi

This won't get you removed from assignment early.

Beg to differ, hope you're showing the boss

Bo, Martine's beautiful, I want to marry her, I'll send you a pic-
ture of us in a second we look really good

Bo, I bought her a drink, that's still professional, right?

I'm going to go meet all her friends, when whatever news the boss
is waiting for breaks, you let me know

I'm going to go dance with Martine come find me when you get here

We're married now, we didn't invite you

Daniel, there's news about Suyana.

It wasn't news. It was terrifying and all wrong, but it wasn't
news. News surprised you.

Suyana had told him as much about seven months
back, when he'd lost his temper—who knew why, it was the
end of a short meeting, he hadn't been patient even when
she still looked like there was a soul inside her—and asked
how she thought this fucking contract relationship was
going to end.

And she'd looked right at him (he'd turned an inch away
from her, pressed his hand against his eye socket so hard it
stung) and said, "Retirement."

A wretched word—a word years away—but it was a
comfort. The worst wouldn't happen; there wouldn't be a

wedding. There was never a wedding. Marriage was much too permanent a statement for two Faces in good standing. You wanted a life of international possibility that kept you exciting to the public, of use to your country, and sold magazines. You had a physical clause to protect each country from accusations of intent to tamper (like Faces were cars whose warranties had to be obeyed; he'd laughed when he read it). Marriage was for after no one cared who you were sleeping with.

She'd looked like she doubted she'd make it that far. Daniel had tried to ignore it. That was seven months ago, when he'd had hope of success understanding her.

This was just an engagement. It was a ring and official portraits and a few sets of candids of them at second base in a nightclub. It was a promise that would keep Suyana out from under suspicion, that was all.

The publicity shit could go on for a year. Suyana planning a wedding. Suyana announcing a honeymoon destination they'd never see while ten thousand people dropped their magazines and dove for their phones to make bookings. Suyana taking the UARC photographers with her to try on wedding dresses for Magnus to look at and debate and decide on, while Daniel stood outside and watched without moving until it was all over.

× × × × × × ×

The third day, Grace came to visit Martine.

Daniel stood across the street and watched her duck into Martine's building, which required a staff badge at too many places for him to sneak around inside. He was debating the best way to make himself scarce and still be able to clock Grace's departure when Martine lifted the shades on the living room window, seven floors up, and looked right at him.

He tried not to laugh. Now Grace on top of it all. She'd probably already known. She'd probably seen him in Terrain a year ago when he made a scene with Suyana, and he imagined even Martine would be loath to keep a secret as choice as knowing where their biggest press leak was always coming from.

Off to the side, beyond the scope of his temple camera, he waved waist-high.

Grace raised her eyebrows and was smiling carefully in another direction as she pulled back and out of sight, calm and practiced as even Magnus could wish for. Martine stared until the shade was drawn. He couldn't tell if it was a warning, or if there were some things she didn't see the point in lying about any more.

It was the marriage news that had required such an off-book meeting, he'd bet money on it. For all they pretended to be above the machinations of C-listers who needed to date somebody to score enough notice for their causes, Grace and

Martine knew what it meant when the American Face was planning an alliance with a country that had risen so quickly through the ranks. Suyana was going to become an ally or a threat, and they were in there deciding which.

"So, before you became a snap and were still crawling around after Suyana," Kate's voice came over the comm, "how many Faces did you actually introduce yourself to? Is this the end of the list, or are there twenty more who would wave at you if they saw you coming?"

"As soon as it costs me a scoop instead of getting me better access to information, I'm sure Li Zhao will be very put out about it all," Daniel said, and turned off the comm.

Bo tapped him on the shoulder half an hour later.

"You're relieved," he said. "They kept trying to tell you, but your connection was down. You can't just take it off-line when you're angry." He looked like a disappointed schoolteacher, which was probably unfair, but so was asking Daniel to keep his comm on all the time if Kate was at the other end.

Then he realized what it meant if Bo was here, and frowned. "So where's Margot?"

"At home. She's covered. Kate apparently had some things to say about you, and I didn't want to listen to it until your time was up. You're off for the night."

"Oh." Daniel's mind was racing. Something was wrong. Someone was missing. "When does Suyana get back?"

"She lands tomorrow morning, early. You're back on duty six a.m., LaGuardia. Get some rest." Bo's mouth thinned to a single line. "And maybe work a little on keeping a safe distance."

"We can't all be invisible," he said.

"It's not their notice we're worried about. It's their handlers hunting us down."

We. Sure. Daniel tried to look solemn. "Okay. I'll stay back from the happy couple. Grace is still up there. No idea if they have plans to leave—Martine's schedule has been strange, but they've been seen in public recently enough that they might not need more visibility. Seventh floor, third window from the left."

Bo nodded, eyes already forward. "Get going. Keep in touch. We'll call if something comes up."

Daniel slid on his baseball cap and took the route that approached Margot's building from the park, where there were more crowds and better cover. Margot's windows faced the courtyard and the garden, but the front door and the freight entrance both faced the street. Any coverage would come from there.

Li Zhao was sitting at the coffee shop at the far corner, sipping on a cappuccino and pretending to read a book, and he knew the line of her back a block before he ever reached her.

He'd thought she considered herself above fieldwork. He'd definitely thought she considered herself above a camera implant. He'd never for a moment imagined she'd ever leave Paris just to keep watch on someone who cut a trip a few days short. This whole story must be something pretty big.

It was nice to feel right about something.

"Martine lives across from a jewelry store," he said quietly, when he was close enough. "Suyana's across from an office and a bank. I'd kill for a coffee shop cover."

"Goddammit," said Kate over the comm, and when Li Zhao turned around, Daniel was still smiling.

"Hey, boss."

Li Zhao was smiling too, that impeccable lipstick tipped up on one side. "Daniel. You look tired."

"You made me look after the Queen of the Night for two weeks, of course I'm tired." He gestured at the farthest seat before he took it, as much warning as he was willing to give. In her office he'd never dare sit without being asked, but the streets of a neutral city felt like a compromise, and his legs were beginning to shake.

"That's why I sent Bo to relieve you."

"I've never been relieved and then told to go home. Do you know how suspicious that sounds?"

She sighed. "I didn't expect Bo to be quite that obvious about it, but that would explain why you're here."

"Sure." He grinned. "But not why *you're* here."

"We have twenty-seven employees in New York. There's been a lot of upheaval. I wanted to make sure nothing fell apart before Paris."

He was too aware of his lips against his teeth. "Yeah, but this is Margot's place, not your office. I think Bo's at Martine's building because something's going to happen soon, and you don't want anyone else hunting your favorite big game."

Li Zhao finished her coffee and tucked her hair behind her ear, fingers pressing her temple.

"Kate," she said, "turn off the incoming sound on Daniel's equipment. I'll contact you to reactivate."

Of course her own equipment could be turned off locally. The benefits of running the place.

"Are you sure?"

"Thank you, Kate, that will be all."

"I'd be nicer to her," he said after a few seconds. "She's mean, but she's loyal. She's been helping you since you changed your name, right?"

Li Zhao kept her eyes on the doors of Margot's building, but she sat back a few inches in her chair, until Daniel could just see a sliver of her profile, and could tell when she looked at him because the white ice chip of her iris would turn suddenly black.

"And don't tell me—you know what name I changed it from."

What a flattering assumption. He wished Bo were here

to listen to Daniel moving up in her estimation. He also wished he had an amazing theory, some detective work he could unfurl to make this moment actually worth it. But after a year of watching Suyana work, he'd learned the difference between noticing things and making connections—the latter was above his pay grade.

Still, he could do what Suyana did, and suggest whatever would get the most out of the mark. Daniel should know how to do that; he'd watched Suyana do it enough.

"No idea. But I figure Margot could probably tell me who you used to be, if she ever saw you."

Li Zhao shifted her weight slightly, uncrossing her ankles for more balance.

"Probably not," she said, after he'd given up hope of an answer. "I didn't make it very long, and Margot doesn't waste a lot of time on Faces who lack stamina."

He knew she'd been IA material—he'd known for a while—but hearing was always another thing.

"I lasted eight months before China went to war with Russia. Nobody told me. My handler nearly fainted when she heard. And Russia had a trade agreement with Norway—it was a long time ago, I forget what it was, maybe a relationship contract or maybe just some understanding. Margot had gotten onto the Peacekeeping Committee already, before the war even broke out."

Daniel glanced up at the sleek tower. Margot was on the far side, free of any prying eyes. She planned ahead.

"After it was over, the Peacekeeping Committee recommended the Faces from China and the Hong Kong Territories be retired, and no new ones be appointed for two years. While those seats were inactive, the Trade Committee passed as many sanctions as they could. Took us ten years to crawl out of that hole."

Daniel's throat was dry. Suyana was in a plane flying across international lines, coming back to present herself as a threat to Margot.

He managed, "As in, retired? Or . . ." There was another inflection you could give *retired* that meant something else entirely, but he couldn't make his lips move. It didn't matter. Her handler had taken her into the middle of nowhere a long time ago, and either Li Zhao had been sent to safety by a sympathetic soul, or her handler had tried to retire her, and he could guess how that had gone.

She raised her hand, asked for another coffee from the waiter when he arrived, smiled at him; her smile alone explained why the young man wouldn't be staying long enough for a coffee of his own.

When they were alone, she said, "Go home."

"I'm not tired."

"If you're not there to cover Suyana at six a.m. when she

lands, you've lost the assignment and I'll give her to someone else. Don't pretend—stop *looking* at me, watch the doors."

But he couldn't move. The hair on the back of his neck was standing up. "You're not following Margot just for the hope of some candid shots when some scandal breaks, are you?"

The coffee came. Li Zhao shook two packets of sugar into it, took a sip, added another.

"Li Zhao—"

"She's excellent. The best there's been since the Assembly was formed, maybe. Born for it. She looks like the sun whenever you hand her a problem. Have you noticed?"

He'd followed for a few hours once, a long time ago. "Yeah."

Li Zhao wiped her lipstick off the rim of the cup without looking at it, one clean swipe. The coffee was half gone.

"But she made a mistake, building the Central Committee into such a monopoly and putting herself at the head. Now there are liaisons for agriculture and public relations and environmental concerns and peacekeeping who all do nothing. And the Intelligence scarecrow retired ten years back, and she thinks no one noticed when she started taking that over, but she's wrong. A dictatorship only ever ends one way."

For the length of a breath, Daniel's nose filled with the smell of glass cleaner from the audience balcony above the

International Assembly audience hall, where he'd stood for the better part of a year at the far edge of the first row because that had the best view of Suyana's seat, and it had the best view of Margot when she turned to look at Suyana like she was waiting for poison to take hold.

"And that's what we're selling."

"The revolution will sell itself," said Li Zhao. "People won't even notice what it does to their countries. They'll just read the news and look for relationships that appeal to them and make bets about who wins."

And a year ago, Suyana had caught their attention out of nowhere when she made a move on the American Face, and Li Zhao got a glimpse of her ambition.

"Wait. You think it's going to be Suyana?"

Li Zhao set down the coffee carefully and spared him a glance—as much as she could without losing the mark.

"No. Whatever secret you two are keeping, it's bigger than her place in the IA. She'll be a martyr. She looks good for that."

A car drove by. It felt like the first car in a long time. How long had they been sitting in silence? The streets were wet; was it raining?

"Does Bo know about all this?"

"Of course. We have to be prepared to record whatever happens."

Of course—Bo knew exactly what had happened to

Suyana, and who was behind it. He'd seen more than any of the rest of them had. And since then Bo had kept him in sight and in line, so he would be calm when the mutiny started and Daniel was following around the first person they expected to die.

Kate didn't know. Kate was sitting in a basement in Paris right now, in silence, waiting for the word that she could start listening again. Was she even waiting? He wouldn't have waited for permission to listen in; Kate wouldn't either. He had to get to her. Or to Dev—Dev might give in and tell him what he needed to know. Dev could help. Someone had to help.

"Bullshit."

"Which part?"

"You didn't fly here from Paris just to take a few night shifts with Margot," he said, and then halfway through he realized and finished, "Because you were already in New York."

Her smile was less victorious than it could have been. "I don't think anything will happen until Paris, but after the last-minute arrangements, I thought something might be happening that Margot was trying to get away from. As it happened, she was making other plans, but still, it's good to see New York again."

Other plans. He'd seen the pictures of Suyana accepting the proposal. Ethan looked almost as confused about why he was proposing as he looked confused about why she'd ever say yes. Suyana hadn't looked confused, not for one second; when she'd reached up to kiss him afterward, she'd wrapped her arms so tight around his neck you couldn't see her face at all.

The coffee cup was empty now, and far down the avenue Daniel could see a glimpse of neon, where some diner or some drugstore was open late. Margot's building blotted out the moon.

Daniel stood. "Well, enjoy your evening."

Li Zhao looked up at him then, the full force of her gaze like he hadn't seen since the first time she'd brought him into her office and threatened his family until he could be convinced to talk business.

"Don't think you can warn her that she's trapped. It's too late."

Daniel went rigid. "Because it's bad form to alert the wildlife?"

But Li Zhao wasn't angry. She looked surprised, and maybe a little disappointed. He didn't know why—he'd never been a strategist like some.

"Because," she said, "Suyana already knows."

12

They landed ten minutes early. By six o'clock they were already on the ground with the door open and the first of the flashbulbs going off from the ground, and it was too late to take off again when Magnus sucked in a breath through his teeth and said on the wobbly exhale, "Oh my God, they've struck the facility."

"What," said Suyana, though it wasn't really a question. It was barely a word.

The American handlers were out of their chairs as soon as he spoke, headed down the stairs to try and make the cameras scatter. Stevens was trying to get Ethan out of his seat, saying, "We should get you inside," and Suyana was vaguely

aware of Ethan's face solidifying into something like deter-
mination as he said, "What's happening?" without moving
a muscle to leave.

"Chordata," Magnus said to him, and then, with a look at
Suyana, "They struck the facility while we were on the plane.
A security guard's in the hospital."

"IA security or local security?" Stevens cut in. Suyana
was grateful; it saved her a question she would have no good
reason to ask.

"Local," said Magnus, and Stevens looked relieved and
beckoned Ethan forward, having cleared themselves from
the last remnants of responsibility. Suyana knew better what
that implied—"Terrorist Organization Disregards Lives
of Locals, Breeds Discontent," the news would say, and
"Murderers Out for Blood on the Amazon," and "Sapaki Has
Sweet Romance Amid National Disaster."

Magnus was looking desperately at his tablet, typing so
fast his fingers were a blur. Suyana's skin prickled; it was cold,
with the door open.

There was a pain in her ribs she could barely draw breath
around it burned so much, and it was so terribly cold. She
reached for the armrest, but her hand was shaking, and she
pulled it back. She felt like she was in an alley, all at once, and
closed her eyes and opened them again just to orient herself.
There wasn't time to panic; she couldn't panic.

"We should get inside," she said.

"Of course," said Magnus, and moved to help her up. (Had he seen her hands? Could he guess? Oh God, she thought, don't let him guess. That was what happened to Hakan.)

But Ethan reached her first, one arm gently around her waist and the other hand resting on her elbow, so light she hardly felt it. "Are you okay to make it down the stairs?"

When she glanced up, she couldn't quite meet Ethan's eye, but his mouth was set in a thin line directed at Stevens, who looked like he was trying not to have a heart attack about all the bad press.

"Ethan," Stevens said as they reached the door, "it's best if Suyana and Magnus handle this themselves."

"Brave sentiment," said Magnus from behind them, but Ethan was closer and holding her close, and when he said, "Suyana is my fiancée," it hummed against her ribs.

It could mean anything. It could just be good PR. These days he was proving better at that than she'd ever given him credit for.

Magnus cut in front of her and lay down strafing fire of "No comment."

"You can let go, I'm all right, it's all right," she said just before she stepped out onto the stairs, just for something to say that would make Ethan stop looking at her the way he was looking at her.

The arm around her waist vanished. The hand on her

elbow never did, all the way down the stairs, as she took careful steps and then walked without looking left or right all the way down the narrow aisle toward the cars that had pulled up out of nowhere.

Suyana looked up at the windows of the airport, where crowds were lined up taking photos and gawping. Some of them looked mortified enough to have heard the news and be pitying or blaming her. Several just seemed excited that their early flights had gotten them the first glimpse of the engaged couple on American soil.

Only a few weren't taking pictures. Only one didn't even have a camera in his hand.

Daniel was a wreck—she could see from a hundred feet away the dark circles under his eyes, his stricken expression, his mouth nearly slack from disbelief.

She dropped her gaze, shook her head tightly, once, at nothing at all.

It wasn't me. I didn't let them. I didn't even show them. I told them not to do it, and they didn't care. They've broken with me; I broke faith with no one, it's just broken.

Ethan guided her into the car and sat beside her, twined their fingers.

"It's going to be okay," he said, like a doctor on a television show—something they said because they were told to, with no idea about the real disease.

She ignored it, leaned back in her seat, and let the cold leather absorb the heat of her anger.

"Magnus. What did Margot say?"

He glanced up at her a second too early to hide his surprise. "She'd like to see us in the offices, immediately."

Ethan frowned. "I can come with you."

She looked at him. "Was she the one who suggested you propose?"

There was a short, deep silence. She pulled her hand out of his, turned back to Magnus.

"I need to go home first," she said. "I shouldn't show up tired and grimy right off a plane; she'd love that."

"There's a risk in delaying."

"There will be statements, probably. If this is going to be my last day, should I look like this? I need twenty minutes at home."

Magnus's skin seemed pulled too tight across his skull, as if even the idea of disobedience pressed against him from the inside, but he was watching her solemnly, and he said, "All right."

It took her one minute to contact Columbina, four minutes to shower, two minutes to claim she needed something personal from the pharmacy and get Magnus to agree on the anonymity of her jacket and scarf, and another minute to make it to the stoop three blocks away, where Columbina was waiting.

"Was it you?" Suyana said while she was still walking, her voice rougher than she'd thought she had in her. Columbina was standing up, one hand gripping the stone rail.

"They told me you'd given them information—"

"That was a conservation facility! It was going to cause problems, there were going to be problems later, but nothing a warning shot right now was going to solve! I told Sotalia—I didn't even give her anything—it was too soon, there were still questions. I wanted to get more information. I told her not to do anything. I *told* her. And now they—it's gone, and I have to go in and—" She scrubbed her hand across her face.

"I'm sorry, Aurelia." Columbina's expression was grim.

Suyana's throat went tight. "Aurelia?"

"We thought it was safest to separate your old contact name after the strike, since—I mean, because—"

"Because you acted without my permission."

"Because it wasn't safe to keep your old name after this. We've never had anyone..."

Who'd lived through something this destructive. They were used to cutting losses and starting over.

"And you named me Aurelia? I see."

Aurelia: jellyfish, transparent and mindless. You took my name, she thought, hollow, and for a second she saw

Zenaida's face as Suyana told her about the viper she wanted to be named for; a snake from home, a risk, something to remember her by.

"They didn't tell me they were going to move."

"How's the man they hurt?"

"He'll make it. I think."

"Jesus." Her fists sank in her pockets, pulled at her shoulders. "If they ask me to denounce Chordata as terrorists, I'm going to."

Columbina paled. "Why would they make you do that?"

"They asked me to do it last time, back when I still thought we were on the same side. I refused. If they ask me this time, I'm going to have to say yes, or they'll realize I know, or I am, Chordata's inside source." She didn't blink, didn't dare. "It's Chordata's fault I'm here. You acted without me, and it ruined an opportunity we needed for the forest. This is supposed to all be for the forest, not for yourselves."

"Aurelia, please."

"Don't call me that."

"You're not the arbiter of those decisions—"

"If my judgment has no weight, neither does my information."

Columbina was holding very still. "That's a dangerous thing to say."

"It's only dangerous to me if Chordata is actually terrorists. That's up to you to figure out—I'm not the arbiter of those decisions." Suyana pulled her scarf higher. "If I don't make it, we'll know why. Tell Zenaida that Lachesis was thinking of her just before they killed me."

She turned and started back for her building. She had four minutes.

Daniel was waiting for her outside a closed storefront, locked and dark, and when he saw her coming he brushed his hair down over the camera.

He didn't reach out for her; he hadn't touched her at all, in a year. He looked her up and down, frowned at the ring on her finger, frowned at the look on her face.

"What do you know?" she breathed.

He smiled without any humor in it, and shook his head, and the words came out less like he was trying to keep quiet and more like he was having to force even this much air through his throat. "Margot will end you if she can. Do whatever you have to. Keep an eye out for Martine. If it's life or death, find Bo."

She nodded, stepped back, wanted to say something (get some sleep, I'm so sorry, stay away from me, it isn't safe), but it was already over and time was going; she broke into a run, didn't look behind her.

× × × × × × ×

Margot's offices were the second-highest floor of the IA office tower, all windows, and big enough for a glass-walled conference room that could seat ten. Margot at one end of such a huge table looked almost lonely, Suyana thought as she and Magnus walked in. Margot probably wanted it that way. More mystique if you struck a tragic figure.

The unsmiling receptionist showed them in—they didn't rate a manager coming to greet them—and Margot raised her eyebrows at Suyana's wet hair and severe gray dress.

"Well, glad to see that no international terrorist incident on your home soil is enough to keep you from looking your best, Suyana. Magnus, always a pleasure."

Suyana made a pleasant face that stopped short of a smile as she took a seat. "We wanted to give the incident the solemnity it deserves. It would have been disrespectful to come directly from the airport in casual clothes, when something so terrible has happened."

There was hardly a flicker over Margot's face—she'd been doing this a long time—but Suyana knew she'd scored a point, because Margot's next words were unrelated: "The UARC has embarrassed itself. This is the second time in your brief tenure with us that terrorists have struck the United Amazonian Rainforest Confederation shortly after one of your visits. What exactly is it you're saying that makes them so angry?"

"It seems hardly fair to ask Suyana what a bunch of radicals think," said Magnus.

"The UARC is still very new," Suyana said. "They're still struggling with shared languages and currency. Some problems clearly run deeper."

Margot looked like she wished she had a document to point to, just to show off the points of her nails. "Some problems run deeper than anyone thinks."

Suyana let her face drop into the blankness of surprise. "Have they checked for explosives anywhere else we visited? At the palace, or the Teatro Municipal?"

Magnus checked his tablet. "Not yet. They're still coordinating efforts on our transit routes, but so far everything's clear."

"Oh, thank God," Suyana said, wishing she'd thought to have Chordata plant an inert bomb underneath her hired car as a cover story if she'd needed one. Wishing she trusted anyone enough to do it now.

"Yes," said Margot. "Only the one target. It seems they have a favorite subject."

"Strange. I'm not even on the Environmental Committee. I don't know what they think they'd have to gain."

"You'll need to denounce this act of terrorism. On television."

"Of course. Who's claiming responsibility?"

Margot blinked twice. "No one, yet."

"Oh." As if adrift, Suyana looked to Magnus. "How would that work?"

Magnus was looking at Margot, a single thin line creasing his forehead. "I'm not entirely sure," he said. "It's not the general practice to speak before someone's claimed responsibility. You could condemn terrorism overall—"

"You'll condemn Chordata," Margot said. "They're likely responsible, and you should publicly distance yourself from looking ignorant of the people behind it. You look ignorant of plenty as it is."

"But that—" Magnus said, and Suyana could practically hear him swallow the rest of the thought—that opened up the UARC to another blow if the group wasn't Chordata, and whoever had done it wanted to make another point.

"It's necessary for Miss Sapaki," Margot said to Magnus, and though it was an old trick and Hakan had taught her to ignore it almost a decade ago, Suyana's palms still went clammy when Margot dropped into the formal. It suggested something different—not even a diminishing, but a removal. "Otherwise, I'm afraid we'll have no choice but to—"

Suyana glanced up at Ethan a moment before the receptionist knocked on the glass wall to announce him, and Margot looked over and went ever so slightly pale.

Magnus looked at Suyana; after a moment, he allowed himself to look relieved.

"Hi," Suyana said, reaching for him as he sat, so the ring would show above the table. "Listen, Ethan, this attack sounds like it may have ruined my credibility. I don't know what—"

"What?" Ethan curled his hand around her hand and looked over at Margot. "Why would it?"

Margot pressed her lips together for a moment. "After being the center of so many scandals—the Chordata strike five years ago, the problem last year, now this—it feels like Suyana has drawn undue attention to herself."

"Making her apologize for it only draws more attention," Ethan argued, at the same time Magnus said, "The problem last year?"

Ethan caught on. "Oh, that's—the kidnapping, you mean. Wait. You're blaming her for being shot and kidnapped because I had asked her to meet me to talk about a relationship and some psycho got angry?"

Suyana watched Margot, looked for anything: the tightening of her jaw, the flare of her nostrils, any tension around the eyes. Nothing. She wondered how Margot did it—if she rationalized it, or made herself forget, or if she was just so good that nothing escaped. It was incredible technique.

"Oh, I—I brought him with me, back home," Suyana said,

like it was just now occurring to her. "People angry about a political union wouldn't like a reminder coming home. Oh God."

Ethan's hand was warm and soft. The ring felt heavy on her finger.

"That's true," said Ethan, leaning forward. "That facility was our project, Margot—the US was the big investor, not the UARC. It probably wasn't even a strike against Suyana. It was a strike against America!"

Suyana looked at him with all the foolish fondness she could summon when she could barely breathe. Come on, she thought; do what I need you to do.

"This is bigger than one country, Margot. This is about the whole conservation project. I should be the one to denounce that."

"No," said Margot, a refrigerator dropped on Suyana's relief. "Suyana needs to be seen publicly refuting this."

Ethan's fingers laced with hers in the moment before he glanced over. "Then we do it together."

I could kiss you, she thought, you beautiful mark, and they stood up hand in hand even as Magnus was saying, "Perfect—Margot, let us know what time you need us to be live, we'll have a script in twenty minutes. Thank you for taking such a personal concern."

× × × × × × ×

Ethan's team made it to the offices in time to berate him and then powder him for the cameras. Suyana would have left him in their care, crowded into the greenroom off the penthouse audience hall, except she worried he'd change his mind as soon as she was out of sight and Stevens started in. Instead Magnus moved to intercept his team with specifics, and Suyana wrapped her arms around Ethan's waist, rested her chin on his chest, and said, "I can't believe what you did in there."

He smiled, but there was no light behind it, and his hand on her back felt tentative.

"Why? Didn't you think I would stand up for you? Why else would you call me for this?"

I needed a shield, she thought, lowered her eyes so it wouldn't show. At best he was a dupe; at worst a spy. Whether he'd gotten observant all of a sudden or was just falling back on the contract, she had to be careful not to make him regret what he was about to do. A public retraction would be damaging. She needed someone she could rely on.

"I'm sorry," she said. "That wasn't kind. Of course you'd help me. We work well together."

Twice he opened his mouth to answer her, with an expression she couldn't read; then his team reached him and it was too late.

"Here's your speech," said Magnus from beside her.

Her speech: The trip had been so wonderful that she chose to remember the kindness and openhearted welcome she'd found everywhere, rather than the actions of an angry few. She wished the injured man a swift recovery, and the UARC's IA budget would be covering his hospital bill. She planned to do her utmost here at the IA to bring peace to the UARC and the world. It was everything expected of her, and still said nothing.

"Let Ethan condemn. He can afford it." Then he cleared his throat. "I assume you called him."

"He offered, in the car. I thought it couldn't hurt."

Magnus was looking at her the way he did from time to time—through her, not at her. It was the same look he gave her whenever someone mentioned the Incident (the Disappearance, the Problem); it made her wonder what he really thought happened a year ago, between losing her and running into the alley where she was standing over the body of the man she killed.

She'd never said a word about what had happened to her. He'd wanted her confidence—he knew it was a lie but not how, and it was always the how that fascinated Magnus— but he was just decent enough not to ask, and she'd never offered. Once or twice she'd mentioned offhand that some public event made her uncomfortable, and he'd given her that look, and then changed her schedule.

He said, "Not a bad move to call Ethan, all told."

"Tell me that if I survive the night," she said. "If we're only making Margot angry by joining forces, I may have wasted him on this."

Someone knocked on the door and summoned them to the cameras, which gave her an excuse to turn away from his expression.

"Oona's on her way, but—" Magnus started, and then fell silent, watching her as she pinched her cheeks and dragged her teeth over her lips while everyone else filed out. After they were all out of sight, she ground her knuckles into her eyes until the sockets looked red and leftover-weepy.

"Is it enough?" she asked, blinking back tears.

He was still watching her. "I wouldn't worry," he said, holding the door open for her. "I think you know what's enough."

At the press conference, she stood behind Ethan and looked out at the bleachers full of people with cameras for heads, and she brushed Ethan's hand as she stepped up to join him at the podium for her remarks, and she cleared her throat but didn't cry, and she fell silent here and there but her voice never broke.

One of the *Daily World* journalists asked her about the last attack on an outpost, and she said, "I was so young, but I remember the toll it took—I hope the next Face of the UARC, whoever they are, will never have to experience anything like this."

One of the American national press asked if it brought back any memories of her captivity, and before she could even summon an expression that neared surprise, Ethan stepped forward and put a hand on her shoulder and said they weren't taking any further questions.

Ethan's team was waiting in the greenroom to drag him to the car. They faded in a cloud of tense advice, with Ethan giving one look over his shoulder, so she caught the words, "... shouldn't Suyana ... ?"

Magnus held out his tablet; their approval rating was up five points in fifteen minutes. She wondered how high the numbers had to be before you were too important to kill. It was hard to tell from the inside. She wondered if you could bring down Margot's numbers enough.

She handed it back to him.

"Didn't waste him after all," he said.

She said, "Let's find out if Grace is free for dinner."

13

"—and I promise to work not just for greater peace within the United Amazonian Rainforest Confederation, but even more closely with the International Assembly, which has put so much trust in me."

Daniel reached up and turned off the television.

"That's not your television," said Bo.

Everyone around them in the cramped counter joint was eating, their faces eclipsed by enormous bowls of noodle soup, and nobody even looked over.

"Yeah, they were all relying on that news. Sorry to cause such an uproar."

Bo shrugged, caught the same noodle at five points so it

made a single tidy knot on the way to his mouth.

"I don't need to see the rest either," Daniel said, like that was what Bo had asked. "They'll answer some preplanned questions about what all this means for her tenure at the IA, and then Ethan will step in and be gallant and that will be the end of it. You don't need to see that. Nobody does."

Bo made another careful tangle of a single noodle and ate it in silence.

Technically he and Bo were still in the middle of an argument that Bo didn't realize they were having, about whether Bo should have told him Li Zhao had come to New York, and why. The argument would officially begin when Li Zhao told Bo that Daniel had spoken with her. Then Bo would have to say something about it and they could get started.

So far, she hadn't said anything. It was proving to be a very interesting argument.

Still, if Bo wanted to keep a few secrets for now, he could. They'd come out eventually. Bo was too much of a company man to hide anything for long.

"Have we heard from Nicodema?"

Bo raised an eyebrow on *we*, but said, "Nothing to hear. She flew out when Suyana and Ethan took off. She's back in Paris, waiting for seasonal work."

"Think Li Zhao's going to start booking overlap for things like this?"

He shrugged. "Things like this don't happen for anyone except Suyana. I don't think the boss is concerned."

Daniel looked over to see if Bo was warning him, but Bo looked as calm and sincere as a lumberjack on a bag of cough drops.

He closed his mouth over the question: Is that because no one expects her to make it?

"I'd better go," he said instead, yanking on his jacket as he stood. "They'll be getting the hell off IA property as soon as this circus is over. Thanks for paying for lunch."

"What? No," Bo said, but Daniel was quicker than he looked, and he was already long gone.

Suyana stayed in the IA building longer than Daniel would have believed she could stand it. At first he thought it was to avoid the ten rows of photographers and reporters who had their faces pressed to the glass. There was a side exit in case of emergency, but he could see it from the corner, and there were so many cameras there he doubted she'd risk looking so guilty unless someone was actually chasing her out.

It wasn't an impossible image. The last time Margot had tried to rid herself of Suyana, she and Daniel had covered half of Paris trying not to be killed. Now her profile had risen, but somehow the danger was worse. When she was C-list, her biggest problem was that no one would have noticed if she disappeared. Now the biggest problem was how many people had their eye on her.

What a waste of a year. Why go through this if you wouldn't end up any safer? Why go through this for a group who ignored you the first time you ever told them no, and put you in this much trouble without caring what happened to you after? Suyana wanted to believe in Chordata; even a year ago, standing in the safe house with people who were waiting for orders about whether or not to kill her, she'd looked like she hoped she was home.

Now here she was, and neither side seemed very interested in her survival.

Daniel wished he was better at looking forward. Suyana always seemed to be able to pluck the future from a tangle of thread and then pull. But he'd only ever been good at noticing when things were more than what they seemed, and that was practically always, with this job—enough instinct to point your camera the moment before the gunshots went off, that was all. Diplomacy was something else, and building a spyglass was a skill he'd never developed.

The foot traffic was light this time of day, when the IA was out of session and most people who weren't desperately conducting state business just visited their embassies instead, to take a few pictures and sign a few asylum requests and then head out to dinner. It was easy enough to keep an eye out across the street from the IA offices for anyone with their head low and their scarf pulled up too high.

When Suyana finally came out the front doors (slowly and without looking over her shoulder, which Daniel chalked up as a mercy), she'd changed from the penitent press conference outfit. Now her hair was pulled back into a messy knot, and she wore black pants and a sleeveless tunic and a complicated necklace of dark stones that made his heart turn over heavy in his chest.

Grace was beside her, wearing something that suggested she'd been called out of the house at the last minute, which meant that choosing her loose jeans and too-big button-up shirt must have taken an hour.

For a moment Daniel was baffled—who headed out for a quiet dinner after news like this, when you needed to be in front of cameras to keep people feeling sorry for you?— but it was time away from Ethan and Magnus, and Daniel imagined it was useful to demonstrate you had allies in the Big Nine when Margot was breathing down your throat. He hoped Grace was in on it; he didn't like the idea of Suyana using her, somehow.

Shit. Was all this an operation? Did Grace know what Suyana was, on top of everything else? Was he the only person ever left out in the cold anymore?

The nationally sanctioned cameras swarmed them as

soon as the doors were open. The photographers didn't ask questions (not their brief), but they were all under orders and took pictures of whatever they were told. Daniel sympathized.

He hailed a cab just as they were closing the car doors, but it cut across traffic so fast it blocked a car that was trying to pull out, and it took twenty seconds for the drivers to give up shouting at each other and slide through traffic.

As Daniel turned to see where Suyana's car was going, he caught sight of Kipa coming out of the offices.

She was ignored by the cameras—she hadn't done anything to earn them except be sweet, and sweet only worked if you were dressed to the nines somewhere near interesting people—but as she crossed the street and hailed a downtown cab at the far corner of the block, a stranger slid in after her. A woman, moving fast, just a glimpse of heeled boots and a bob that swung in a curtain across her face as she ducked inside.

He couldn't think about it—he had to focus, to think about how many places Suyana and Grace could go if they started out heading downtown, where they would be most likely to be left alone except for key people, and decided if Suyana had walked out looking like that, she was going to play some politics over dinner.

By the time Daniel was settled in his own cab, he'd decided. "Follow that car," he said, and pointed at Kipa's taxi.

He suspected where Suyana and Grace would be for the next several hours, and there was time for him to catch up there. If he waited any longer, Kipa and Columbina were going to disappear.

Sometimes you knew a Face was going to go underground because they wore the same thing two or three days in a row, so the press couldn't run any story on it without looking like they were spinning tales. If the Face vanished for a day or two, it was hard to make it a story when your audience remembered you making shit up about them twenty hours ahead of time.

It wasn't going to work as a tactic for long—readers were starting to get wise to the trick, and now a good photographer could tip his magazine off to illicit vacations a day early. It was amazing, though, what the mind skipped over if it saw the same person wearing the same thing. It made you both more distinctive and more invisible, so by the third day everyone recognized you but you could almost get past the cameras before anyone remembered they were supposed to be taking pictures.

Daniel wasn't going to pass up any trick that worked. He wore black pants and a charcoal button-down, no matter what, and a coat whenever it was cool enough to warrant one. It was a smart move—it looked expected pretty much anywhere you were, and no one ever gave him a second glance.

Kipa and Columbina were walking through Central Park, and Daniel hung back just far enough that they didn't notice his pacing them. (Just in case, he bought a hot dog from one of the park vendors and took occasional thoughtful bites while staring at nothing on his phone. In this crowd, it was close enough to blending in.)

Kipa had grown in the last year. Suyana didn't see her often, so Daniel often went months without really noticing her, but she'd seemed to square her shoulders in the IA. She appeared at parties where you least expected her; he must have half a dozen shots of Kipa in a floaty skirt and impossibly charming top gliding into the VIP section as Suyana carefully never looked over. Daniel had suspected something was wrong—that Kipa knew more than she should, maybe, that during that fight in Terrain a year ago Martine had made a lucky guess and now Suyana had to manage three more people who knew.

But he'd never considered Kipa as Chordata material, which he realized now had probably been the point. Kipa was on an environmental subcommittee that voted to save whales and owl habitats once a year, and never said a word otherwise. She made herself forgettable, and then showed up and listened.

Daniel was impressed and embarrassed. It was one

thing to miss the person Suyana had come to save in the middle of a loud nightclub a year ago, as a stranger was explaining what your life would look like now. It was another thing to keep missing a connection for a year. That's what tunnel vision got you.

He got as close as he dared and moved as quietly as he could.

"It doesn't sound like her to not want to know the reasoning behind anything." Kipa was frowning.

"Hi, Daniel," said Dev over the comm. "So, what the hell is happening, exactly?"

Columbina sighed. "I thought so too, but she was so angry—you know how angry Aurelia gets."

"Aurelia?"

Columbina looked long-suffering. "Lachesis."

"Oh, sure," Kipa said, and if the hair on Daniel's neck wasn't already up, the tone of Kipa's voice would have done it, as they realized in the same moment that Suyana's old name had been blanked. There was a replacement, but no one recognized it—that name meant nothing. Daniel knew how easily people disappeared: even Suyana, even Chordata. He cleaned his hands three times on a napkin.

"Yes! And she accused me! Like a setup, like that is something we would do."

"Mmm." Kipa stared past Columbina into middle space

for a second, as if remembering something. "And of course you never would."

"Daniel, repeat, you are off target. Can you read me? Where are you? Where the hell is Suyana?"

Smack between them, he thought, right in the center of it all; can't you tell?

"Of course we wouldn't just abandon her—we'd never betray anyone kind enough to help us," said Columbina, very nearly as politely as she'd sounded before.

"Oh. Good. I thought so. I don't like to think of you—of us—being that sort of place." Kipa's thumbnail was picking at the polish on her index finger, on the far side of her body, where Columbina couldn't see.

"I'm just concerned that's the impression she has. She seemed very upset, and she wouldn't even listen to me when I tried to explain. I was hoping you might be able to help me talk to her."

"Sure. What did you say, when you explained? I mean, what would you be saying differently now?"

Daniel buried his smile in a napkin.

"I'm not kidding," said Dev through the comm. "This is off assignment, seriously. If you think this is a story of its own, alert us and we'll get someone on it. Suyana could be launching a rocket to the moon right now and you'd miss the story."

"This is the story," Daniel murmured. "Don't worry about her."

She'd never go to the moon without saying good-bye.

"—so we can speak to her tonight," Kipa was saying. "I'll find out where she's going from her handler. But I don't know if this will carry much weight unless there are—I mean, it's a big apology. Do they have plans to show they're sorry? If I bring you to her, can you make this right?"

Columbina drew up to her full height and looked straight down at Kipa, who had actually dug the heels of her hands into her skirt like she was a precocious nine-year-old who knew she was in the right and was going to be adorably staunch about it. It crawled up Daniel's spine to look at it—she was too young to be looking so young—but he supposed that whole affect had the potential to be disgustingly effective in the right room. Old men with savior complexes. Handlers who liked the idea of anyone too innocent to have a hidden agenda.

And, apparently, women who were playing the big-sister control agent on the side. Columbina's shoulders softened and she hooked her thumbs absently into her pockets, mirroring Kipa, as she said, "Yes. The Norwegian outposts have promised to see what comes of it before they do anything. At least a year. It will look like another local problem, if it has to be handled. We'll help it blow over, however we can, and she'll have plenty of breathing room while we try to fix this."

Daniel wasn't hungry anymore; the rest of the hot dog went in the garbage as he turned and walked back to Fifth. Whatever happened next, Suyana was setting the destination, and that was his primary concern.

She wouldn't be safe for long, the way things were going. Bo was her best option; ex-killers made the most useful snaps in situations like this. (Daniel could pull someone out of the crosshairs once, but doubted he'd be dumb enough to do it again.) Daniel just had to get himself fired before they left New York, while Li Zhao was too focused on Margot to let Bo have her. With Bo doing swing shift, it would be easy for her to move Bo to Suyana—a steady eye instead of the guy who was going to pieces. Bo liked Suyana more than he'd say. That was all Daniel needed to know.

"Dev, what the hell's going on?" he said as he cleared the line of trees. "That wasn't Suyana! Why didn't you tell me? Now I've lost her, I can't believe this, I rely on you for this intel."

"I'm going to kill you," Dev said, and Daniel pulled his lips back from his teeth in a fuck-you smile as he peered into the tinted windows of the parked cars along the sidewalk, just to make sure Dev would see.

x x x x x x x

Turned out those well-cut clothes worked for you even when you pulled up in front of the Concordia Club, where you were not and never could be a member. So long as you looked sharp, you could dawdle long enough to check the windows and the license plates without any of the door staff asking you your business.

Grace's car was in one of the rare parking spaces in the gated courtyard, looking exactly like the other two cars beside it, and something around Daniel's throat loosened when he saw it.

Then he calmly moved around the corner and staked out the staff entrance until someone ran out with a shopping list in their hand, and Daniel could catch the door and go inside like he'd done it every day of his life.

Suyana had pulled the same thing when she wanted to stay beneath notice in a place where she wasn't welcome. Daniel wasn't going to pass up any trick that worked.

The Concordia Club, established on a date important enough to write in stone above the entrance, was exclusively for IA employees. (You could sometimes usher your family in with you for dinner, according to Bo, so long as they kept quiet and seemed suitably impressed.) Faces, handlers, and those in administration who could afford the membership fee got to use the facilities inside, which Bo said included a restaurant, a lounge, a library, a pool, a gym, massage, and complimentary dry cleaning. Daniel was laughing by the end of the list—something about the combination of dry cleaning and the pool made him imagine handlers sheepishly floating in the water waiting for clean clothes as diners watched them coolly from over their lunch salads—but he'd never questioned the reconnaissance. If anyone could get inside without being noticed, it was Bo.

Daniel hung his coat on the first hook he found and grabbed three glass bottles of seltzer—no way Concordia Club members would settle for tap. And as it turned out, the kitchen had a rhythm that was easy to parse. One staircase heading from the kitchen up to the dining room, another for bringing dishes back down. To avoid collision, but he liked knowing there were two possible exits if he needed them.

"Daniel, what is this?"

"I'm observing the news, Dev." Daniel moved for the upward stairs.

"Daniel, I've ignored your personal meetings because nothing came out of them except you getting your heart broken, and I figured that was your business. But she's with another Face—oh my God, you're in the Concordia Club, that entire room is Faces. Daniel, absolutely not. Pull out of this right now, or I'm going to call Li Zhao."

"You should. I'd love to see her come down here."

The dining room was busy and dim, and he paused a

moment to get his bearings before he set two seltzers down and headed over to Suyana's table with the third. He didn't have to look to see where she was; he'd known before his eyes adjusted exactly where she was.

He stopped at the table next to them and poured, smiling at the two men sitting there (one of Egypt's handlers, and someone Daniel didn't recognize).

"You were nearly at the end of your contract," Grace was saying. "I was beginning to wonder what was going to happen between you two."

"It was such a surprise. I can't imagine how he ever got that idea in his head," said Suyana in a voice that some people might buy.

"I'll bet," said Grace, who was not one of those people.

A photographer, UK national credentials, stepped up to their table, and Daniel stepped smoothly back until he was out of frame. Suyana bent a little forward, rested the fingertips of one hand on the table between them—bridging the gap visually, or looking as if she was in serious discussion, Daniel couldn't tell. Grace turned to her and looked sharp, surprised, for half a beat before she could smooth it back into the sly, beautiful canvas the UK always wanted her to have when she represented the nation: always present, never involved.

When the photographer had moved on, Suyana said,

"I'm not sure how I'm supposed to look after a press conference like that. Without Ethan soaking up the sincerity, sometimes I forget what to do."

Grace smiled around her wineglass, the edges of her arms softening, her body easing an inch forward along the table.

He couldn't blame Grace for believing Suyana's lie; he wanted to believe it himself.

Daniel moved to another table in their line of sight and poured for two of the administrators he recognized vaguely from the IA offices.

"Listen," Suyana said. "If anyone were to ever . . . require a press conference from you where you had to admit things you didn't think, what would you say?"

"If you mean because of personal developments, I'd refuse. Nothing to address. And we're in enough wars at the moment that the UK has template speeches ready for allying with one country and vaguely apologizing for striking another. Colin and I just write press releases without me having to stand there and answer questions about things I can't help. I'm not sure I'd ever agree to give a press conference like one of yours, actually."

A muscle in Suyana's jaw flexed and disappeared. "Sure. But you're Big Nine. I'm not sure I'd survive another disagreement with Margot."

It was spoken like hyperbole, but her face was serious

as stone, and after a moment it looked like something was falling into place for Grace.

"Well, of course, if Margot made the request, I suppose that's quite another thing." Grace picked up the wineglass with slightly shaky fingers. "Then I can see the advantage of a press conference with your fiancé."

Daniel stepped back to let two waiters through. Neither of them glanced over—a waiter didn't have to concern himself with what the water boys were wearing.

Suyana glanced around the room, and Daniel was already half smiling despite himself, the instant before she saw him.

Absolutely nothing crossed her face—the mask never dropped, and when the waiter came by she turned toward him and smiled placidly and ordered dessert and coffee and joked with Grace that she'd need all the caffeine she could come by, and when she laughed, the Egyptian handler looked over and smiled faintly, like it was nice to see someone trying to overcome adversity over dessert.

Suyana didn't look back at Daniel. She didn't turn her body an inch toward him, like she'd done in the early days. (Sometimes even when it wasn't a signal to meet her—sometimes it just seemed like she wanted to be that much closer to him, for no reason at all.) He might as well really be some water boy, instead of the only friend she had. His knuckles were white around the bottle.

"Excuse me a moment," Suyana said as she stood, and tilted her head toward the hallway to the restrooms. Grace nodded and reached absently for her tablet.

Daniel moved for the ladies' room.

It was empty, thankfully, and when he heard her coming he opened the door, threw the lock behind her. She frowned over her shoulder. Then she turned the faucet on, her fingers trembling a few inches above the water before she turned to look at him. It drowned out the sounds they made, white noise shielding them.

"Not my first time meeting this way," she said, and he realized he must have been staring.

Dev had gone silent in Daniel's ear. He couldn't remember the last time Dev had said anything—maybe nothing since the threat to call Li Zhao. She needed to see this if it was going to work, but God, how many people were watching this feed?

"Everyone can see us," he said, meaning it as a warning, but it came out ragged and at loose ends.

She waited a beat, and he realized he should have dragged his hair over the camera by now to keep her expressions away from prying eyes, so that even if she had to watch her words, she could be human for a minute or two.

He was still holding the bottle. He didn't move.

When Suyana caught on, she looked him in the eye

(the hair at the back of his neck stood up, always), and then looked right into the camera. Her throat sounded dry when she asked, "What should I know?"

It shouldn't have infuriated him that this blowup was going according to plan, that her focus on what he could do for her would work to his advantage. It really shouldn't have.

"Wow. Cut right to the fucking chase, don't you?" He crossed to the counter, pretending not to notice that she pulled back from him just enough to keep a clear path to the door.

"Daniel, this place is high risk. You wouldn't be here unless something was really wrong."

"Yeah. Kipa's bringing a friend to wherever you're headed after this. I'm not sure it's a friend you want to see, but what do I know—she's a *mutual* friend, though it would have been nice if I hadn't had to find that out from Kipa."

The meaning landed on Suyana. Then she glanced in the mirror and back at him, and it took him a long, heavy heartbeat to realize she was looking for options in case the worst happened and she had to fight him and run. The whole place suddenly smelled like lemon polish; he could hear his shoe squeaking on the floor as he moved closer to her.

"I'm sorry. I'm just—just don't go wherever you're supposed to go. They could have anything planned. We know they could."

She cleared her throat, looked at the floor. It sounded like she'd gone a week without water. He imagined her drying up all at once, like everything he'd seen in the last year had been her slowly pulling away on the inside; maybe she was just a husk now that did as it was told.

"Thanks for the warning. I'll be careful."

He took a step back. "You'll be careful . . . when you go?"

"I can't change plans. Magnus will be suspicious; it's not worth the risk. I'll be all right. They wouldn't try anything that could make me a martyr."

It felt like all the blood vessels in his jaw were going to burst. She was better with information than this. He knew she was. He dragged his free hand down his face. "Suyana, every time I speak with you, I'm risking everything. My boss is probably on her way over right now—they're all listening to this goddamn feed, all the time, any time they want. They might be outside the door waiting for me. Why the fuck am I risking everything to help you if you won't even keep yourself safe?"

Suyana looking at him always left a scorch mark. Her eyes were so dark, and just at the ends there was some deep-purple shadow that made it look like she hadn't slept in years, and he couldn't even tell if it was on purpose.

When she spoke, she dropped her eyes again, and her voice was the one she used during the contract negotiations to date Ethan, in a room full of American men who had to be carefully explained to.

"And I appreciate it. But I need to know what's happening—it's more important for me to know than to be safe."

Not to me, Daniel thought, the words a hot lump at the base of his tongue, but he didn't say it. Li Zhao should be listening by now; he couldn't imagine her face if she ever heard him say something so lost. There was a snap being overly involved with his mark, and there was someone who'd gone pitiable over someone they'd already lost, and he had to be careful. Suyana was a loss he had to accept, but a lot of things were less important than pride.

"Fine," he said, with the sense of tipping off a ledge, falling closer to something he'd tried not to think about. "Good luck. I'm headed to Paris, probably, since she's going to reassign me the instant she sees this footage, but since you're going to ignore warnings anyway, it doesn't much matter."

The hiss of the faucet pressed against his ears. When he looked at her again, she wore the expression he remembered from that long day a year ago; the Lachesis he'd seen in the moment she wanted him dead.

"I can't imagine why you're so angry," she said, the edge of her voice like a blade she was slowly drawing. "I don't want to think that you imagine I'm ungrateful because I don't simper for you like I do for strangers—I can't believe you'd think that.

Or that I don't appreciate your warnings. And even your witness, despite the details of your watch."

Her gaze flicked to the camera, and Daniel wondered if, three thousand miles away, Dev was recoiling from the contempt on her face.

The gunshot scar shone under the lights as she stepped forward. Daniel fought the urge to look around him like she had; it would be giving in. (To what, he didn't know. This had started out deliberate. Now he was afraid.)

"But more than anything," she said, and the knife was out in every word, "I wouldn't want to think you resent me unless I'm covered in blood and begging you for help."

They were nearly touching. Three strands of hair that had come loose from the knot were floating near enough to cling to the static of his shirt. He didn't know when she'd moved closer. He'd never have let her. She was warm; her eyes were two black circles, dark and deep.

She'd killed a man this way once, standing this close. His body remembered it without his permission and went cold, his wrists heavy. If he wanted to brush the three hairs back behind her ear, he couldn't lift his hand.

"You should get going," he said. "Grace will be waiting at the table for your next photo op."

He'd leaned in to intimidate her, he thought as the door swung closed behind her. He'd leaned in to force her to move away, because of course she would have, because she'd bluffed him and he'd called, that was all. There was never any question what she'd do.

He threw the bottle into the sink so hard it broke, and took the exit stairs without even a look around to see if she'd ratted him out. It didn't matter if she'd broken their confidence. It didn't matter. He didn't give a shit where she was. She wasn't his problem any more.

"Dev," he barked as soon as he was on the street. "Is her new tail in place?"

There was a long pause that would have sounded like dead air except he could hear Dev holding his breath.

"Yeah," came over the line at last. "I can't tell you who—"

"I don't care who it is. I just want to be gone. I know you've talked to Li Zhao. Who's my new assignment and where are they now?"

Miserably, Dev said, "Um."

"Dev, just—who is it?"

"Grace."

14

Grace always entered a nightclub looking like whatever she was wearing was a lucky plume of smoke from which she had just emerged via some other, better realm.

Before the assassination attempt, Suyana had mostly been concerned about scoring invitations to enter the night-club at all. Since the assassination attempt, Suyana knew she entered clubs like she was daring them to throw her out. She couldn't help it.

She'd worried at first that it looked too aggressive, that it looked like she was hiding something and she was sure to be found out, but it turned out that in pictures it just looked like she was a stocky newcomer, suitably aware of how close she was standing to Grace or Martine—a lucky C-lister raised up through the goodwill of others until she could stand next to her betters.

As she and Grace posed on their way into Empire, Suyana cheated her scar forward.

The Empire ("That's terribly pointed," Grace said on opening night, at the same time Martine said, "They cannot fucking be serious," and all along the gauntlet of photographers on the red carpet, the three of them were careful to pose so that no one got them and the sign in the same shot) was a nightclub of the old kind. Inside, it was a comforting maze of small tables and dim light and breaks in conversation as the bandstand introduced a singer for a handful of low-key torch numbers at a time. It was the sort of nightclub you could go to right after an explosion on your home soil, and magazine readers would believe you'd wanted to go there to think.

Grace headed for the bar. Suyana headed for the tables on the low, deep mezzanine, where she could sit facing the door. One chair she left open opposite her for anyone who wanted to take their chances.

("You won't want to be involved in what happens," Suyana had explained in the car, and Grace had looked at her, the thin silver necklace at her neck casting a constellation against her dark skin, and said, "A bit late for that, don't you think?")

It was relatively early in the evening, as IA parties went, and Suyana could rake through the crowd for Kipa and Columbina. Not that she could prepare for much—if Kipa had fallen in this tightly with Chordata, there was little Suyana could do without disaster—but there was no allure in being taken by surprise.

Suyana wished she'd ignored Zenaida's warnings and been closer with Kipa. They talked at a brunch here or a charity bowling tournament there, but it was dangerous for anyone to connect them, so Suyana had never connected. And Kipa had done her one better; while Suyana had been hurling herself into the limelight, no one knew anything more about Kipa than they had a year ago. That took a kind of quiet skill you had to be born with. Suyana admired it and feared it in equal measure; there was something thrilling about someone she couldn't read.

(Grace and Martine had seen the connection between them a year ago, but neither of them had ever mentioned it since—not even Martine, not even as a joke. Suyana pretended along with them; she was happy to pretend.)

If Kipa sat with her and Columbina kept her distance, then Kipa was in control of the situation, and was still her friend. Suyana could manage that; she could smooth things over and tell Kipa whatever Chordata needed to hear in order to take her name off the list of liabilities.

If it was Columbina—and Suyana could see it happening, Columbina's dark hair swinging as she took a seat, Kipa standing behind her, nearly swallowed up by the gloom—then Kipa was just an accessory to someone else's wishes, and all Suyana could do was make sure Kipa realized the trouble she was in before the worst started. Before she called Suyana by the name of something that had no spine. Whoever had chosen it had been deliberate; Chordata had so many heads there was no knowing. So long as it wasn't Zenaida; Suyana let herself imagine that Zenaida wouldn't let her be erased without a fight.

So much would go wrong if they really turned on her. But her anger at Daniel had burned away the last of her fear, and the inconvenient flickers of self-preservation were gone. Some habits were hard to shake, and the first thing she'd ever done when she looked at an enemy was to imagine them vanishing.

She saw Columbina first—clumsy, moving into a puddle of light—and before she'd decided whether it was more strategic to pretend not to see, Suyana was staring. Then it was too late, and she decided she might as well level a look at them as they crossed the room through the pockets of the crowd, Columbina occasionally glancing at Suyana and then away.

But the first person who actually approached her was

Grace, who delicately dropped two glasses on the table and availed herself of a third chair she seemed to conjure at the edge of her fingers.

"Grace." Suyana didn't look over, nearly sorry for how rude it looked. "I thought we had a plan. That wasn't even close to an hour."

From the corner of Suyana's eye, Grace stabbed the lime wedge in the bottom of her glass with her straw and pulled it out, wringing it to death between two fingers. "It's not that I don't believe you when you say you're in trouble—last time you told me that, Colin had to rescue me from IA Peacekeeper custody in my own bolt-hole flat, so trust me, I damn well believe you."

Grace had never mentioned that before. She sounded like she hadn't wanted to mention it now, like nerves had wormed it out of her. Suyana's stomach turned over absently, like she was sorry for someone she'd never heard of.

"But," Grace went on, her pleasant smoothness back in place, "I'm increasingly worried about being kept in the dark, and I'm not sure I'd be much safer at the bar than I would at this table."

"It's worth your life."

Grace looked at her, on the verge of saying something, and Suyana waited for her good sense to win out. But she only settled her back against the wall. "Being caught in your wake has a way of altering one's evening," she said, and flashed one of the grins Suyana used to think was masterful practice and turned out to be just the way Grace smiled. If it weren't for the tightness of her hands in her lap, you'd never know she was nervous.

Grace had always had more faith in Suyana's reasons than Suyana's reasons deserved.

Kipa and her guest had paused when they saw Suyana wasn't alone, and the back of her neck started to itch. She looked over at Grace.

Who was staring at Columbina.

She'd always been a bit slow about where people's hearts lay, so it took Suyana a full ten seconds to guess why Grace's lips had parted slightly like she was about to call a name, or was having trouble breathing.

"How long ago?" Suyana asked, trying to keep an eye on Grace and still watch Kipa and Columbina approaching.

"Two years. It was in Paris."

She wondered why Columbina had gone to Paris when Chordata had a presence there and probably some operatives who would have been ready to seduce an asset, but it was better not to guess how far Chordata would go for that kind of thing. It was enough to know they'd found someone who fit Grace's tastes (beautiful, cold, hurts), the way they'd found Zenaida to take Suyana aside and mother her in drops.

By the time Kipa took the empty seat, Grace was lounging so deliberately Suyana heard something in her back pop, and Suyana could feel the heft of Grace's breaths through the few inches that separated them.

As she sat, Kipa whispered the all clear, "Violet," with a glance at Grace.

"It had better be. Don't look at her."

Then Kipa smiled—too small to register unless you knew her. "No worries. You have them running scared—she wants to make sure you're not angry. They think something's wrong and they're going to lose you." Kipa's face never broke its gormless sincerity.

Suyana couldn't believe it. "*That's* why she's here?"

"Yep. Columbina must want to keep the peace something terrible to risk this. She said you wouldn't talk to her?"

Grace's fingers twitched a quarter inch, brushed Suyana's knuckles as if she wanted to grip Suyana's hand and lost her nerve.

"Oh, I'm sure she did." Suyana let her face relax, let herself look halfway between smug and charmed. Chordata wanted to make good. She'd loved them all her life, even when she knew better. Of course she'd let them apologize. They were expecting it.

She'd settle, back in the fold and out of danger. They'd all walk away clean. Suyana could swallow her tongue and agree; there was less than a week until the Paris session, and plenty to do until then. Better to bury the hatchet and not have to look behind her.

Grace breathed in too long, out too long.

"Take Grace to the bar," Suyana said. "I'll talk to Columbina. If I put my right hand on the table, hit Grace's panic button and get out."

Kipa blinked.

"Good idea," said Grace a beat too late. "My throat's gone a little dry."

When Suyana was alone, she indicated the chair, and Columbina moved forward and sat.

"Grace doesn't know what I really am," Columbina said. "It was just reconnaissance. Didn't work out."

"Interesting. Did you ask?"

"No point." Columbina shrugged, and Suyana watched her try not to look over at the bar, where Kipa was doing her routine for Grace, telling stories younger than she was to get smiles out of people old enough to know better. Grace was letting her pretend it worked.

She waited, let the silence and Columbina's blinders settle, until Columbina said, "Some people just aren't looking for a cause."

So Columbina had a soft stomach after all. Suyana tucked her right hand farther under her, sensed more than saw Kipa relaxing at the bar.

Suyana made a small, sympathetic noise and waited until Columbina remembered herself. The pause was longer than she expected; Columbina must be very sure of her success.

"I'm very angry," she said then, without venom.

"I understand," Columbina said, almost good enough to be true. "We made a mistake."

"That means a lot." Suyana let a smile of relief flicker around the edges of her mouth until Columbina was matching it. Then she began negotiations.

Suyana looked appropriately solemn for the camera on her way out, not quite arm in arm with Grace, who made a vague approximation of a smile that would have looked a little queasy if they were holding still.

As soon as the car door closed behind them, she called Magnus.

"Ethan and I should take some engagement photos," she said. "Go to Paris a few days early, play up the romance. It'll be good press."

After a moment Magnus said, "All right. I'll get started."

Suyana must have been biting the inside of her mouth; she could taste blood. "It should look like his idea."

"Oh. Of course. Why?"

The silence went on too long. At the far end of the seat, Grace was looking at her like a pin at a moth.

"I'll be home later," Suyana said, hung up.

The divider was up and the speaker was off, but Grace was still careful when she said, "So what did I escape, when Columbina left me?"

She blinked. Columbina must have been sure of success to give Grace the operative name. However Chordata had lost Grace, it had been a near miss.

"A lot of trouble."

"Suyana."

She looked at the speaker switch, at the reassuring OFF she never believed.

"I was young, and they gave me a cause. I never betrayed my country—I tried to protect it—but."

But she had betrayed Hakan, and betrayed Daniel and Grace and herself, and by now it was a lie so precisely constructed that she'd betray everyone who knew her as long as she lived.

"This last problem"—and she paused a beat for Grace to catch up to the "this" she meant—"was against my will. The rest has only been against good advice, and the problems I've had I made for myself. Not everybody's born wise."

Grace watched her through three stoplights. Suyana looked away after the first one, could only look sidelong at Grace's reflection in the window and wait.

"I'm not sure how wise it is to fall for someone who turns

out to be a covert agent," Grace said after a while. "I don't know about the UARC, but for the Big Nine you have to watch movies about it in training. You go to seminars about organizations they think are recruiting. We're targets. It's why Colin had to fight so hard for my privacy; the UK wanted to make sure no one was taking advantage of me."

"Did she ever plead her case?"

Grace huffed, cleared her throat. "I don't remember. I never got the sales pitch. It felt like she was waiting for something, I thought a declaration, maybe. Then she stopped waiting."

She had been waiting for a declaration, Suyana was nearly sure. It would have been a sign of dissatisfaction with the Assembly, some glimmer of rebellion she could have tended into fire. She nearly said, Columbina left because it was something you'd never give. (There might have been something else—Columbina might have seen what Suyana had seen in Grace, and realized Grace was someone not to be wasted on their line of work—but it was better not to make guesses about lost causes.)

"Then you were smarter than I've ever been," Suyana said. "And you won."

There were shadows passing across her eyes, but at night it was easy to find shadows, and otherwise Grace's face never changed. Later, she said, "All right."

Even in her sadness, Grace had some essential surety that Suyana missed, a tooth that had rotted through. She made kindness look sincere, and mistakes look noble, and watching her, Suyana's dark thoughts had no name.

It had surprised Suyana, in the last year, to realize how much of being a Face was just muscle memory. There was strain in building up the endurance to reach as high as she had reached, but beyond that climb your body was honed for what you found at the top. You looked the way you were meant to and said great things that meant nothing, and you shook hands with anyone presented to you and slid your hand in the crook of your boyfriend's elbow, and eventually your body could do all of it without you.

You could disappear inside yourself and never come out again, if you wanted. No one would notice a thing.

She had fallen under the eye of an organization she could never fully trust again. For their sake, she'd put herself under the eye of the most powerful politician in the world. The last time she'd chosen between them she'd nearly died, and now she had lost an asset.

Sloppy to have cut Daniel that way; embarrassing to expect him to linger. She knew better than to hold on to pride when there was something you needed. Pride you only used when you had the luxury of losing.

She hadn't been thinking, though—she'd been relieved

and terrified and hot-skin angry, and hadn't treated him like an asset should be treated. That had always been the problem with Daniel: He made her want to be honest.

At the door of her building, four photographers had settled in to photograph her homecoming and Magnus was hovering just inside, waiting to take her arm and remove her from other countries' unwanted eyes. She risked a glance over her shoulder to see who was watching from across the way. (It wouldn't be Daniel, of course—Daniel was long gone.)

Then she tucked a loose strand of hair behind her ear like it was getting in the way of her dignified thinking, and headed up the stairs and inside.

Maybe it was better to lose Daniel. Too much history, habits that were hard to break. She could start over with the next one and be who they expected her to be. That one wouldn't know to look for anything behind her ambition; she'd deliver nothing less. She had the muscle for it now.

15

Grace was astonishingly balanced. Daniel spent four days in New York following her on shopping trips with her handler Colin and dinners with promising B-listers and nights at clubs that had memberships. She was better at ignoring Daniel than Martine had ever been, but without giving away any tells, she nearly always managed to be facing away from him, or moving too much, or silhouetted too brightly to make a decent shot.

"God, what happened to you?" asked Kate over the line, which was as close as she got to complimenting his usual work.

They still made second-page news—the shops she'd

visited had paid top dollar for them and planted them in news stories right next to ads for their stores. Diplomacy at work. Good money, anyway. Li Zhao was happy.

But Grace greeted fans openly; she argued openly with Colin about matters of state.

"This dress is a little insulting," she said in Bergdorf, putting back a gown in Union Jack colors, and when he said, "But a little nationalism—" she cut him off with, "Is unnecessary between two free countries who are trading well."

"Well, white is surrender," Colin said, thumbing the rack, "purple's too obvious, gray is depressing."

"I'll wear blue—*plain* blue—or wear those enormous gold and emerald earrings with the gray. Can't call it depressing then."

"Independent Scotland has a lot to prove. They're going to be easily put out."

Grace's face softened a little. "Colin. It's just Annella. A week ago I held her hair back in the bathroom at Hypatia. She's going to hug me no matter what color I'm wearing."

"Or else," Colin muttered, but he was mostly joking, and Grace grinned.

She had a real smile—not always, but often enough. Daniel had always wondered if Faces hung on to those, but she'd been in the IA going on ten years, and there it was.

He realized after a few days of covering her how Li Zhao

could afford to have so many Faces followed. He'd assumed the whole network looked like him and Bo, strung out on lack of sleep and racing after their assignments and desperate to avoid disaster. If most of the Big Nine were like Grace, the snap might not even need overlap coverage. She was in bed by midnight, most nights, and never left the house before ten. That was nearly a day job.

Daniel would have mentioned all that free time to Bo, but Grace never went to see Suyana, so there wasn't much chance. Daniel doubted he'd have the heart to mock Bo much even if they ran into each other. He knew what it was like to look after Suyana; Bo needed all the rest he could come by.

The Paris travel prep meeting was held in Bonnaire offices on two continents at an hour in New York when everyone's Faces were probably asleep.

Bo wasn't there. Suyana was probably at Ethan's and would be sneaking back home just before dawn to play her other part with Magnus. Maybe Suyana was just now concluding a farewell meeting with Columbina before she got on a plane to Paris and the IA session and let Chordata betray her again on the first continent they'd tried it, for old times' sake.

On the television, Kate and Dev and a dozen strangers sat in the Paris headquarters, all trying to look serious while arranged around a single velvet sofa in camera range. The chair Li Zhao occupied had been kept studiously empty. When he saw it, Daniel—who was crowded with the New York snaps in what pretended to be a dining room—shot Li Zhao a look that she returned with such wickedness he tore a divot of skin off his lip trying not to laugh.

"Our sources at the three major airports have confirmed everyone flying commercial," Kate said. She and Dev were still at their stations; they had no interest in being anywhere near the Paris also-rans who were only good enough to cover the session rush. "We're reassigning so no one's cover identity ends up on the same manifest as their usual assignment. For charter flights, all we can do is have someone at the airport as close as possible to the most likely times of travel. Scheduling and assignments will be finalized as they happen—obviously it gets tricky."

It sounded like they were planning a rendezvous with one of the space stations, but not even Daniel thought it was very funny. He looked around at the bleary faces of the Paris team and wondered which poor soul would be living in the airport until the Faces started to show.

Li Zhao added, "Four New Faces will be flying directly to Paris from home countries: Sweden, Indonesia, Iran, and Ghana. We'll assign from there if necessary."

No names were attached to new recruits. They hadn't

earned any until they did something noteworthy. Dev had shown him the archives once; everybody had cross-checks once the footage got back to Bonnaire, but it got sent in tagged by country, not by name.

Daniel did it too. There was no difference after a while, and it was easier to talk about Norway than it was to think about Martine's hand shaking around her cigarette.

The meeting went on and someone in Paris actually had a question, which made Li Zhao look like spoiled milk, and by degrees Daniel stopped paying attention. Grace was already scheduled for a charter flight with Martine, so Daniel's schedule would burn out soon. He'd hop a flight and pick up again when he landed. He hadn't seen his new flat, which he'd be sharing with Bo because life was a joke, but that was his only concern. Everything else was settled.

Bo would get there first. Suyana was traveling by private jet, thanks to Ethan, and getting photo shoots out of the way in Paris before the stores started keeping lists of who wore what to avoid repeats. Daniel hoped Nicodema would be her interim snap until Bo's plane landed. The last thing Suyana needed was more strangers. (He had utter faith she'd made Nicodema. If he'd been good for anything, it was teaching her how to look for people who were about to betray her.)

Daniel ducked out—he didn't care about introductions,

if there were any—and was at Grace's building an hour before she was scheduled for anything.

Columbina had beaten him there; she was hovering at the breakfast cart across the way, picking at a doughnut with the expression of someone who'd eaten four doughnuts already just for an excuse to stay nearby.

Daniel's stomach dropped out from under him. Chordata here for Grace—goddamn, he couldn't imagine what for. Grace didn't have so much as a toe out of line, and you didn't recruit for your covert organization by ambushing a stranger at ten in the morning.

When Grace came outside, she must have thought the same thing, because when she saw Columbina she looked over her shoulder like someone who knew what her snap looked like. Daniel glanced away a degree or two, as if it would help. Colin took the UK national photographer aside and began a list of questions about the condition of her equipment.

Columbina gripped a notebook and approached like a fan, pen in hand.

Grace said, cold and a touch louder than necessary, "You're bloody joking."

"I just wanted to tell you," Columbina said, then ran out of words. She shook her head a few times, held the notebook in a death grip. "I never—I didn't tell anyone that—it's all forgotten."

Grace smiled (a false one), plucked the notebook from Columbina's hands, and signed. "You stalking me to say so hardly fills me with comfort," she said pleasantly. Grace's thumb trembled, just at the point it met her hand.

"I'm sorry," Columbina said. "I would have told Suyana—I would have talked to you, you and I were friends once, but...things are different with her now."

Grace looked up. "Is that what was between you two?"

It sounded every inch the scorned lover, and Columbina reached for Grace's elbow as if to comfort her before she remembered herself and settled for taking back her notebook instead.

Daniel put together a lot of things in short order before he decided that whatever else happened after this, he could say he'd seen how it went when a real diplomat conducted an interrogation: the mark never even noticed.

"No. Nothing like that, ever, with anyone—"

"With anyone but me? It's enough you lied to me once, Columbina."

"Grace. Please."

Grace hesitated, relented, shrugged. "You're right. Hardly does any good to be jealous now. I don't know what it was I saw. I know how charming you can be, and she's a pretty enough girl."

"Not my type. And the thing we had in common is over."

"Flatterer," said Grace as she stepped back, shyly, an attitude so alien Daniel was surprised Columbina swallowed it. "It's good to see you. Thank you for—well, for the reassurance."

Grace gave her one more, "Take care of yourself," with half a glance over her shoulder, before she met up with Colin, waiting politely beside the photographer, who looked ready to quit.

The photographer hadn't taken a single picture. The last thing the UK wanted was pictures of their Face with her old flings.

It was masterfully done. Not even Suyana could smooth-talk someone like that; she tended to just make you feel lesser until you wanted to prove yourself, and half of that was probably by accident. Ethan just had his team take care of whatever it was and showed up to smile and shake hands. Only Martine delivered her threats with that kind of finesse. The IA was a nervous bunch.

Grace had angled Columbina so subtly that Columbina had come back to deliver a message and ended up right back on whatever hook she'd slipped off. She'd also given away how Chordata felt about Suyana, which was pretty clumsy for a solitary agent. Maybe sleeping with Grace had that effect on a girl.

Grace had breakfast with the retiring Face from Sweden, who looked ten years younger now that he was off the job, and it was just enough time that when Grace stepped outside a moment before the car pulled around and made a phone call, Daniel wasn't thinking much of it.

"Listen," Grace said, "the weather's getting awful here. I hope you can still get on the plane today? Good. Well, it's not any better in Paris, I hear, so be careful what you bring with you to keep the rain off. I'm moving up my flight as well, so perhaps we could have dinner before you turn into a married woman. Right. Exactly. See you then, Suyana."

She said the last with her face turned not quite toward Daniel the way it had been not quite turned to Columbina, a thing she wanted to pretend she hadn't meant you to hear.

16

The first time Suyana had flown to Paris, it was business class. It was the first time she'd been on a plane outside the UARC, and it had all impressed her terribly—the seats that reclined nearly into beds, the food that came on real plates and was tailored to her needs (Hakan wanted her to look as if she minded her figure; it was good publicity, even if she never lost a pound).

Her first act as a diplomat had been pretending it was something she'd expected. She thought she'd done all right until four hours into the journey, when Hakan said gently, "It's good never to seem better than your company—that sort of populism goes over well. But it's best for most things to pretend you expect them. Doesn't do to look too grateful. We're selling the dream of a nation."

"I thought I was supposed to be playing things innocent for my first Paris session," she said, and had the thrill of startling him by being right.

"Just let them underestimate you for a year, until you understand the geography. But Suyana, with eyes like yours, you're never going to be seen as young. Better to pretend like you know what to expect."

It was a good lesson, as those went—she'd saved face at a lot of parties by walking in as if she was expecting something more lavish than she got. It didn't do you much good after the first few minutes, but the first few minutes were all most people ever saw. She got invited to more events her first year than she did any year after.

On that plane, at breakfast, she'd thought about sending her omelet for reheating just to prove a point, and hadn't. Hakan hadn't asked her to—he preferred the gentle correction when it was least likely to do her harm—but she'd lost a chance to show him she understood the lesson.

She thought about it sometimes, when an impossible trade-off presented itself (the poor man's lady and the tiger, at thirty thousand feet), but she'd never imagined another outcome. A lukewarm omelet was nobody's fault, and Hakan's praise would have come and gone, and she was still too hungry then to turn away anything that would feed her.

What she had learned since—that the praise would have fed her better, and for longer—she wouldn't have wanted to know, back then. She wouldn't have wanted to know anything that was coming. It was better for her to imagine Hakan at her side. The rest of those years were decisions she wouldn't want to think about taking back.

Six years after that first flight, sitting next to Hakan with a French phrase book and a single suitcase, she took Ethan Chambers's private plane to Paris, alongside her handler and her stylist and so many people from his team that the plane's bedroom had been turned into storage.

"Sorry about this," Ethan said as they pulled out one of the bench couches in the lounge into a bed. "I didn't realize how much space we take up."

"I just feel sorry for Grace trying to travel on the same plane as Martine," Suyana said, and he smiled.

Usually he laughed at anything that had to do with Martine. Nervous about the engagement shoot, maybe. Still shaken up from the spotlight in New York, maybe; it had improved since the press conference, but they both knew she owed him for that in a way she couldn't explain to him.

(He'd tried to make her, with one long searching look in the elevator on the way out of the Assembly building, and she'd said, "Thank God you came," and held him tight, her chin tucked so her face was out of sight of the cameras. She pressed an open hand to his chest, where his heart was beating, steady and solid and wrong.)

"Are you all right?" she asked, before she could stop herself. Never ask a question someone can best you by not answering.

Ethan worried his lower lip with his teeth, then steeled himself. "Yeah. No. There's something we should talk about."

She sat on the edge of the makeshift bed and waited, breathing in for a five-count and out for a five-count. But he didn't say anything—he cast a glance farther up the length of the plane, where Stevens and Magnus were bent over an itinerary. Both had refused to sit facing away from the happy couple, so they sat side by side. Suyana wasn't sure what Stevens was trying to keep an eye on, given that they were sleeping in full view of a dozen people. She had a better idea what Magnus was watching for.

"Maybe not now," Ethan said, with a smile that had no light behind it. "But it's not something to talk about on the ground, either."

It must be Stevens keeping him quiet, though Ethan had no trouble doing as he pleased. The only time others had won out against his own inclinations was the proposal, and even then, he'd stood behind it more than he had to. Maybe that was the problem.

"Ethan, if you're having second thoughts, I understand. This has been a lot of trouble for you. You shouldn't have to get caught up. If America is asking you to back out—"

"No, nothing like that." He picked at his cuticles when he was nervous. He was so rarely nervous that most people never realized the tell. "I just want everything to go well in Paris, with us, and I'm—I don't know how to do it."

Wrong, she thought, something inside him a sounding bell.

"I don't know either. There's no way to make sure everything goes well. It will be nothing but trouble for me on the ground—I'll be working so much just to get back to where I was. Magnus is trying to sell fashion editorials of me to the wedding magazines that called while we were in the UARC. Nobody's calling him back."

Ethan nodded; no surprise. "Do you need help?"

"Oona has a plan to have our engagement photo shoot be me in jeans and a T-shirt and a veil. It sounds terrible, I know, but if you don't mind going along with it, that might catch some editor's eye."

(It had sounded like Kipa's photo spread a year ago, a tutu in the sand; Suyana had objected to Oona's idea of the engagement outfits for a shoot that was designed to be positively toothless. Magnus told her, "You could stand to look a little toothless.")

"I didn't really mean the photo shoot," Ethan said after a second, and it was so unexpected—he took any out she gave him from the truth—that she waited in surprised silence for what he actually meant.

It never came. Stevens said something that half carried down the plane, and Ethan shook himself like a dog coming out of the water, and it was gone.

"Let's get some sleep," he said. "We have to look rested for the cameras, and it's going to be hard enough without Stevens and Samuelsson yelling at us that we've stayed up too long."

"You know, I'm the Face of a country. I make my own bedtime, this is not what I signed up for," she said as they lay down under the thin blanket and settled in side by side—Ethan with a little wave to the rest of the plane that was still awake, and one arm chastely around her waist.

That one got her a laugh, at least, which was enough that she could fall asleep.

She dreamed she stood in the center of the green, Panthera Onca on one side of her and Zenaida on the other, a kerchief pulled up around her mouth so that only they would know that it was her. Chordata had the research facility surrounded; in the dark, with nothing but the dim lights on inside, it looked like a sleeping beast. There was movement inside—the security guard. Suyana held up a fist.

"Wait for me," she said, and ran for it, and she knew it was a dream because they waited.

In the silence of the forest (that silence that teems with the clicks of insects and the calling of birds and the rustling of animals through the leaves), Suyana's feet made no sound even as stems snapped under her feet and animals scrambled from her path, and though her heart pounded in her throat, she didn't so much as take a breath until she was slipping inside through a door that opened in the wall without any searching, like most doors do in dreams.

There was no security guard pacing in the open central pod. There was no sound from upstairs, either; the only light came from a side office Suyana remembered.

The door to the preservation room was thrown open—what had he to fear, alone in the wild?—and she watched him for a long time as he sorted and plucked and muttered to himself, and when she said his name, Ethan turned around with nothing in his hands but an envelope of seeds.

If she would be surprised to be seeing this awake—and she didn't think she would be—

"I hoped it would be you," he said, and the knife she wasn't holding went through his ribs without her ever coming closer.

x x x x x x x

Magnus was awake—Magnus hardly slept, and would never risk being disconnected from the news after this latest disaster. As soon as he saw her stand, he followed her into the bedroom and closed the door behind them.

(There were people to whom something like this would seem clandestine, sneaking off from your boyfriend's bed in the middle of the night alongside the man you live with. Sometimes she tried to picture it, to see if she could imagine life after all this, where you did only as you wanted and had solitude as your regular state. She never could. She'd stopped thinking about it; better not to worry about things you'd never see.)

Magnus said, "What do you think he knows?"

She couldn't answer that, and he knew it. He smiled thinly, a saint accustomed to suffering. "Apologies. It's late."

"Of course."

"Starting over. Let's try this. How are you feeling about him? About all this? Did you—had you two actually considered the marriage as—"

"No," she said, as lightly as she could. "We never discussed it. But you never know when someone will get nerves about aging out of the job and try to go out with a bang. Do we know who's in line after him?"

He looked through her, not at her.

"Leili," he said. "Sixteen; old enough that Ethan

should be concerned. Charming in the Kipa mold, from the photos. Chosen partially for ethnically ambiguous appeal, I suspect, given how ready they are to get the spotlight on her the instant Ethan retires. Right now they're on the brink of having her tap-dance on TV, they're at such a loss as to what to do with her while Ethan's still going. But I've looked into her grades before the Face mentorship program, and if someone isn't getting her an advanced degree in the sciences on the sly, they're wasting her time."

There was a flicker of jealousy somewhere—she hadn't heard that much praise for herself in their entire joint tenure—but she was too tired to hang on to it. She wanted the information; he'd had it ready. Faithlessness wasn't worth worrying over.

"Sounds like I'm marrying the wrong American Face."

"No argument." Magnus folded his arms, dragged his lip over his bottom teeth, and glanced at the door like Ethan would be opening it to see what Magnus thought of him.

"So, you say she's ready. How ready would the Americans say she is?"

He looked at her a long time before he said, "They've bought her a ticket to Paris."

A long time ago, Suyana had heard Grace's handler, Colin, talking to her when he thought they were alone. He knew things a handler always knew; he guessed the rest; he was very good.

Sometimes the things Magnus knew felt like things he had gathered through means he shouldn't have, because he knew she'd need them.

She was still trying to decide if that was an asset or a warning when he said, "Tell me what needs to happen before the session starts."

"That depends on your wedding priorities," she said with a smile, an open gate. "We have a lot of photo shoots to get through."

"Suyana. You know what my priorities are."

His brows had been knotted together, exhaustion and concentration pushing his face in on itself, the words rolling out uneven, like they hurt. But his expression opened and softened—pale skin shifting back across the bones, blue eyes fixed on her. It was that same bliss of being cornered he'd worn when she'd pressed him to a wall a year ago and threatened to kill him for keeping secrets.

It was hard to look at him. He was staring at her—she felt its weight and warmth like a palm pressed to the back of her head—but she looked at his mouth, then his ear, then the door behind him, before she got up the nerve to meet his eye.

A smart Face forgave what they were asked to

forgive—most of it was above your security clearance, and the rest was out of your control. But Suyana had never stopped seeing him as the man on the edge of Hakan's desk where there were still rectangles of dust from vanished things, Magnus in his impeccable suit holding her file half-open like it stung him and looking her up and down to decide if anything could be done with her.

He was young, still; when she got in the habit of hating him, she tended to forget.

Her fifth thought, which was the one she told him: "We'll have to find out if Ethan will really go through with this."

Her fourth thought: Ethan was a spy, he must have been on Margot's side to believe he could win against her, and I can't tell if that's changed, and I need to do something about it while there's still enough time for little Leili to fly across the ocean and be what I need her to be.

Her third thought: My new snap is the tall one with red hair, and I'll need to make sure he's in Paris before we do the shoot with the veil. They'll make six figures off the candids, and I'll need a favor to remind them of when I come asking for their help.

He second thought: I need to decide once and for all whether I can trust you, because not knowing is going to kill me.

Her first thought, deep and vicious and impossible to say: If I'm going to live through this, Margot has to disappear.

× × × × × × ×

They took the outdoors engagement photos two days into their stay in Paris, just long enough for everyone to be rested and for national press to "accidentally" be present wherever they ended up.

"It's so phony," Ethan said with real distaste as they settled onto the wall overlooking the Seine, Suyana in the crook of his arm.

About fifty yards away, one of the bookstalls was selling some of its most artfully beat-up books for Suyana to hold. (Ethan didn't need to; wherever he went, everyone assumed he had all the education he needed.) Ten minutes earlier, the stand had sold a book to a man who'd vanished into the sparse crowd despite his height and his hair. She wished he was easier to track—she angled herself toward the narrow alley where he was mostly likely to get a clear frame. It was all she could do.

Oona handed her the books and reached to affix the veil, but Suyana whispered, "Leave it," and gave Oona a conspiratorial look.

The veil would fall, and she'd catch it in her hands and turn to Ethan and grin at him. He'd laugh, and he'd curl her hand over and across his knuckles, and maybe if she could keep close enough, he'd lean in to kiss her temple and make the only photo of them that would matter—the one that

Margot would be unable to decode, whenever she was deciding whether Ethan was still a willing soldier.

"Look at these," she said, held up one of the books.
"Thomas Hardy, *A Manual for Secretaries*, and a book about
how to sail. What exactly am I studying for?"

Ethan raised his eyebrows, smiled just enough not to
ruin the line of his jaw. "Just don't go sailing if you're sad. You
know how that ends for everyone in Hardy novels."

"I do now," she said, and when the breeze picked up and
tugged her veil out of the slip of her hair, she pressed the
novel flat to his chest and caught the veil with both hands,
and as Ethan clutched the novel and looked over the wall at
the fallen books and Suyana angled her arms to pull away
the veil without blocking her face, one of the photographers
started his shutter.

They did an indoor shoot in formal dress four days later,
when no inconvenient breezes could ruin what the Americans had in mind.

They'd rented out a wing of the Louvre so she and Ethan
could stand under enormous paintings of royalty and mythical
garden parties and look both diminished and everlasting. Some
were so big that a single whorl in the gilded frame was the size of
Suyana's head, and the photographer was forced to remove to the
adjacent gallery just trying to get it all in the frame.

"Not facing each other yet, please," the photographer called. She saw Magnus's lips form *Too marital*, but was too far away to know if he'd actually spoken.

Suyana hadn't been aware they were facing each other, but they were, that forty-five-degree angle they'd been practicing for a year.

Ethan rolled his eyes and plucked at the edges of his collar to make sure they were tipped outward—he'd gotten a round of instructions before the stylists would let him tend himself between shots. Suyana envied him. Her dress was so complicated she wasn't allowed to touch it; Oona had to reach under the bell she made and confirm structural stability and correct drape of fifteen layers before Suyana was allowed to do anything more than shift her weight.

"Side by side, straight and tall, please," the photographer ordered, and they stood an arm's length apart and looked straight ahead. Suyana felt like the first time she'd ever had her picture taken, waist-deep in the river in front of a forest she'd never seen, young and already tired and refusing to look as inviting as she was meant to.

"All right, take hands," called the photographer, and they reached out at the same time without looking. Something else they had worked on.

"No, I mean step closer," the photographer said, but Magnus was looking up at them on the verge of moving for the camera, and saying "No, don't, hold it," with an urgency Suyana hadn't expected. But he was a handler, and for a few heartbeats everybody listened. The photographer's camera went off three times automatically before he could make himself disobey, or before Ethan could recover from the out-burst and step closer.

That was the frame she and Magnus insisted go out in the press package, despite American objections that it looked awkward among all the handclasps and the single chaste kiss on the cheek Ethan was giving her in one of the frames, her eyes closed in polite bliss.

"It's our only request, and if it's so awkward, then none of the magazines will use it and you've won your point," Magnus pointed out finally, after which it was difficult for them to argue.

Four magazines used it. Two made it the cover. Suyana's random-sample image recognition went up by seventeen points in the weekly polls.

In the UARC's cramped flat, which had no adornments, Suyana pinned both covers side by side on the wall across from their bedroom doors—the candid cover closer to her door, the formal cover closer to his. His insistence on that pose had felt like loyalty. Strategy, she told herself every time she opened her bedroom door and saw them.

Suyana and Ethan stood an arm's length apart, hands

connected by the stiff V of their arms. Ethan was just beginning to frown, which made him look troubled in an intrigu-
ing way, and Suyana's face was set as grim as the queen above
her head, her dress taking on some majesty that went beyond
meeting him at the altar; two statues made of stone, dwarfed
at the foot of a painting that would outlive them both.

17

For the first week Suyana was in Paris, everyone at Bonnaire avoided saying anything to Daniel about the engagement.

Suyana and Ethan were running around outside posing for pictures before he even got there, which meant handlers everywhere, news outlets desperate for orchestrated behind-the-scenes kissing, and black-market IA types desperate for any unnatural collusion between representatives of the state. Notices went out over the wire at all hours.

But no one ever asked him what he thought Suyana would do if there were four parties and she and Ethan could only make it to two each but would attend at least one together, and he never offered because it wasn't his business anymore. For a week he followed Grace to burger joints and the Diplomatic Corps building and clocked when her light went out and never had to think about anything he didn't want to.

But by the time Daniel landed in Paris—two days after the first round of engagement photos—Bo had spent three twenty-hour days in a row following Ethan and Suyana around and trying to track which of them went home when from what party. He'd put in a call for late-night cover that Li Zhao hadn't granted, and Daniel thought it was only good business to swing by Bonnaire straight from the airport just in case.

"Good morning, Daniel, absolutely not," Li Zhao called from her office as soon as he was at the top of the stairs. The echo of a laugh floated faintly up from the elevator shaft, which meant Kate was on duty.

"I'm here as a motivated member of a crucial team that monitors international relationships with the public," he said, crossing his arms. She was working; the screen gave a blue cast to her red lipstick and reflected in her glasses, and it erased any truth in her expression.

"I never talk like that about the work."

His tongue was heavy behind his teeth, his throat a little dry. Long flight.

"No," he said, more quietly than he'd meant to, "you just

make us sound like hand-selected martyrs whenever you're signing us up."

After a moment, she looked up over the rim of her glasses. "You flatter me."

"I'm afraid I don't."

"Grace lands in thirteen hours," Li Zhao said. "Kate has the address for your flat and for hers. Take a shower, get some sleep, do your job."

And he did. Grace ate a sandwich at a café packed with students and met with Colin for dessert crepes on the street like father and daughter, their conversation drowned out by the crowd. Grace stopped by Martine's apartment, which faced a courtyard except for a corner living room, but by now Martine knew better than to turn on the light and let them be seen, which meant Daniel spent an hour reading the newspaper in the square across the way. Grace was home in bed by eleven.

Daniel walked north and sat for a while near the stairs in the shadow of Sacré-Coeur. After a while Dev came over the comm and said, "Time check, two a.m.," like it was something Daniel had requested, and absently he answered, "Thanks. Is Bo covered?" as if there had been a reason for him to be out so late, waiting for something that wasn't coming.

"Yep, uh, they're all set." Dev never said her name, but there were holes where it should be, which was worse than Kate's laughing somehow.

So Daniel stood up and went home before anyone could think to ask why he'd been at the bottom of a staircase in the middle of the night, on a bench five streets away from an apartment he'd never dare look for, where some people who might help her had been living, a long time ago.

Bo got three engagement photos into *Closer*, and nearly thirty seconds of footage onto the New York nightly news. It was incredible money—so much that Li Zhao called in the usual suspects to watch the broadcast, and Kate and Dev and a few faces Daniel vaguely recognized gathered around the velvet couch to watch their salaries being made.

But any candids of an event this big were going to be valuable, and the mood of the room was the general understanding that Bo was good and had just lucked into the right shots at the right time. Not even Kate said anything cutting to Daniel about it, which was about the time he suspected that he was being deliberately handled when it came to Suyana.

The footage was in four-second bursts of Ethan laughing and Suyana taking back books from someone on the other side of the river wall and them kissing for the cameras as they grinned chastely against each other's lips; they were played between talking-head debates as analysts looked at their body language and decided how in love these two really were. Verdict: Very. Daniel ignored the commentary. Rules of the game; he'd been doing his homework, and these things were easy to rig. Those same experts had also decided Grace was Very in love with the guy from the Hong Kong Territories when she'd dated him for three months a few years back. She'd fallen out of love with him shortly after Hong Kong had given the UK preferential trading rights and a stronger promise of mutual aid than it did to mainland China. She and he were still friendly—once a year they went out to dinner at some restaurant with big windows. Magazines occasionally name-checked them in articles about IA relationships, as an example of a best-case breakup.

Afterward, everyone who had a late-night follow filed out for the evening shift. Bo hadn't even been there; his shift had started at dawn and wasn't going to be over until Suyana got home from the Deneuve Theatre Awards after-party, close to two in the morning.

"Daniel," Li Zhao called.

He stepped inside, kept his hands in his pockets.

"How are you liking Grace?"

"I sleep more. Works out for me."

"You still try to see her?"

"You know I don't."

She took off her glasses and set them on the desk (not held in one hand like when she was making a point, and Daniel didn't know what point she was making now).

"I'd like to make the assignment permanent. There are going to be some changes this session. Grace is in line to get a committee position in Humanitarian Aid. And Suyana's out of the question—you know you can never go back."

He didn't bother answering. Some things were clear. Any shot at Margot? he almost asked—big game, and though Daniel was a monster, he was a monster who made plans— but the glasses on the desk distracted him, and he only nodded. (It meant something; she was considering some- thing she couldn't quite bring herself to ask.)

In the main room, Kate's chair was pulled up to the dining table, and she was picking at some flaw in the carv- ing along the edge. For Kate, it was practically vandalism. He slowed down.

"What's the matter?"

She looked up. "What? Nothing."

"All right. Good night, Kate."

"Has Margot landed yet?"

He sank his weight on his back foot, like her question had nailed him right through his boot. "I have no idea."

Kate was watching him. The tips of her hair were bleached-out aqua now, and made her look like she was still sitting in front of a glowing computer in a dark room. Every time she picked at the table, a little silver star earring on her right ear shivered.

"You should keep an eye out for her," Kate said. "You'd be surprised. Bo always knew where she was. He was excellent at it."

"That was Bo's assignment."

A flake broke away from the table under her fingers. "She wanders if you're not careful—you've seen it."

That felt like a bigger vote of confidence than he deserved—he'd only seen Margot once, when she'd gone to a museum and met up with a hired gun and he'd risked his life to get Bo to follow.

Then Daniel understood, and his knees went heavy.

From the open door to Li Zhao's office, Daniel could hear typing. He could hear Kate's nails scraping the finish off the table in places Li Zhao would never see.

"I'd love to," he said, "but sadly my camera makes it hard to pursue outside interests."

"Cameras malfunction," Kate said, with her hair falling in front of her face. The silver star in her ear had gone perfectly still.

Cold slid down his spine. Whatever Kate was suggesting, if she was willing to help him, it was bad news. "I thought you were loyal."

"I am," Kate said. "I'm loyal even when she isn't."

He nodded, once, slow enough that the camera wouldn't quite register it. "I'd better go," he said carefully after a second. "I feel pretty tired."

"You look it. Sweet dreams. Take rue Palmatier home; you'll avoid the traffic."

Kate texted him a number and a name from her personal cell before he had rounded the corner. He'd halfway decided to ignore her warning about Margot and go home, but the name changed his mind. He was a sucker for a good story.

So he walked half a mile out of his way and sat in the café across the street from the unassuming building on rue Palmatier until Margot left.

It was another half hour's walk to the small art nouveau building she disappeared into. And whatever happened inside must have been engrossing, because by the time he gave up and turned for home, the light had been on for an hour, illuminating the room right through the filmy curtains.

He wished he could narrow his guesses; he wished he could look into the future and understand it like Suyana did, or be Bo and disappear. But it turned out all he could do was stand casually across the street and dread the dark as Kipa and Margot sat across from each other like a pair of shadow puppets waiting for their cue.

Global ran one of Bo's candids in a feature the week after it ran a cover with America's official photos from the fucking Louvre, with Suyana in a gray dress she couldn't sit down in and Ethan in a tux that made him look like the president of something. Bo's snap was the polar opposite— practically a new story—but it only enhanced the party line and made them look more earnestly in love than the stately photo had.

The candid drove the engagement story right back up the ladder, but it was just long enough after the official parties had had their say that no one from the American team felt scooped enough to start demanding the magazine's sources. A smart play.

It was a smart photo, too. Suyana's veil had slid from her hair (she looked markedly less surprised about it than Ethan did, which markedly did not surprise Daniel), and she was reaching for it with her free hand and grinning sidelong at Ethan, who was too busy staring love-slack at her and leaning in to help to notice yet that she was pushing her book against his chest for him to hold, held fast against him by the wide spread of her hand.

It looked truly candid. The veil puffed out just at the edges like a ghost, and the pearl-covered comb had vanished in the crunch of Suyana's hand and left just the clean line of the net against the stones of the river wall, and the book was almost out of frame against Ethan's body, like something you weren't supposed to see.

"Good shot," he admitted once, during one of the brief

moments he and Bo both occupied the flat and were conscious. "Really good shot."

"Yeah," said Bo, shrugging on a jacket of no particular color. "You'd almost think she didn't know I was there."

Daniel tacked it up on the wall in their living room, to remind them to be frightened.

Grace didn't like late dinners. The small places got crowded deep in the evenings, and even among the chic sort, getting a glimpse of one of the Big Nine was a thrill. To avoid pictures and autographs, she had to be seated by six, out by eight. ("I hate you," Bo said as they passed in the apartment hall, the last time Daniel had seen him.)

When she was going out with Martine, the evening started at ten, and the bodyguards showed up half an hour ahead of time and opened the service doors in the building lobby and stood in the bottom of the stairwell as she took the elevator down.

Grace came out in heels and a dress that looked carved from granite, which meant a nightclub with dancing—when dancing was involved, Grace planned for dresses that stayed where she put them.

Daniel feared they were headed for Terrain (he didn't have a quarter-million-dollar necklace in his pocket this time, and that sort of entrance only worked once), until they pulled up in front of somewhere dark and low that had a bouncer reassuringly open to bribes. Daniel barely lost sight of them on the way inside.

He was preparing his lie for the VIP area when he realized they'd taken a booth off the dance floor instead. That alone was a concern. There was no way Martine didn't go for the most exclusive possible seating; she liked a pointed remove.

"—in the goddamn Central Committee," Martine was saying as he slid into the nearest booth.

Grace laughed. "That's terrible. Since when do you want Committee work?"

"That's what worries me," Martine said. She sounded nearly like she had outside Sessrúmnir in Norway, as haunted as anyone since Suyana, and for reasons he didn't understand.

(If Margot had her eye on Martine, Daniel could only wonder that Martine was so calm. Maybe she had yet to turn Margot down and realize the price of Margot's disappointment. He thought about the shadow of a small hotel and the sound of gunfire, and wondered—slipping, he was distracted, he worked hard not to think about it—where Suyana was now.)

Grace was quiet for a second. "Don't you think she's just trying to punish Argentina a little after how they voted on the environmental amendment? It would make sense. So would you, as replacement. You did do that tour of their new toy in Norway."

Daniel held his breath until it hurt before Martine said, "Yeah, I guess it's because of the tour."

The song changed, and people applauded. It was an excuse to look over at the cloud of vapor smoke above Martine, and the way Grace had gone still, looking at the dance floor and not her friend, so when she spoke it seemed a less piercing question than it was.

"What are you worried about?"

Daniel wondered about the odds that Kate would be true to her word about cutting his signal when it mattered, and then thought about Suyana holding a knife in her hand and doing what no one else had been able to do for her, and the thing in her eyes that had shifted and shuttered when she realized she'd been so alone.

By the time he was thinking of anything else, he'd already slid into the booth beside Grace, and they'd frozen the conversation to look at him, the combined force of their stares nearly enough to send him scrambling back out.

"You should ask Kipa," he said. "She's the one getting late-night visits from Margot."

"Why on earth?" Grace asked, at the same time Martine said, "What the fuck's your problem, On the Record?"

"Not tonight," he told Martine, hoping it was true. "And I don't know why, but if Margot was going to see her late at night, I'd be curious, wouldn't you?"

"It's more than I'm worth to be curious," said Martine. She sat back pointedly, turned her face to the dance floor, and hissed out a stream of smoke.

Grace was still looking at him, and if it didn't seem like she quite believed him, she looked as if she wanted to. "What would Margot even have as a hold over Kipa?"

Don't lie, he thought, even he knew better than to lie now, but there were true things he didn't dare say. He settled on, "Whatever she had a year ago, against Suyana."

From Grace's face, it was close enough to what she needed to hear. Absently she curled one hand into a fist, perfectly painted nails vanishing under her knuckles, as she slipped into the hundred-yard stare he knew by now was a Face running through their options and calculating odds.

Martine was watching them sidelong, the tips of her fingers bloodless against her cigarette.

"If Kipa's begun to pull away from the public," Grace said, "we'll need to—"

"You sure you're off the record?"

They both startled and looked at Martine. Daniel said, "I hope I am, but that's up to somebody else's kindness."

The song over their heads was thumping into his bones. Martine shook herself once, sequined dress moving like a fish, and looked at Grace.

"In the car on the way back from the airport, after Norway, Margot was checking her tablet every few seconds, and I thought how funny it was—it was deep night, all the press from our visit was over. I figured she was looking for vanity mentions. But she checked over and over, for a long time, until she saw something and sat back and turned out the light."

Beside him, Grace had gone perfectly still. Martine, who was no longer looking at either of them, ground the cigarette onto the table like that could snuff it out.

"When I woke up later that morning, I heard the UARC outpost had been destroyed and Suyana was in the wind for it, and then I forgot it as hard as I fucking could, because that means I sat on some hotel stairs drinking myself stupid while Margot, the chair of the goddamn IA, was looking the place over so she could tell somebody how to blow the other one up."

Chordata. Daniel couldn't imagine the entire organization in Margot's pocket, but he could see her convincing one or two people—Columbina maybe, maybe a mole in the UARC branch of Chordata—to do what they could, and report whatever possible. There had probably been enough desire to blow the place that anyone with information would have been of use. Maybe someone in Chordata had even admitted to Kipa the new IA recruit they'd scored. If Daniel was in Margot's shoes, that would be what he came over unannounced at night to find out.

The world had been a singular fool. The IA Central Committee didn't have a head of intelligence these days—a sign of transparency, they'd said when the position was dissolved, a sign of international trust—but of course there was one. She'd just been good at her job.

A beautiful plan, really. Have a mole or two anywhere there's dissent. Make waves whenever you need someone to be swallowed. Everyone on the Chordata side probably thought they had acted for the best in all this. Even the moles might believe they were outsmarting the system. Everyone did, until they learned better; he remembered that.

He needed to go—everything was falling apart—but he felt as heavy as Martine in her scales, as heavy as Grace, who was looking at the dance floor without seeing anything, with her hands pressed at the edge of the table.

The music was a booming line that never stopped, and Martine's shoe came to rest beside his shoe to keep him from falling over or from running, and they sat for a long time as if waiting for the truth to fall and crush them.

× × × × × × ×

He buzzed at the door of Bonnaire until someone tripped the lock, and took the cellar stairs two at a time.

"What's Margot going to do to her?"

Kate looked up and over at Dev, who had startled and was looking back and forth between them. Then he turned to a computer that faced away, reached for headphones, and slapped them on with great deliberation.

Kate handed him a data card. "Everyone she's spoken to in the last two weeks," she said. "No idea who might be your man. I hope you find him before he finds Suyana."

He slid it into his pocket, fought off a sense of déjà vu from the last time he had pictures in his pocket that he hadn't wanted anyone to see. (That had been for Suyana too; people got caught up with her somehow, the way a slow flood could carry away whole houses before you noticed anything wrong.)

"Did I have a camera malfunction last night?"

Kate look back at her screen. "Seems like you did. But it looked like a boring night anyway; they went into the club, they came out again."

"Don't suppose I get to know what made you change your mind about Li Zhao."

Kate flinched, set her jaw. Dev turned up his music so loudly it bled through his earphones, off-key and tinny.

"I haven't changed my mind about anything," she said

finally. "I'm giving you a story. We get headlines no matter what happens. What headline it is, I'm leaving to you, that's all."

"Good luck," said Dev, without looking over.

After a little silence, Kate said, "Good luck."

When Daniel wrapped his hand around the data card, the edges stung the pads of his fingers, just like old times.

18

"Do you remember the time we went for pizza in New York?" Ethan folded his arms and glanced at her.

At the far end of the table, Magnus and two of the Americans were going through contract negotiations for post-marriage obligations and benefits. Magnus was winning nearly 70 percent of his points, which meant the Americans didn't expect to have to honor it. She wondered what they'd bring out when they wanted to break the engagement. It would have to be oblique; she was so rarely without Ethan it was impossible to pretend she'd been in a compromised position.

"Of course I do," she said. "You risked mushrooms. I was

very proud." It had been weeks ago, and she had wanted to make sure of him.

Ethan said quietly, "I think that was the happiest I've been in a long time."

If she hadn't already suspected him as a spy, this pointed nostalgia would have done it. She'd offer him lessons, if he was going to last long enough to need them.

"I'm really glad we did," she said instead. True enough.

"No, she's entitled to that security beyond any limitation of tenure," Magnus was saying. "If they both retire somewhere—"

"Yes, of course, fine," Harold said, making a note.

Ethan said, "We could do it again."

She looked down the table, where Stevens was dutifully entering changes. Magnus was folding up his paper copy (always paper, she didn't know how he came by so much paper), and a printer was whirring quietly in the office.

"As soon as we sign this thing," she said, making a binding international agreement sound as much like a chore as she could, "we'll sneak out for gelato."

For a moment he hesitated, and she wondered if he was going to risk it and ask her to leave before they signed. It would be tipping his hand. He'd have to be sure of Margot, to do it.

"Sounds perfect." He took her hand, smiled one second too late.

She smiled back, as calm as she had ever been, until the contract was in front of them and their signatures were on it.

She sent Magnus a message in the ten seconds it took Ethan to put on his shoes.

So Ethan tucked her under an awning and out of a mist of rain, and she grinned and brushed droplets off his coat as he looked at her with hollow eyes, and just as the first tourists were asking for photographs and the gelato was dripping down her hand in sticky ribbons, a sedan pulled up and two of Ethan's bodyguards got out.

"Oh, come on," Ethan said as he reached for someone's map, more resigned than put out. "Hi, yes of course, and your name?"

"It's fine," Suyana said, smiling for a photo with a teenager who scampered back to her friends, raincoat fluttering behind her. "Thank you for the thought."

Ethan fought a scowl. "I just—I wanted one nice thing."

She looked at him sidelong, watched him sign the glorified glyph that passed for his autograph. (You never signed with anything that looked close to legal. Your real signature was the stamp of a country. The doodle was your celebrity.) His hands never shook. She envied him.

"Guys, thanks so much, but I gotta go," he was saying, and someone *ooh*ed as he reached for Suyana, and she tossed a laugh over her shoulder as he folded her into the comfort of his arm and walked away to scattered applause.

"Smooth," she said, aiming for a compliment that could sound earnest.

But his face had closed up in some benign, untouchable way, and he said, "The car's probably around the corner. We should get to dinner," and prepped his smile for the American photographer who would be waiting as soon as they came into sight.

They didn't drop Suyana and Magnus off from the celebratory dinner until the photographer had gotten a shot of Suyana and Ethan kissing candidly in front of the silhouette of Notre-Dame, which took nearly twenty minutes thanks to the barely-there rain that clouded the lens and made the shot look more like an Impressionist painting than a sneaked classic.

Magnus clutched his tablet in one hand and looked anywhere but at them, as if it all bored him beyond words. Ethan glanced up a few times too many, scanning the bank for someone he never saw.

Suyana didn't look around. Bo was wherever served him best, and no one else was of particular importance. Ethan's lips were dry and warm, and with every kiss, she thought, This one's the last.

It wasn't the last until midnight, and Ethan's kiss as he helped her out of the car at her building was so distant he might as well already be on the phone with the enemy. It was so quietly decisive it took Suyana a moment on the sidewalk to get her breathing under control, as Magnus shook hands with a group of handlers she hated and wished them all farewell. (This one's the last, she tried to think, but it didn't hold; she knew it wasn't true.)

Ethan was already in the car and pulling away, and at this hour the traffic wouldn't hold him long, by the time she'd committed to what had to be done and admitted no one could help her but Magnus.

"Follow him, please."

Magnus raised an eyebrow and glanced at Ethan's car. "What exactly do you think he's doing at this hour?"

"Meeting Margot."

She might have escaped suspicion if it had sounded more sarcastic, or more angry, or more studied. Instead, she'd been distracted by the car, and now Magnus was staring at her, less in shock from the suggestion than that she'd admitted it without an agenda.

There was no recovery. She met his eye. "You're losing him."

Magnus made some genteel wave with one hand without ever looking away from her. Because he was Magnus, a cab pulled up out of the smoke, ready and waiting.

"Keep me posted on where he goes and who he sees," she said. "Do nothing till you hear from me."

With an expression more sincere than he probably intended, he said, "Yes, sir," and vanished into the cab and around the corner.

And just like that, she was alone for the first time since the engagement.

She started to look around for Daniel out of habit, before she remembered. Instead she put on a smile and waved at the two bodyguards who had lingered behind Ethan to look out for trouble. But she wasn't their brief until the wedding, and they waved good night and slipped back into their sedan and headed home.

Suyana breathed in and out for a moment, just to savor a breath that had no expectations in it. Then she wondered if she could risk a quick walk to the Seine—four streets, maybe five—and spend a moment at the water, looking over at the glimpse of Notre-Dame before she went back upstairs and waited for news. She'd just as soon have nice scenery for that. She'd just as soon be suspended a little longer in mutual pretend, like Ethan was a man she really cared for, and she was someone he could be loyal to.

She was nearly in view of the river when she felt the man step out behind her, and her stomach soured as soon as she saw his shadow in the streetlight—some shadows you just knew had trouble behind them—but before she could reach the café two doors down or the open walk along the river, she felt the knife along her ribs.

Whoever it was, he was enthusiastic; the blade pushed through her clothes and scraped her side, and she'd hissed at him before she'd registered the whole of the danger.

"Stop moving," the stranger said quietly, tightly, and she did. It wasn't the voice of a professional. He was nervous, angry. He must be a believer—no telling of whom. Both Chordata and Margot recruited their killers from far afield. Very urbane.

She breathed in slowly so that her voice would be a little steadier when she asked, "Who sent you?"

Behind her, he actually froze. Then she could feel the blade skim the edge of the cut to her rib cage as he craned his neck to get a better look at her.

"Jesus," he said, halfway between respect and disbelief, "how many enemies do you have?"

Through the fog of panic, she could feel her face smoothing into complacence, the affable expression you put on when you were trying to find common ground with someone at the start of a difficult negotiation. She had enough enemies that one would call her Suyana and the other Lachesis, and if this stranger would hold still and listen, she'd tell him everything as she waited for a name and her chance at the knife.

"Let me give you a list," she said, as professionally as she could. Her elbows had been trembling, but as she spoke they went perfectly still as if she'd given them some outside signal. (She couldn't do anything from within, somehow.)

"Sorry," he said, cooler and calmer, "no time, I—"

Then there was a crack, and something muffled and rotten and metallic as the knife hit the ground, and she waited for the pain that would tell her what tendon the man had severed, which way her head would fall as she bled out.

But a moment passed and she could still breathe and she was still staring out at a sliver of the street, and she realized the man at her shoulder now wasn't the one who'd been holding the knife.

That one was on the ground, on his stomach, looking up at her too directly from a neck that had been wrenched until it snapped. The other one was taller and silent, and though it took her two breaths to be able to turn around without shaking, he waited.

It was Bo. His hands at his sides were still slightly spread open, ready for all comers.

It fell into place quietly, the last tumbler in a lock: Daniel picking a fight with the camera pointed right at her, the substitution to a man Daniel had promised she could count on (she'd never questioned it, it was something he seemed to mean, and that happened so little with him), the man in a lump at her feet.

"Good to see you again," she said, for lack of anything else. Fall back on manners, Hakan had told her; diplomacy is manners more than kindness.

The last time she'd really seen him was a year ago, when he was showing her pictures of the assassination attempt to prove Daniel was a liar. He'd been there when she stood above the body of the man she killed, but his wasn't the camera that had concerned her then.

Bo must have reasons. He owed Daniel or he loved Daniel or he'd seen more of Margot's methods than he liked and thought this time was the same as the last. She set it aside for later.

"You gave me a good picture," he said, as if she'd asked.

Absently—her tongue felt heavy and thick, the man had started a word that could have been Lachesis, and the knife was on the ground and she couldn't look at it—she said, "I gave you three."

He looked at her as if she was a spider. One corner of his mouth turned up.

"You're welcome," he said.

Her heart was slamming into her ribs. Daniel had sent this man to look out for her when he knew the worst was coming. The dead man's arm was across her foot; he was already going cold.

She chased possibilities up and out the branches of the tree, but they were narrow. Margot had sent the killer—under the canopy of Chordata or as a personal errand, it didn't matter. Either way, there was no more careful maneuvering left to her. That branch had been sliced off clean.

Now it was strike or nothing. Grow so large no one could rip you from the foundation without collapsing the ground under their feet. The mudslide that consumed the forest.

She looked up the long way to Bo's face, held his gaze until she was sure of him.

She said, "I'd like to speak to your employer."

The employer was waiting for her in the living room past the dusty shop and the creaky stairs that Suyana couldn't imagine Daniel taking seriously. She imagined Daniel took the woman in charge very seriously. Despite the hour, her black suit was crisp, and she sat with her shoulders canted just backward from straight, the position you learned when an IA trainer came by twice a week to strap you into the yoke until you lost the will to resist it. Hakan would have been proud of posture like that.

Suyana could have asked Bo to relay this over the line; she was sure enough of her offer sight unseen, and Bo would have just nodded and it would have been agreed. But there had been enough unseen things. Sometimes you wanted to look the enemy in the eye.

Suyana's instinct was to wait through that first edged silence until Li Zhao introduced herself properly, but one look at Li Zhao changed her mind. They'd stand all night in silence waiting on information they both already knew. Suyana didn't have the time.

"I'm here to offer you an exclusive," she said.

"For how much?"

"Let's not make this about money," Suyana said, as pleasantly as she could manage. Money spent too easily. It was better to be owed.

Li Zhao raised her eyebrows and stood. "Then what are we making this about?"

Bo shifted beside her, little more than an inhale that wavered on the way out, but the hair on the back of Suyana's neck stood up when Li Zhao stopped moving and glanced at him. Suyana didn't dare look over; whatever Bo was suggesting, it was between him and Li Zhao. Suyana could do nothing but go on.

"I'd require open communication with every snap currently in Paris, including Daniel Park."

Li Zhao folded her arms across her chest—carefully, practiced. If her thumbs weren't trembling, you'd never know she was nervous.

But this wasn't a challenge; it was merely a defense against poor negotiation, and that much Suyana understood. Li Zhao was still listening—she was a professional—and tonight Suyana would rather deal with business than ideals.

"He's been forbidden to contact you. He can't maintain objectivity."

Suyana imagined the floor of the Assembly, a year of not quite looking up at the balcony so he wouldn't have to not quite look back.

"I didn't ask for his life story," she said, hoping it sounded as arch as Magnus. "I asked for his contact and cooperation."

Not unkindly, Li Zhao said, "What could you possibly be offering me that would mean opening up my employees to such dangerous exposure?"

Suyana tried to smile, but she was tired, and it came out like it had when she was thirteen, sitting in a jail cell and listening to a stranger explain the rest of her life; lips pulled a little tighter over her closed teeth. She'd become a decent diplomat, for someone whose first instinct was how to make her enemies vanish.

She said, "I'd like to start a revolt. You'll want to be there."

Magnus's message had come in while she was at Bonnaire, and reading it gave her the same muted, infuriating calm of his cadence as if he'd told her in person.

He made a phone call. With him now.

He and Ethan were sitting at opposite sides of Ethan's dining room table, and though both Magnus's hands were visible, she had the sense Ethan was at gunpoint when he turned slowly, deliberately, to look at her.

There was no way Magnus would have announced his intentions. He'd have let this play out with her here, for maximum effect. But Ethan's eyes were red and glittering—the wait and his guilt must have worn on him—and he looked exhausted past the point of defense.

She was thankful for the hired killer. The wait had done more to break Ethan than she could have. (She wasn't sure what she'd have been willing to do to break him; it was better to leave some lines untested.)

"Evening, Suyana," Magnus said, without looking up from his paperwork. Of course he'd found paperwork somewhere.

She pulled off her silk shirt. It was a single motion, too fast—she hissed when the yank on the dried blood tore the wound on her ribs open—but it did what it was supposed to do. Ethan stood up and stepped toward her; even Magnus rose halfway before he could stop himself, and pressed his palms to the table.

"Suyana, Jesus, that's—oh God, there's blood everywhere—Suyana, what happened?"

She closed the distance, so Ethan could reach out and touch her whenever the last of his dignity left him.

"Margot sent someone to find me, after you called her and told her you'd left me alone."

Ethan had been reaching out a hand toward her, but it dropped like she'd cut a string. "No," he said. After a moment, less certain, "No."

"Ethan." She took another step; he shrank away as much as he could without stepping backward. "You know it's true. You knew it was true when she encouraged you to sign the contract last year, after I got shot by someone they never traced back to his employer."

The sound of his mouth clicking shut punctuated her last word, a door closing behind him.

She didn't dare look away—this was important, it was important to look at him while all the parts fell into place—but she was sorry to miss Magnus, to whom this was also occurring (maybe not for the first time, one of them was cleverer than the other), and who was realizing the depth of his mistakes.

"Oh. Oh my God." Ethan was so shaken that he practically pushed himself back into his chair as his legs gave. He wiped a hand over his face, eyes to jaw, like it could keep the truth from coming out.

But it wouldn't, and she waited.

"I'm so sorry," he said finally, the words wet and scraping.

"At first I thought it was just—I mean, just Margot, you know how she is, a suggestion from the chair making sure I went through with it so America looked good—but I was going to offer you the contract anyway, Suyana, I promise."

"I believe you."

"And then later, when she asked me to keep an eye on you, I thought she had to be mistaken—I mean, you never did anything under the table. I thought she'd gotten you all wrong about just being in this for the cover story." As he trailed off he was looking at her, and as close to resentful as she'd ever heard him, he said, "That'll teach me."

The scratch on her ribs was beginning to ache.

"By tomorrow she'll know Magnus has been here, Ethan. Leili's already got her plane ticket. Whatever happens now, you're finished."

His eyes were lit practically gold when he looked up at her. Barely, still; she was barely taller even when he was sitting down. He'd spent the last year absently tilting his head lower, the better to hear her.

"Yeah," he said, in a tone she'd never heard from him. "She cuts her losses."

Magnus was already in the living room, having gotten someone on the phone. She guessed who he was calling; he was hard to trust, but he'd never been slow to catch the direction of events.

Her eyes stung suddenly. It had been a long night and was only going to get longer, and her stomach was a bag of acid, and for a moment she forgot all her dignity and put her hand on Ethan's hands, as loose and open as those of a man whose life wasn't forfeit, just to feel his fingers closing around hers like a fly trap.

Ethan's fingertips were warm, and damp as if from tears, and his voice was gentler than she deserved when he said, "So what happens now?"

She said, "You're going to marry me."

19

"Daniel, if you're not planning on a threesome tonight, Li Zhao has a new assignment for you."

Kate had waited until Grace was already back home to say anything; relatively gentle, as Kate went. It must be time to test bringing his camera offline. He turned up his collar against the rain, wished there was a mirror where he could fix his hair with his middle fingers so Kate could get the message. "Go ahead, Kate."

"Suyana got attacked a few hours ago."

The next seconds were a little fuzzy; he knew he didn't make a sound, mostly because he tasted blood from biting his lip, and he was at the edge of an intersection with people looking at him like he'd nearly walked into traffic.

He knew why she'd had to put that on the record. He took a deep breath, let it out; Li Zhao would be watching to see how he handled the shock, this wasn't a betrayal by Kate, he knew why. He swallowed around a sour lump in his throat.

"Does Grace know? Should I go back?"

She huffed, disbelief down the line that made him angry until she said, "Negative. There's been a change of organization."

"Oh shit, you killed her?"

In the background, Dev coughed.

"You might wish," Kate said. "We've all been redirected to a single assignment."

"Oh. For the session?" Proceedings started in under forty-eight hours. It would make sense to wrangle them all together beforehand.

After too long, Kate said, "It's preparation, sure. You should look at the attacker first, in case you have an ID."

He stood in the doorway of a town house and watched the footage on his phone—a smear of a face and then a jerky step forward and then Suyana slowly turning to look into the camera as she realized she'd been spared. There wasn't a good look at the attacker's face until he was already dead and Bo looked down at the corpse. Probably for ID purposes. Bo didn't miss a trick.

"So, Bo—"

"Don't finish that sentence, please," said Kate, and he remembered a discussion a long time ago about what sort of work hired guns went into if they lived long enough to retire. "Was he one of the men Margot met with?"

Daniel shook his head as he tried to decide which lie would keep them least suspicious of Suyana.

"Margot must be hiring out the job to new people," he said. "We'll have to be careful."

"Well, then keep a lookout on your way to the church."

He put a hand out for no particular reason, nearly jammed a knuckle against the stone wall under his fingers.

"The church?"

"Saint-Merri," Kate said slowly. "For the wedding."

Four heartbeats knocked against him so hard he swayed. He pressed his hand harder against the wall, the stone rough against his palm. The doorway was too cramped—his breath echoed in static.

"Daniel?"

"No. No, yes, I read you. I don't—sure. We're all being called in, fine."

"Daniel, she asked for you specifically."

"Oh, I bet." Li Zhao knew how to bring a lesson home, he'd give her that. He was going to get his shit together before he showed up at the parish, though. She wasn't going to get the satisfaction.

Kate ground her teeth together twice, like she was chewing her answer.

"I mean, Suyana asked for you."

If he was shaking when Bo opened the red door and ushered him in, Bo was too nice to mention it. He only said, "Are the others in place outside?"

"I recognized two," Daniel said—tourists sitting near the fountain.

"That might be enough. So. You can sit anywhere you'd like. The city clerk who's making it legal is sitting in the front row, avoid her. I'm nearer the door, in case the groom tries to run."

Daniel couldn't feel his hands. "What?"

"Suyana has plans for how all this is going to go," Bo said, caught somewhere between business and concern. "I'm not sure who shares them."

The answer almost burst out of him—it doesn't matter, once Suyana has plans—but Daniel closed his mouth. He wasn't good at predicting the future. The past was a dangerous place to draw conclusions from.

They were already at the altar, Suyana and Ethan and Magnus and a priest. Suyana was saying something to Magnus in a voice too low to carry, but Ethan was sniffling into his sleeve, and the soggy, despairing sound bounced off the ceiling every so often.

"Daniel, think about this," Bo said, but he was already moving forward, past the hulking columns and their paintings, toward the altar.

She stopped and looked at him even though he didn't think he'd made any noise, and it was the stupidest thing in the world to imagine she'd known it was him before she looked up, but damn if she didn't meet his gaze like she knew just who she was expecting to see.

He'd only been apart from her a few weeks, but when she walked toward him (midsentence, and Magnus stared after her a moment), she looked like a different person. The circles under her eyes were a sunken purple, the unhappy lines around her mouth like a battle carved into a stone. Her dress was the pale gray of a storm, and she wore no makeup, not even on her scar.

No wonder Ethan was terrified; Daniel was fighting the urge to run for it, and all she'd asked him to do was watch.

But it wasn't a surprise to Daniel the way it must have been for that poor asshole. This wasn't the first time Daniel had seen what she looked like when she was preparing to turn a story around.

He was angry—he was furious, a year of disappearing inside the act and where had it landed her, what good was all this—but somehow the only thing he could think to say was, "Are you all right?"

She took in a low breath, like now she had to recalibrate, and for a second the mask slid into a face he almost recognized. But it passed, and whatever answer she might have been looking for escaped her. Instead she said, "After the wedding, Ethan's on his own for a while. Li Zhao is arranging for someone to cover him just in case he decides to make a run for it, but it won't be live."

"Live?" He resisted the urge to cover the camera.

"We're sending a feed of the wedding ceremony directly to *Closer* TV and half a dozen news stations."

It took him a second, but he caught up. "So the IA and the Americans can't pretend it didn't happen. With six stations competing, it will have aired somewhere by then. Fuck."

"The new American Face is on a plane taking off in five minutes," Suyana said. "Margot has America's blessing. She's retiring Ethan before the first day of session."

That was the day after tomorrow, and a wedding wasn't going to save him from being kicked out if Margot had made up her mind. "So why—" He stopped as he realized.

Ethan. That big, dumb grinner. All that attentive care of Suyana, done for the benefit of someone else.

"But he stood with you when the UARC bad news broke."

"He thought he was using leverage against her, for my sake. He didn't understand her."

The church's scattered points of light floated in her dark

eyes, and when they moved, it was his only sign she was still thinking and not just delivering conclusions. "After we drop off Ethan, we go dark while I talk to Grace and Martine."

"Jesus Christ, what about? Who's we?"

"You and Bo and me."

"Fuck you, why don't you ask me first?" It was quiet—he didn't have the breath for more—but it was a year of anger all at once, and she flinched. Good, he thought, somewhere deep and horrible.

He expected some rejoinder about how she'd assumed he was used to following her around. Maybe something about how Li Zhao made the decisions, not him.

Instead she just said, like she hadn't slept in two years, "I have to go get married," and it turned out that was the worst thing she could have said.

She was moving to go; she was already the sliver of her face he always caught when she was trying not to be seen.

He picked the name that would sting. "And Magnus?"

"I don't know what he'll do," she said, and before he could point out what a terrible fucking idea it was not to be certain about people's loyalties before you decided to stage a coup with them, she was back in front of the gold-plated altar, taking Ethan's hands gently away from his face and holding them in hers, gazing up at him as steadily as any other snake with something it's decided to kill.

Magnus was looking sidelong at Daniel. "Who's that?"

"My brother. Let's get started."

The priest was confused, but at least it made him brief, and it was going normally until Suyana said her "I do" with such quiet, warm conviction that Daniel startled. He shouldn't have, he knew what kind of actress she had become, but still, he was happy Bo was over his shoulder and out of sight. (He hadn't looked around for any of the others. He didn't care where they were.)

At least he wasn't alone; Magnus looked twitchy about her sincerity until Ethan took a heavy breath and echoed "I do," and it was too late for second thoughts, at which point Magnus started typing into his tablet, because of course he would.

Ethan's voice was steady, and his hands closed around hers as she spoke in a gesture—apology, acquiescence—just for her. One edge of her mouth twitched with her effort to hold it still, and suddenly the eye contact turned into something softer, something shared instead of a demand. Daniel wished he'd been looking elsewhere.

But the priest was invoking God, and the pronouncement was echoing in the rafters of the silent church, and everything around them was gleaming gold, and that was a moment to end a broadcast on. Just as well Daniel had gotten it. He'd take any victories he could come by.

He missed the kiss—he was looking up at the golden

sunburst and didn't want to drop his head too fast—but it didn't matter. He'd gotten the shot that would sell. Anybody could kiss. Didn't mean anything.

It was nearly dawn when they filed out of the church, almost like a real wedding procession.

"Blackout," Kate said on an exhale that sounded like Li Zhao was out of hearing. "Comms are clear."

A woman who had been having a lively conversation on the phone slid a packet into Magnus's hand as she passed by, and Ethan (with Suyana's hand tucked into the crook of his elbow like this was a real wedding) took it from Magnus without even feigning surprise that he was going to have a ten-second honeymoon.

"It's a Canadian ID," Magnus said, "and enough money to make some people forget you. Decide which ones."

"It's impossible to disappear when you're me."

Daniel didn't even begrudge the guy his ego. It was probably true. One thing for Li Zhao to disappear after a few months, back before the network was so fast and the Faces so ubiquitous. Another thing for Suyana to disappear, when she had played parts so long and people were inclined to make assumptions and feel superior and let themselves forget. Trying to get the American Face to drop off the edge of the world was going to be a different problem.

Bo was talking to the pair near the fountain, and Daniel was the only outsider within earshot when Ethan turned and asked her, "If I wanted to stay, would you stand with me?"

Daniel winced even before Suyana answered, as soft, but with the knife behind it. "What was the thing you told Margot most often about me?"

Ethan didn't even go red at the ears, which meant he'd kept his bedroom secrets, but he let her hand drop. "I mostly told Margot you seemed unreachable. I didn't mind looking like an idiot so long as it kept her from being curious."

Daniel thought two things at once. First, that Ethan was a fool to have answered, and second, that was the most interesting thing anyone could have told Margot. He didn't have to look at Suyana to know she thought the same.

It struck Daniel, like the thin end of a wound he'd feel later, the series of disasters they'd gone through to make Suyana even this knowable to him. She'd been designed otherwise. She didn't trust unless circumstances had utterly abandoned her. Daniel had been a lunar eclipse.

He kept his eyes on the fountain a little longer, until the sounds of the embrace were over. They didn't know the cameras were off; it seemed polite.

When one of the tourists by the fountain had disengaged to follow Ethan, Daniel risked a look at Suyana. Then he wished he hadn't, but an assignment was an assignment.

"Magnus," she said. "Go home and call anyone you think has Margot hanging over them. We'll need a majority vote of no confidence and support for the new candidate. Whatever you can do would be of use."

Magnus glanced up from his notes, hiding his abject horror just in time. "And . . . who's the new candidate?"

Daniel smiled. If he thought Suyana wanted herself in the limelight, he knew a different woman than Daniel did.

"I'll let you know when she says yes," Suyana said, and headed toward the river. Bo fell in behind her, and after a moment Daniel joined her.

"Magnus might turn on you," Daniel said.

"He might."

She was wearing a light parka now, nondescript and long enough to cover the dress, and a scarf that covered her jawline. Her hair was pulled back—he supposed the long, straight weight of it would attract more attention loose, but it was strange to be able to look right at her.

"Shouldn't you have him followed?"

"We did," Bo said, and Daniel had never wanted to punch him so much in his life.

"Surprised you didn't send me," he said.

There was a pause that no audio recorder would have thought much of. Then she said, "I wanted you here."

The rising sun stung his eyes. He couldn't bring himself

to actually make an apology—he wasn't wrong, there was nothing to apologize for—but he was quiet when he said, "Right. I had forgotten what you're like when you cut your losses and start doing the smart thing."

"I never do the smart thing," Suyana said. She wiped a hand once, viciously, down her face. "I just carry the losses."

She sounded aged, and like she didn't expect to live until tomorrow, and it was close enough to the truth that for a moment he leaned close enough to brush against the scar from the bullet she'd taken when they'd first been in Paris, a long time ago.

20

Bo didn't let her stop moving to make the phone call until they were already along the Seine, where he could keep an eye on all directions and they had options for escape if they needed them. Then he said, "You're clear," and motioned for Suyana to get going.

Daniel snorted as Bo glanced in every direction as casually as he could. Suyana frowned. "He was your idea," she said. "Let him be the hero if it helps."

The look she got was something unreadable, and she nearly clarified that she was grateful, not offended, just before Grace picked up.

"Hello, darling."

Either Colin was there or Grace was rehearsing for a propaganda film. "I need a favor."

"Makeup? Oh, I'd love to, I need some as well. Lyta is nice, as stylists go, but if I ever want decent lipstick, I'm on my own! You know how it is. What's going on?"

Suyana imagined Grace's trajectory from the living room to the privacy of a locked bedroom door. "We have to talk before session tomorrow. You, Martine, me. Now."

"You should talk to Kipa as well," Grace said. "Margot's been at her."

Shit. "Fine. Somewhere public and loud."

"There is no way I'm about to discuss whatever this is in public."

"Private places aren't safe."

"Well, I don't know," Grace said after a moment. "I have a place I can offer."

Suyana's heart turned over once. Her safe house. Grace was offering her new safe house. (It's going to be you, Suyana thought, sudden and fierce, so much she nearly said the words.)

"That's . . . very kind, but we'll want sound cover."

Grace huffed a laugh. "I've taken precautions since last time, thank you. The windowsills in this place are disgusting and the floors are a disgrace, but at least I know if anyone's been in there but me."

Suyana knew those precautions. This life turned everyone into a spy.

There was a moment's quiet. Daniel raised an eyebrow at her.

"Send me the address, I'll meet you there. And pick up Martine. It's better than either of you being alone."

"What about you?"

"I'm not alone," she said, and then, for no particular reason, "Thank you."

She hung up before Grace could ask what the thanks was for, so she wouldn't have to say, For believing me without me having to explain. That was something you saved for when you needed someone to tip in your favor. Like telling someone you were grateful, she thought with a pang, meeting Daniel's eye.

"It's all right," he reminded her. She must have been looking for the camera, out of habit.

Bo said, "Unless you're having the meeting here, we should get going."

Daniel rolled his eyes, and a rejoinder to Bo died in her mouth when she thought about being on the banks of this river twelve hours ago. "Good idea. Who's covering Margot?"

He paused while someone fed him the answer. "A relay team of three."

Something in his voice made her skip the interim

questions and go right for, "When did they lose her?"

"About fifteen minutes ago."

"Who would be most likely to know where she is?"

"Big game hunters," Daniel said with a shit-eating grin, and then looked at Bo. "Best man for the job."

Suyana did the math about who was the most dangerous and the most in danger, fractals spreading into possible disasters. She said, "Margot will be gathering all the support she can. I need details. Bo, if you can find her, you should find her. I'll be all right."

"Are you sure?" The frown was audible.

"Of course. I have Daniel, for luck."

When they were alone, Daniel took a step closer to block out onlookers and said, "Is there . . . anyone who can help you?"

It stung to hear him sound so hopeful—like he knew, like they were in this together and Chordata was still on her side. For a moment she was back in the perfume department, picking up bottles and setting them down again and waiting for Zenaida to appear in her bright hijab and heavy silk coat and smile and embrace Suyana with one arm, like a daughter gone just long enough to miss.

"No," she said. She cleared her throat. "Some of them acted without my consent, in a way they knew would work against me. I thought I had handled it. Last night might suggest otherwise. I have to become too powerful to disappear."

Daniel had gone pale at the edges. "So . . . that . . . was them?" He gestured vaguely at her torso.

She rested her hand lightly on her rib cage, so he'd know where the wound was.

"No point worrying now. We have a meeting."

As they set out side by side, he said, "They might be two sides of the same problem. Martine thinks Margot set up the research facility to blow. Once they knew Margot came after you last year, it must have made sense. Maybe Margot's infiltrating Chordata."

She didn't need to ask how he knew—he'd learned since last year, and he'd been busy these last few weeks—but her pride was eclipsed by the news.

Of course Margot knew Chordata was looking for alternative sources. Of course Margot was working to eliminate a problem. If you had the chair of the Central Committee in your pocket, even Suyana was expendable. Fools, whoever had listened to Margot and believed her, but Suyana supposed Chordata had to have its fools the same as any other organization with five hundred legs.

Fine. She let the anger build. She'd use it. She'd need it; Grace and Martine would need to be more afraid of her than of Margot.

x x x x x x x

When she knocked on the door of the unassuming flat in the unassuming side street of an unassuming neighborhood not far enough from Montmartre, Daniel said, "Blackout," so solemn that when Kipa flung the door open it startled her.

She covered her surprise with gruffness. "What did Margot tell you?" (Beside her, Daniel was rubbing his forehead with a thumb, like the introduction pained him.)

Kipa shook her head, shrugged. "You know what she tells people when she wants things handled. It was decisive."

"But you're here anyway?"

Her eyes were wide and serious. "Of course," she said, and Suyana ached to believe her.

When they shuffled into the cramped studio—feeling even smaller in the dim of closed curtains—with a table and a quorum of rickety folding chairs squeezed beside the bed, Martine and Grace were sitting in a haze of nervous smoke from Martine's cigarette.

Grace glanced up first. When she saw Daniel, her eyes went wide for a heartbeat before she could smooth her face back to a polite nothing. Martine barely spared either of them a look; she must know Daniel better.

"Suyana," Grace said, "you know he's surveillance."

"He's with me," Suyana said as she took a seat. Daniel, after some silent negotiation with himself, sat gingerly on the edge of the bed, hands in his lap. "And he's not taping this. I've struck a deal."

"Oh, *well*, if you've struck a *deal,* then I suppose that's all sorted out."

"Martine."

Kipa raised her eyebrows, and Suyana tried very hard not to do the same as she leaned forward and said, "It's about Margot."

"So he told you?" Martine said, casting an unimpressed look at Daniel.

Daniel hadn't told her much, really, and for a moment her fingertips stung like she'd lost blood. She ignored it. He'd sent her a lieutenant, and he'd followed her when she gave the word. She'd asked nothing else of him.

"Do you mean the attempted murder last year, or the attempted murder last night?"

"Last night?" Kipa had a hand on the table, staking her claim to talk—not a bad move, but her nail polish was chipped. Suyana would have to break her of that habit.

"Margot sent someone after me last night. The knife got me. My snap saved my life."

It was a bit much—"took care of it" would have worked just as well—but she had brought a new press order on all of them, and sometimes you had to oversell. Sooner or later, everybody was susceptible to a good headline.

Kipa was the first to summon an answer. "So what are you going to do?"

"Shit," Grace said a moment later, as it occurred to her. Martine shook her head tightly, once.

Suyana said, "I want her out. Tomorrow's the first day of session. Everyone will be gathered, but there won't be anything scheduled for vote or debate. National press will be present. I want a vote of no confidence in Margot before she can say a word. Call in your allies, whoever you have who would be willing to second a motion."

Martine narrowed her eyes. "Who did you say was going to lead this stirring *cri de coeur* in front of every country in the world and a hundred of the army?"

Suyana smiled, all teeth. "I will. Don't worry, Martine, I never mistook you for a woman of action."

In lieu of an answer Martine sucked in a pirate's breath off her cigarette, and if she looked like she was on the verge of regretting something, the smoke made it hard to tell.

Kipa broke in. "But then wouldn't the vice chair just step up?"

"That's in case of death or emergency. Otherwise it's a vote. We'll need a new candidate for chairperson. Immediately."

Grace blinked and frowned. "Who, exactly, did you have in mind?"

"Not me," Suyana promised. She never could. As soon

as she was under the lights, the truth would come out, and maybe Chordata deserved it, but she wasn't going to make a decision for the entire organization. She knew what it felt like for decisions to be made without you that couldn't be taken back.

Kipa said, "Not me either."

"So what?" Martine blew smoke through her teeth so hard it looked like the edge of dragon fire. "It'll just be someone else on the Central Committee. She's groomed that whole place to do just as she says. She'll be replaced by herself."

"Not if a majority backs an outside candidate. The Committee can't risk making the wrong appointment themselves in the middle of no-confidence upheaval. It taints by association." She risked a look at Grace, who seemed staggered but was paying attention, and pressed her luck. "An outsider will be the best solution—they'll take her on to see if she'll fail, and by the time she succeeds it will be too late to remove her."

Martine frowned. "How the hell do you know she would succeed?"

Suyana looked across the table with deliberation and met Martine's eye without blinking. "If I put her there, I will make sure she succeeds."

Martine opened her mouth to refute it, smoke rolling across her cheek. But the words never came; she looked at

Suyana like she was remembering something, and then her face shifted a centimeter and she sat back.

"Well, I'm not doing it. I've seen what happens to anyone who ends up on top. I'm out." Her voice trembled; her hand trembled. "You're wasting your time if you want to change anything."

True in the long term—how could it not be?—but Margot had been on top for nearly twenty years, which was a good enough run to offer her successor, and now wasn't the time to lose focus. Suyana turned to Grace, whose hand was already a fist on the table, knuckles down. "Grace, do you want to be chair of the Central Committee?"

Grace tried a smile—one of the canned ones, one that wouldn't fool any of them. "It's not that I doubt you, Suyana, but this is dangerous business."

"It is. And it won't be easy. But I've seen your face when we're expected to vote No on something important. You have things you want changed, Grace, I know you do. With the right support—"

"That sounds like a threat."

"If you feel like it is, Martine, you're welcome to abstain from the voting."

Grace raised a hand off the table an inch and stopped them both. "So, this is the plan? I say yes, and you somehow make it work to oust Margot on camera?"

Suyana looked at her, tried to summon whatever conviction she still had about anything. "Grace. Do you want to be chair?"

Behind her, Daniel took in a slow, heavy breath and held it, like he was trying to get a steady close-up. If he was, Suyana thought, and this camera was rolling, she'd kill him, too.

After what felt like a long time but couldn't have been, Grace said, "I'll accept the nomination."

She would have kept pushing—accepting wasn't the same as wanting, they'd all done nothing their whole lives but accept, and this had to be different—but there was a glint in Grace's eye as she spoke, hunger looking to be fed.

With power there was a far-off chance of justice; Suyana knew what that felt like. The first time someone suggested it to her they took a picture of her standing in front of the green, and the International Assembly had sworn her in beneath the official photo of her staring out at them all and already making plans.

"We need two-thirds," Kipa said, reaching into her bag for a notebook. "Do we have it?"

They looked at one another. To discuss something like this was dangerous. To write it down was treason; to begin a list like this was putting your head on the block.

Kipa said, "New Zealand." She wrote with the concentration of someone whose letters were usually written for her, and Suyana felt a pang. She couldn't fail—not if it would put Kipa in danger. (That had been part of Grace's thinking in bringing her, Suyana had no doubt. Kipa might be an ally, but Suyana wasn't a fool.)

When she glanced over her shoulder, Daniel was looking at her, the shadow of a smile on his face. She returned it, just for a second.

Martine said, "Norway."

And because it was important, and because it was important that they saw it as soon as possible and recognized what she had done (what she was capable of), Suyana held up her hand with the engagement ring and said, "The United States."

21

The list took several hours to put together, which only surprised Daniel because he'd figured there was going to be a harder time finding people who were willing to move against Margot on someone else's word.

Martine had a list he believed. She was brittle, but that kind of sharpness got results. No surprise if she had three dozen countries who owed her a favor.

"Denmark," she said, pointing to the paper like it would know exactly why Denmark was a lock, and even Kipa smiled as she wrote.

He'd underestimated Grace. He suspected a lot of people had underestimated Grace—except Suyana, expert at taking someone's measure—who had appeared affably diplomatic, but was actually concealing an impressive network. Daniel had images of her getting elevator doors unstuck like a comic-book hero just before it plummeted, while a dozen Faces shook her hand and promised they owed her one.

Every so often, Suyana glanced at him sidelong and looked ready to smile, which meant she was enjoying the surprise of being believed. He smiled back; he was angry with her, still, but he worried for her more. The fight could wait until they had the luxury of a fight.

"If you're not sure, don't list them," Suyana said. "We'll have half an hour, at most, to talk to people before they call the session to order. There's no time to convince the undecided. Lock down anyone you can, and ask them to talk to people they trust. Margot's had a whole day on us to shore up support for whatever she's planning. I don't think it's enough, but we have to be efficient."

Kipa glanced up from her notes. "How will the people we talk to know who else we need to talk to without implicating themselves in treason?"

"The people we talk to have people who owe them favors," Suyana said. "Call them in. All of them."

Grace glanced at Suyana's left hand.

"Doesn't anyone have anything on Iceland? This seems ridiculous," Grace said, and Kipa smothered a giggle, and

Martine said, "It's a fucking miracle, a country that can stand alone," and they all seemed on the verge of fellow-feeling just before Bo cut across Daniel's feed and said, "I have something you and Suyana should hear."

When he stood up, Suyana looked over, and it was the biggest, most awful relief of his life that she realized what had happened before he had to say a word.

The front door of the building faced a little row of shops and felt too exposed for what Daniel knew this was, so he took her around the corner to a side alley, where Bo was waiting.

Suyana's first words were, "How did she do it?"

"Ferry from Calais to London. He bought a ticket in cash, paid someone to go with him as his boyfriend. The guy found him in the engine room just before they pulled into port." Bo took a breath that seemed to rob him of two inches of height. "The body's been identified as Ethan, through teeth. Just a few minutes ago. London police don't know what to do yet."

Suyana nodded twice, then held her head stiffly still as if afraid of over-accepting. "What are they saying happened?"

"Mechanical accident."

She made a low, agreeing noise that scratched at the skin on his neck. For a moment, she rested one shoulder against the wall; the shoulder she'd been shot in.

"I thought she'd wait," she said. "I thought she'd at least

want to see how tomorrow went before she decided. She must—she must know what we're doing. Of course she knows, sorry, that was a stupid thing to say. She wanted to make sure Ethan could never admit she'd asked him to be a spy on his own kind."

There was a little quiet, because Bo was a quiet person, and because Daniel had no idea what you said at a moment like this.

Then she said, "Whoever's with Magnus now, tell him to put in a claim for the body."

Even Bo made a face. "Are you sure?"

"I'm his wife," she said, edged. "I need to put in a claim for the body to start paperwork. The Americans can't let this look like he died before they called Leili in. I want time stamps." She looked up. "Bo, does Bonnaire have anyone in London?"

A beat. "Li Zhao's dispatched someone from that office. Should be ten minutes."

"She should call the BBC and deal, now," Suyana said. "I want broadcasts before Margot can make this disappear. They can say whatever they want about him, so long as he's too famous to vanish."

She was twisting the ring on her left hand absently; Daniel wondered if she knew.

"Where is she now?"

"She's been visiting a lot of old friends," Bo said.

If Suyana thought it was odd that Bo knew who Margot considered friends, she didn't betray it. "Good. If she was confident of her chances, she'd be calling Committee meetings. Keep Daniel apprised of who she sees."

Bo nodded, and had already taken a step back when she said, "Thank you, Bo. This is invaluable information. It will make the difference for us."

He nodded again, more warmly, before he vanished, and Daniel tried not to think about how often Suyana had handled people this way in the midst of some disaster that should have knocked her sideways. How many times she must have handled Daniel, that he hadn't even noticed.

Her nails were beginning to scratch her ring finger with every twist. He reached out slowly, his hand over hers—an inch away, not touching her. (It was unimaginable to touch her right now, for reasons he was carefully refusing to examine.) "Do you want to go back upstairs?"

She nodded—more slowly this time, like she was actually considering it and not just unable to keep still. "Daniel. When this story breaks, I don't—I don't know if I want to see the body, if it's too horrible. I need to see it eventually—I'll have to talk about it, make it important, how he died—but not . . . not today."

It sounded so broken that at first he thought something ugly and beneath him, but when he didn't answer, she didn't get any more calm or any more upset; she just looked down the street like she was expecting someone, and after a while, it unnerved him enough to say something.

"We'll get news via Kate," he promised. "No TV."

When she'd gone back inside, Kate said, "Shit, this is a mess."

He said, "Can you confirm I'm blackout?"

"Dev turned off the feed collection," Kate agreed carefully. "But the camera's still got physical memory, a few minutes at a time that get constantly overwritten. We're overwriting it as soon as it comes in."

"But Li Zhao can look at me in real time. Goddammit, Kate—"

"I wouldn't blame Kate for a situation you've single-handedly brought on us," Li Zhao answered.

He barreled through before he could start worrying about being seen. "And I wouldn't like to think you're looking the biggest story of the year in the mouth. Don't blow this by trying to capture the moment too soon. That could kill all of them."

She said, "I'm glad you remember that, Daniel. You'll want to keep that in mind."

She'll be a martyr, Li Zhao had said. *She looks good for that.*

He switched off the comm and took the stairs as slowly as he could, so that when he opened the door, they all knew he was coming.

× × × × × × ×

By the time Bo got back in touch with his list, it was already nightfall.

"Ready for this?" Kate asked, and Daniel's stomach plummeted before she even started.

Daniel repeated a list of names that, frankly, impressed him. How Margot was moving so fast was a mystery, but you couldn't say she didn't have a contingency plan. It went on so long, and Kate's voice got so grim as she read them out, that he felt like the bed was tilting and he was going to be dumped onto the floor.

Kipa, working to keep a steady hand, drew lines through name after name. Suyana was doing silent tallies, and he watched the muscle in her jaw come and go as she began to realize what they were up against.

"Well, this is a rousing game of we're-fucked bingo," Martine spat, standing up and raking a hand through her hair. "How can she move that fast?" A flurry of Norwegian that had to be profanity, and then she said, "I'm going outside for a real cigarette. If I don't come back, tell Ansfrida I wanted to vote in favor."

As she stormed out, Suyana tilted her head in Martine's direction. Daniel wasn't surprised by the request, but he still sighed as he stood.

Martine was waiting for him just outside. "Calm down, I'm not getting a real one," she said, craning her neck to the sky. "Terrified of them. My grandfather died that way, in some hospital room with a stranger. Not me."

"All right."

"And you can wipe the concern out of your voice. She might think you hung the moon, but I've seen you when you think you have a story, and it doesn't impress me."

The flush of her first words had utterly vanished by the end. "What, exactly, doesn't impress you?"

The cigarette in her hand twirled vaguely, pointed up. "That you think this can last."

He opened his mouth, closed it.

"It's not that I doubt your loyalty, as far as that goes when you're a snap," she said, so crisply he almost missed the compliment. "But I don't doubt this outcome, either."

Daniel was on the verge of replying—something awful, something way too honest—when he noticed that the man at the *tabac* across the street hadn't moved since getting his paper, and was trying to sneak looks at them above the edges of the finance section.

He looked down at her, put on his biggest grin. "We're being watched."

She raised her eyebrow and looked at him without any sign of tension or distraction (of course, he thought, that's what she is, but still he was impressed). "So what are you suggesting?"

"Kiss me," he said, and wasn't sure how deeply he meant it. From her smile as she slid her arm around him, she had a better sense of it.

When they broke apart, the stranger looked less certain of who he was watching. Daniel murmured, an inch from her mouth, "We should go get some food and a bottle of wine to bring back, until this guy decides we're together and gives up. Plus, we'll need to eat, and after this no one's going anywhere until morning."

"Why, Daniel," Martine said, and it was awkward how good his name sounded in her voice, "that's the closest thing to a plan I've heard all day."

He frowned despite himself. "Really? All day?"

She never moved, but her face clouded, and he had the sense of her pulling back until she was on a shore so remote he'd never find her.

"This is what you don't understand," she said, as kindly as she'd ever said anything. "People like you and me make plans—take our best shot and hope we walk away from the worst. People like Suyana don't. They push until something cracks and then they fall in. They don't care."

For a moment he felt like his fingertips had turned to ice. Then he tried to answer, but his throat closed so tight no answer could ever get out of it, and he felt as numb as he had watching Suyana give orders for her husband's body; the first moment Li Zhao ever spoke to him; the first time Suyana ever looked him in the eye.

After a little while, Martine took pity and slid closer to him, shifting them until she blocked him from sight of the stranger, and guided them down the street toward a little cluster of restaurants. They walked side by side with their arms around one another, silent and in no hurry, like two people who knew what love looked like.

22

Martine took with admirable calm the decision that they'd be using the flat as a safe house overnight, until Suyana specified that no one would be allowed to drop off supplies.

"You can kindly go fuck yourself. I'm not going to appear in front of the International Assembly with dirty teeth in a shirt I've been wearing for twenty-four hours. Some of us have standards."

"You'll do better to look a little like you've been on the run," Suyana argued. "Make them wonder if she's after you, too."

"She wasn't, until yesterday when you got us involved in this."

Daniel said, "Martine, we both know that's not true."

Suyana looked over her shoulder at him; Daniel made a tiny leave-it motion.

"And it's not Suyana's fault you picked an ugly shirt," added Kipa, who had grown less afraid of Martine with every comparative page of allies, as their number of supporters nearly matched.

Grace said, "I have some clothes here. Martine, you can borrow a shirt. Something formal, so the jeans look disrespectful and not just careless."

"Fine. Perfect."

"I'll change too," Grace said, halfway between Suyana and nobody. "I should be wearing something a bit more serious, I suppose, if we're going to nominate me to lead the free world. Jesus Christ."

"Nothing fancy," Suyana said. "Don't look like you expected it. First day of session, with a six a.m. call time—it makes sense to look subdued."

"Oh God, I'll be a no-show at Lyta's for styling. Colin's going to realize. I'll have to tell Lyta I have a woman over for the evening and hope she buys my apologies without telling Colin." Martine winked at her, and Grace gave her a look that suggested a decade of silent understanding. Suyana's envy passed; no time to linger over small things.

"I told Elizabeth I was spending the night," said Kipa.

"No one ever looks for me until the afternoon junket anyway. But won't Magnus be worried?"

Suyana said, "We're in touch with Magnus."

Martine looked at Daniel like he was an open window in a rainstorm. "How awful."

But Daniel was looking at Suyana. "What are you going to wear? Do you need anything?"

Shame on him for asking, if this was coming from him; shame on Li Zhao if it was coming from her. They would never do better than this. Suyana let her hand drop along the front of the gray sheath.

"My wedding dress."

Bo had been waiting somewhere, and in between one corner and the next he appeared at the edge of the procession.

"Li Zhao says she's got everyone she can in the gallery, and eyes on the ground. Whatever you need."

Suyana looked into the camera. "And how is she feeling about this?"

Bo paused as Li Zhao's response trickled in through the comm. Daniel looked increasingly mortified. After ten seconds Suyana said, "Thank you, Bo, that answers me."

"You're welcome to the details."

"Should I, though?" she asked, and when he smiled at her there was a little ease behind it, which was all she'd wanted.

Paris in the predawn was the most beautiful Paris; even Suyana knew that, and when Bo asked the four of them to walk ahead in silence for a moment, Suyana understood. In this light they looked like ghosts or witches, something powerful and untouchable and lovely, even in pencil skirts and jeans and sequin tops and Kipa's sensible cardigan with the top button on her blouse left undone.

"This isn't a clothing commercial," Martine snapped finally. "Can we actually talk or what?"

Daniel grinned. "Sure, Martine. We've grown so used to your dulcet tones, what would we do without them?"

"Keep it down," said Bo, glancing around.

The streets here were narrow, and the roofs low enough to climb onto. Suyana walked faster. After a moment, Kipa and Grace moved to keep pace. Martine sighed, long-suffering, before she caught up. Daniel and Bo kept two or three paces behind, catching two angles that might pass for a single camera if the public were gullible enough.

No one spoke until they passed an intersection with enough early shops—a florist, a baker, an awkward family of tourists arguing about the Metro—that the noise covered Martine from the mics as she leaned in toward Suyana. "I'm sure you'll take this as an insult, but if this doesn't work, do you have a plan?"

It was a startling show of concern, and Suyana must

have looked it, because Martine said, "Withdrawn," just as Suyana said, "I'll be all right. Daniel and I will do something if we have to."

"Good," Martine said with a twist of a smile, "because if this doesn't work—"

"Daniel!" Bo shouted.

There were two gunshots in quick succession.

Suyana was moving already, but without knowing where the shooter was, it was no better than last time, outside a hotel, where something was wrong and she was helpless. She was scrambling to cover Kipa as she tried stupidly to look at the rooftops for the gun, and someone knocked into her, forcing her hard to one knee.

Bo was pointing his gun (he had a gun?) straight ahead, and Suyana followed the line to a man who'd dropped on the sidewalk. She'd knocked over Kipa, Grace was crouching beside Martine—they were shaken but she saw no wounds, and she was looking down at herself with the first cold wash of shock when she heard Daniel make a wet, horrible sound.

No, she thought, like that would make any difference, but as soon as she looked at him she saw the blotch of glossy red he was covering with one hand.

"Get to the Assembly," Suyana said. "Now."

"Come on," Grace said quietly, reaching for Kipa, and then all three of them were running for it, against the stream of people who had come outside to see what the noise was about.

"Not here," Daniel said.

Bo said, "Don't move him, it will make the bleeding worse," the gun hanging from his hand like an extension of his fingers, but Suyana looked him in the eye as she took Daniel's hands in hers (numb but working, they could be numb so long as they worked) to pull him staggering behind her like something broken.

It was a gut wound. If he wanted to die out of sight of strangers, she'd make sure he did.

He sank to the filthy pavement as soon as they were out of sight in the alleyway, melting back to rest against the wall.

"No," she said, "lie flat," and after a moment he tilted his head so it dragged him slowly sideways and toward the ground.

She arranged him as best she could (a funeral, no, not a funeral). She'd never seen him disconnected from himself; the lying down worried her more than the wound did, in some childish useless way. She rested a hand on his shoulder, moved it toward his neck, moved it back. He followed the motion with half-lidded eyes; his head was as still as if he was recording.

"Don't fall asleep," she said.

He said, "Soon."

"Not yet."

He inhaled (it rattled somewhere inside him that made her hands unsteady), said, "You'll be late."

She knew—part of her was calculating how fast she'd have to run to catch up on a knee that burned, every passing second making it impossible, she'd miss her chance to call the vote of no confidence and nominate Grace—but she couldn't move. He had one hand braced against the wound, and she rested her hands over his; blood slid over them both.

"Ambulance!" someone shouted in French. "Call an ambulance!"

"Fuck that."

Suyana pressed against his hand. "Don't you dare," she said through gritted teeth. "I got shot twice, you're not allowed to die from just one."

"You win," said Daniel. He wrapped his free hand around her wrist, and she worried she'd hurt him, but it felt more like something for him to hold on to.

"I'm with you," she said. "Help's coming. I'm with you."

Footsteps echoed into the alley as someone ran into the café next door. There was a flurry of conversation from someone inside, and then the television flipped channels to an English broadcast.

"—has just accused Central Committee Chair Margot Larsen of attempted murder," a reporter was saying breathlessly.

A burst of chatter drowned out the next few sentences, and when Suyana could hear it again, the announcer was saying, "—and the chamber, as you can hear, is in an uproar, but Grace Charles and a witness to the attack, New Zealand's Kipa Forsyth, insist that—one moment, I'm receiving reports that we have obtained footage of the shooter via an anonymous source—"

There was a crackle, and then the uncanny overlay of the sounds at the mouth of the alley echoed on the television; bystanders breathing heavily, panicky sounds leaking around the edges, as someone was calling in French for police. Shadows moved slowly on the pavement under the streetlights—gawkers, or snaps looking for a better angle.

"As you can see by the footage, it appears that there is, in fact, a wounded man who may have been in possession of the weapon we can see there on the ground—"

Boots charged past them, and Suyana pressed harder against Daniel's stomach. He wheezed.

"Ow, fuck, stop, that—that won't make me invisible to cops."

"Try harder," she said, though her voice sounded thick. Bo was speaking with the police; she caught "Hired security for Suyana Sapaki" and "My license," and wondered what exactly he'd done all day when she'd told him to follow Margot and prepare.

"As we get someone on the ground down there," the announcer said, "we take you back to chambers, where Martine Hargaad, also from Norway, has demanded a vote of no confidence in Margot Larsen. This seems to—I mean, this is coming as something of a shock after Martine and Margot went on a homecoming earlier this year to visit the Norwegian environmental initiative, where they seemed very friendly."

"There might be more to this story than we're getting at the moment," the other announcer said.

"Oh my God," said Daniel, faintly but with admirable venom, "can't I die without listening to this?"

He wasn't breathing heavily any more; whatever struggle he was going through was ending.

But the announcer was drawn in now. "It looks like Sweden is standing up, and now two standing at the same time, and across the hall it appears—oh, wow," and then there was utter quiet from the studio, with nothing playing but the feed, as the sound of five hundred people in chambers rose and swamped the microphones with voices.

"You have to go," Daniel said. He was shaking, trembling so hard the words barely made it out. She couldn't tell if he knew what was happening or if he just didn't want her to see.

She swallowed around *I can wait* and settled on, "I'm here."

He tightened his grip on her wrist; his teeth ground together with something he was deciding not to say. He squeezed tighter, once, then let her go.

She nodded. She could hardly move her head, her throat was so hot with tears.

When she stood up, she saw her dress had a band of grime at the knees from the Paris streets, and her hands were gloved with blood. Her breath froze in her chest.

"It looks good," he said, with no air behind it. "It'll sell."

She tried a smile that didn't feel like anything, and he mirrored it with a smile that looked like a rictus.

Then he closed his eyes. He said, "Run."

She did—out the far side of the alley, away from the police (no time for questions or ID), and when two people fell in behind her, she panicked before she realized how smooth their gait was and how they spread to cover two angles; Li Zhao had planned to cover every exit.

"Watch Daniel," she shouted, and after a moment of waiting for orders over the line, one of them peeled off. It wasn't any easier for Suyana to breathe—her heels jarred and stung and her knee creaked and her ribs were too tight and her heart was in her ears—but when Daniel died, he'd die on-camera, and Margot would fucking pay for it.

She took the side entrance, smacking against one of the walls out of sheer velocity as she gasped to the guards, "A guy just tried to kill me." No point invoking Margot. If they were loyal to her, Suyana might not make it to the stage. Better to make it sound like a damsel in vague distress. "My security detail was involved. One of them's wounded—please get help."

They were looking at her hands. "But you've been—"

"It's his," she said too loudly, cleared her throat as she passed, and shook off her shoes as she bolted for the stage.

It was an uproar. Handlers were shouting at one another, Faces were shouting to be heard. Margot stood on the stage near her chair, hands folded like she was waiting out a tantrum. Grace and Kipa stood side by side onstage. Colin, and Kipa's handler, Elizabeth, stood on the ground below them, staunchly blocking two handlers who were trying to pull them down. Magnus stood just ahead of Suyana in the wings, his back to her, looking very studious and not at all like he was blocking Margot's way out.

And halfway between Margot and Grace was Martine, grinning at Margot over her shoulder like someone feeling bulletproof. Margot was glaring daggers at her; Martine opened her mouth and let the smoke roll out.

"Excuse me," Suyana said to Magnus.

He turned around, went terribly white, and stepped aside.

Without shoes her feet made little noise, but as she walked past Margot someone gasped, and as she walked past

Martine, someone started to cry out something that melted before it turned into a word.

There were pockets of silence after that, as some people leaned forward, waiting for their cue to help, and others (the smart ones) recognized what must be happening and froze.

By the time she took her place on the far end of the stage from Margot, the jeering had quieted down, and the arguments left were scattered, thin with panic. She couldn't see where they were coming from—stage lights and flashbulbs were everywhere—but they were easy enough to drown out. A camera could only absorb so much sound.

"I second the vote of no confidence in Margot Larsen," Suyana called, and though her voice was rough with tears at the edges, it went out barrel-deep across the hall, and the shake in the last words was still all right—it would make sense, when people realized she was a widow. (The Assembly hadn't had a Face wife in chambers in forty-five years; the novelty would impress them.) She tilted her left hand slightly, so the ring would be more visible under the lights, if you could see it through the blood.

She called out, "I second the nomination of Grace Charles on behalf of my murdered husband, Ethan Chambers, the Face of the United States, and on behalf of the United Amazonian Rainforest Confederation."

There was a moment of utter silence, as the room took her in, and almost as one glanced over at Margot, and then across the hall at one another, trying to determine if, once they started, they would have enough votes to finish.

"All in favor, say aye," Martine said, and it was smart—her voice was pitched nearly hopeful. Martine knew how to create a story on the fly.

(Suyana thought, Make her a member of the Central Committee, and then keep watch. We'll have to be sure.)

Suyana fought not to clench her hands in the silence. This blood had been visited upon her; fists would make it look like blood she'd deserved.

"Aye," someone called from the back of the room, where Malaysia sat.

Then, "Aye," called Bin Mee-yon, and even when the volume rose past Suyana's ability to make them all out, the sounds were of countries calling out the second, and not the jeering of a crowd past controlling.

Security was moving through the audience hall and in the wings of the stage; in Suyana's peripheral vision, Magnus stepped aside to let them get to Margot. He was staring at Suyana with a look she could feel. She didn't look back. She was afraid.

Part of her wished she could summon tears—it would sell Grace as a savior; they needed a savior and not just a replacement if she was going to hold her tenure through the transition—but for everything she'd handed the IA, there were some things she couldn't give.

Six streets away from here, Daniel was dead.

As members of the Central Committee began to call for calm, and country after country shouted their votes, Suyana stood unmoving, her fingers slightly separated like Bo's when he'd just killed a man and was still expecting enemies. The sound of camera shutters filled her ears, and the sea of ayes filled her lungs until there was nothing inside her but a deliberate emptiness she could hone into whatever needed to be done.

(Bo was here, standing in the back of the auditorium where the view was best, his face gone blotchy with tears. It was over.)

She kept her gaze out and steady across the crowd without really looking at anyone and rested her hands as close to her dress as she dared, where the light-gray column would set off the blood, and she would make a better figure for the cameras.

23

"Two more," the photographer said, and Suyana held her position on aching heels until Grace's new assistant, Amira, signaled the all clear, and the Committee broke from their formal poses. Except Grace, of course, who always stood like she was posing for a portrait, and who took the break as a chance to check in with the photographer and look at the results on his screen.

That was for Amira's benefit. She was Grace's embedded snap, courtesy of Bonnaire Fine Tailoring and a promise Suyana had made in exchange for Grace's crown.

Suyana had already lost Grace; as soon as Grace met Li Zhao and realized the kind of woman Suyana had signed their futures over to, a door had closed.

("Coverage of . . . everything?" Grace had asked, so polite that frost formed on it, and Li Zhao had smiled and said, "If you're concerned you might have some secrets left, don't be." A fist had closed around Suyana's stomach, and she very carefully didn't look at Bo or Kate or Li Zhao. She looked at Grace, as Grace realized that off-line didn't mean invisible, that she had a flat Li Zhao had already seen, that it was too late to hide anything.

"I want a woman," Grace said, "and I want her on-site so I can dismiss her properly when I have overnight guests, none of whom will ever appear in any newspaper for any reason. You'll give me assurance in writing."

Li Zhao smiled and shook hands on it. Suyana decided she'd need to find the sort of people you called when someone like Li Zhao broke her word and needed hunting.

Grace never looked at Suyana. Suyana never looked at Li Zhao. A deal was a deal; you dealt with one devil at a time. It cost Suyana a friend, but everything cost. What did it matter?)

Amira was young, and had the look of someone Li Zhao had found on the streets who was happy to play the middle ground so long as she had a bed to sleep in. She adored Grace, Grace made sure—she laughed at Amira's jokes even when it wouldn't make a good picture, she pulled Amira aside sometimes as if she just wanted to be away from it all, and now when Grace needed privacy, Amira turned her face away on some cue not even Suyana could see. When Amira watched Grace planning, it was with the faithfulness of a handmaiden. Amira had an eye for nobility; she could get a shot of Grace reviewing photos into *Closer* for a piece about Grace's first days, some behind-the-scenes sidebar in which no task was too trivial to deserve Grace's attention and care. Smart. Harmless.

It was still early enough in Grace's tenure that she was trying to be both. She had a social secretary for outside appointments, and Kipa as her liaison to other Faces, a newly created post that did wonders for the position practically overnight. Grace had already met with every Central Committee member for long dinners, and was starting the rounds with the countries that had stood up early to cement her vote.

"Never underestimate how much people like you just for seeming to like them," Kipa said sometimes to Suyana with an apologetic smile as she nudged an Intelligence meeting off Grace's calendar in favor of lunch with China, a museum trip with Argentina, a film festival with Turkey.

Suyana supposed Kipa would know: as it turned out, nearly everyone wished her well. Countries she'd never mentioned on that long night were only too happy to see her rise in the ranks. Fair enough; plenty of people were happy to see an acquaintance in a position of usable power. And Kipa never got less kind, merely more cautious.

But Suyana sometimes watched Kipa walking across a room to greet someone and marveled at how much she was like water, filling whatever vessel someone expected to see.

Kipa was still good, Suyana thought in her generous moments. She had schemed no more than she needed to keep herself safe; she gave an ear to anyone who asked. The distance that had grown up between them was nothing wretched. It was only that Kipa was good, and she also might still be Chordata, and for the sake of appearances she had to lie to Suyana for the rest of her life.

Suyana thought about Columbina sitting on a stoop in New York, knee to knee with Kipa, listening to Grace's secrets. She thought about a snap filming it all, about the basement in Paris and its smooth rows of servers loaded with footage Daniel had taken of Suyana and Columbina. Suyana pictured Li Zhao approaching Columbina with her hand out, a pillar of opportunity, her face eclipsing the sun, the sound of a camera shutter no one could stop.

Suyana wished she'd asked Kipa more about Columbina, in those last moments with Kipa when honesty was possible, just before Daniel was shot. But it was gone and she'd never get an answer now. That's what came of being distracted when you had a job to do.

She made an appointment with Columbina. It had to be at night, Suyana said like always, so she wasn't followed; it had to be somewhere quiet, where no one would see.

The Central Committee settled in quickly. Those who were invited to remain (most of them, after they'd supported the vote—tenure was too precious a thing to give up for something so small as personal belief) had seemed just as happy to provide input to Grace as to Margot. Maybe more, since Grace was still listening to outside counsel. Even Grace adding Suyana to the newly minted Director of Intelligence seat didn't ruffle many feathers, and Suyana had looked around the room as her appointment was silently accepted and wondered how many of them had suspected Margot all along and never said a word.

"Promise me you'll tell me if I start turning into Margot," Grace had murmured once on her way out of the meeting room. "God knows none of them will."

The only vote Suyana had really lost was Grace's. In a perfectly reasonable, perfectly kind, perfectly pleasant way, Grace disappeared. She was terribly busy, and she was terribly grateful, and when Suyana met with her alone for briefings on the shifting loyalties among member countries,

Grace always took the seat closer to the door.

She was kind about it; Suyana imagined it was impossible for Grace to be cruel, and if Grace never quite looked her in the eye, then that could be useful too. The work still had to be done. They could do the work; they were practical.

The only rough patch of the new ascension—it got Grace accused of favoritism, and two of the lesser Committee chairs resigned in protest before they were promptly replaced with Faces from two of the earliest countries to have seconded Grace's nomination—was the appointment of Martine as Central Committee liaison to the Defense Committee.

"This is a reminder that the International Assembly has not punished Norway, only a criminal," Grace said in a filmed statement that got released over the evening news in seventeen countries. "Norway remains a longstanding ally and valued member of the IA, and we are certain that with such a long record of working toward global peace, Norway will treat this appointment with the highest respect and consideration."

Martine got no words in edgewise on that filmed statement. Nor on the next one, about plans for developing a new protocol for deploying peacekeeping troops.

"If she keeps me out of one more, I'm going to start taking it personally," Martine muttered. Suyana was sitting close enough that it might have been intentional, and she'd felt enough sympathy to say, "This position attracts warmongers. There are probably six countries lined up outside her office wanting to claim the position. She just doesn't want anyone to realize someone sensible has their hand on the button until it's too late for anyone to kill you and jump the line."

"You don't think I'm a warmonger?"

Suyana had no answer. She wasn't used to Martine asking questions that sounded open-ended, and these days her words dried up at the strangest times around people she knew.

Martine got to speak at the annual Rally for Peace, flawlessly sincere as she read someone else's statement about peace being layers of sediment that built a world, so in the end all the discontent about her came to nothing; most things did.

Suyana was embarrassed that she had imagined, even for a moment, Margot vanishing behind bars as punishment for her crimes. It had been what kept her staring out past the crowd the day Grace was elected—a picture of Margot lit by shadowy stripes as the door clanged shut, like one of the revival movies she and Ethan had seen at Cannes last year. It was a child's hope. (She could just imagine Hakan's face if he'd lived to see it and she'd been fool enough to ask him—that cloud that gathered every so often, when she'd done something so stupid he was reconsidering his choice.)

In the wake of the emergency election, Margot was charged with conspiracy to commit murder, conspiracy to commit fraud, and conspiracy to disrupt government procedure. But somehow, after such a long and fruitful friendship, America couldn't find much legal fault with Margot over just one corpse. Even the countries that had wanted her gone were wary of any precedent that could come back to haunt them; this was a circumspect group. They objected just enough to make sure her removal from the public sphere would be too permanent to make good on any spite. She might have had to go to prison for the murder conspiracy if the UARC had agreed to bear witness, but Suyana had known as soon as they read the list of charges that she wouldn't. To prove Margot knew about the bombing ahead of time, they'd have to track down Chordata, and an investigation of Chordata would turn up Suyana's name.

She swallowed a stone, and shook her head, and when Magnus looked at her long enough, she realized someone would need a reason and managed, "Our country's been through so much, the last thing I want is for us to look like this is petty revenge. We put our faith in the International Assembly's judicial procedure and thank the world for their support."

The statement got on the evening news in five languages. Her reputation was spreading.

After the closed-door trial, so short they didn't even pretend not to have come to a deal beforehand, Margot was barred from public service. She was serving a sentence for fraud, under house arrest in her Paris apartment for ten years. She had retained her personal aide—on the civilian side—and her private chef, who was forbidden from speaking to Margot and received her instructions through the aide. The two guards stationed outside her door wore suits rather than uniforms, out of respect for the residents in her historic-landmark building.

If you wanted to go see her, all you had to do was have your name on a list. Suyana's dress had a skirt like a bell, but the guard at the door only patted her thighs once from the outside, not quite looking at her, and went back to his conversation. She could have stored a pistol three different places and still made it inside. There were probably no cameras, then, to review their security performance and interrupt Margot's privacy.

She could kill Margot and both the guards, and be gone before anyone knew what had happened.

In the first moment Margot saw Suyana, she looked as if she had the same concerns. Her hands curled around the arms of her easy chair (Suyana thought of Li Zhao), and she shifted her weight a little forward, so it would be easier to stand in case Suyana started shooting.

"You can sit back down," Suyana said. "I've never needed a gun to deal with you."

Margot raised an eyebrow. "So it's going to be one of those visits."

"I've never made a visit like this."

"You will," Margot said, indicating a chair opposite her absently, a hostess gesture that had yet to die. "Now that Grace has saddled you with the official title, you'll have to make official visits to endless people in disgrace to decide if they're enemies of the state. Always a mistake to be transparent. I only had to visit people worth my time."

"Maybe someday I'll visit one of those."

Margot laughed like a door unlocked. "To what do I owe the pleasure?"

The chair Margot had offered had no arms. Suyana sat in one that did, let her fingers drape off the edges.

"I wanted to know when you first got involved with them."

"The attack on the mining office. It suggested a mole in the UARC delegation."

"But they never would have just let you join up."

"If you want to be in this job for long, you'll learn how to be the sort of person people approach. They found me when the first plans were being drawn up for the joint research facilities."

"So those were bait."

A flicker of surprise. "No. They're conservation efforts that look good to the press. God knows the IA needs it. Chordata just approached me because they think like you do. I let them, that was all. Their missteps are tragic. You're well matched."

Margot had probably done her a favor. If they really turned on her as soon as they had another avenue of information from someone they should have suspected, it was because they were looking for a replacement, not an addition. Suyana had outlived their loyalty. Just as well it was over.

Suyana was careful to avoid any mention of herself; it seemed important to be as far from this as possible. "And then you just let it burn?"

Margot half lifted a hand like she was dropping garbage. "They're less expensive than you think, and I didn't expect you to turn to stone with Chordata. Something had to make you look guilty. Early results that came in from the facility were promising, though—the program should be continued there. I'm sure Grace can help you."

Suyana's throat had swollen; she had to force a breath

to get the words out—a mistake, the wrong time to ask for something when you had nothing to give, but it was too late. "How long after you killed Hakan did you realize the mole was really me, that first time?"

It took a moment for the silence to settle; Margot's expression was so foreign that Suyana couldn't name it as pity until the center of her chest had already started caving in.

"He knew it was only a matter of time," Margot said eventually, like it helped—kindly, like it helped. "Every handler who chooses their own delegate gets myopic about them. He'd always wanted someone to rise."

And she had. He had been her check, and he had been removed, and this was what she'd become. (In some corner of her mind where nothing mattered, she wondered if Hakan had guessed what she'd been willing to hollow out just to lighten the load for the reach upward.)

She thought about asking where the body was, but even if Margot knew, she didn't want to hear it. It would be like asking if Margot remembered Li Zhao from twenty years ago just to see if she flinched. The body was where it was. You can't bring it with you. Keep going. Reach up and pull.

"So you tried to kill me? Twice?"

"I thought this time, with you, Hakan might be on to something." She glanced around her pretty prison. "I was right."

Three knuckles cracked against the arms of her chair. Don't lean forward, she thought, whatever you do. "Why couldn't you just fucking leave me alone?"

"Suyana. You've been a terrorist agent for a decade. They didn't even have to wait for you to make it to the IA to recruit you. Was I supposed to trust your mercy and good sense?"

She wanted Margot in a prison. She wanted cement walls and a gated door and a long corridor empty of inmates so that Margot would hear no human voice but hers for the next ten years, and every time Suyana turned her back, Margot would have to decide if today was the day she begged.

"Who else have you disappeared?"

One corner of her mouth ticked up, dropped. "I've been in the IA thirty years."

"And now?"

It was both sides this time, curling up like smoke. "Oh, I'm just a private citizen. That body count's yours now." Shadow crawled across the green carpet in front of Suyana, until Margot's apartment looked like the edge of the sea.

(Suyana had hung placid in the water as Grace took her seat. Suyana had stretched a hundred threads with stingers at the end of them; she'd asked Bo how you hired killers.

The police had found Columbina a few weeks back. Mugging gone sour, they'd said. They'd never found who did it.

"I'm concerned about Columbina," Grace had started a week later, and when Suyana said, "Don't be," Grace had understood, and looked at Suyana the way she'd looked when Suyana had promised to put her at the head of the table and keep her there. Suyana suspected it was the only way Grace would ever see her again.

Margot would understand, when they talked about it. It would happen someday; who else did Suyana have?)

"I have to say, if you plan to make it very long, Miss Sapaki, I would suggest a little subtlety."

She'd gotten everything she wanted from Margot without any subtlety at all, but that wasn't something you brought to someone's attention when they were giving you information. Poisonous knowledge was still knowledge. She pressed the side of her tongue in between the wide comfort of her molars until the skin gave way.

By the time she was calm again, it was too long a pause to fill with a cutting remark. She could have blown up in temper and sworn never to come back, just to give Margot the satisfaction the next time she came, but that would require a better liar than Suyana was. Martine could do it, maybe; Kipa could do it so well no one would ever find out she'd been playacting. But Margot had apparently always been beyond Suyana's ability to fool.

So she stood up and left without a word or a look behind

her. There was no convincing her this was the last time (Margot had too much information Suyana wanted, and it would be doled out until the day her sentence ended), but let Margot wonder how long it would be before she came back—whether she was leaving in shame or in anger or if something had suddenly occurred to her that would burn someone's tenure to the ground. Let Margot decide how much she'd have to give up next time to get Suyana to stay.

No point in making a scene. Margot was a resource. This was a conservation effort.

She picked the splinters from under her fingernails before anyone else got home.

Grace sat at the meeting room table in the chair closest to the door, next to Martine. Suyana sat where she could see all the angles of entry; no point pretending it wasn't her place. Kipa came in a few moments later and said something in Grace's ear before she took her seat and pulled out her tablet. Kipa must have a new contact too. Suyana couldn't ask her. Kipa hadn't looked at her in weeks. It didn't matter.

"Where do we stand with Argentina?"

"Hello to you, too, Suyana," said Grace, with a smile and a glance at Martine.

"Hello, Grace. I'm concerned about Argentina. They were late to stand up for you during the vote, and since then they've gone suspiciously quiet on the floor. I want to make sure they're not regretting their vote. We can't afford any sense that people could be drawn into some other recall vote on the side."

"I'm sure not," said Grace, but this time when she looked at Martine, Martine looked at Suyana and then out the window, and said, "They have been quiet."

"I'll schedule a dinner as soon as I can," said Kipa, scrolling through.

"Not tonight," said Martine. "She's having dinner with me."

Grace laughed. Suyana didn't know why; Martine was dead serious.

Kipa was smiling. "Well—she knows you, Martine, and she's so busy."

"I bet," said Martine.

"I want to make sure everyone feels they're being heard."

"Sure."

"So maybe we could look at next week?"

"Kipa, you'll keep my dinner with Grace tonight or I'll poison your food."

Kipa grinned for a second before she laughed, like Martine had passed a test, and the laugh was as genuine as Kipa's laugh had ever been. Grace laughed too, and leaned in to look at the calendar Kipa was holding out. Across Kipa's turned back, Martine looked over at Suyana with a face

Suyana was coming to know, and sparked the fake cigarette in her pocket before it was even all the way to her lips.

"Stevens sent me a very polite, horrible message wondering how long you intend to wear the ring," Magnus said.

They were at home, and nightfall made her feel almost at ease with Magnus, so she was able to give that notice the expression it deserved.

"That's what I said," Magnus assured her. "In the nicest possible way. You're a widow until you decide to stop."

She heard the question in it. "I'll give it up in New York next year, when everything's settled. Right now it's useful for Grace, and for Leili."

Leili had arrived in the middle of the chaos that first morning in chambers, and Suyana realized Magnus had been right about her when Stevens caught her up on what had happened in a few breathless sentences, clearly guiding America away from the mess as soon as some method could be established, and instead Leili had walked onstage in front of live worldwide cameras to meet Suyana.

It had been a hug rather than a handshake—Suyana didn't blame her, with the blood—and Leili had said, "On behalf of the United States, I'm so sorry for your loss. He was always so kind to me," with her voice trembling at the end, and looked down at Suyana's hands like it was

Ethan's blood. (Suyana would have ruined it, if she'd been able to speak.)

The cameras had loved it all. If Margot had stood a chance at defending Ethan's disappearance at the tribunal before that, it vanished after the new American Face consoled the grieving widow.

Suyana was planning a trip to Tivoli with Leili after the Paris session broke for holidays. There was no question of Suyana going home; they were sending a new Face to replace her (Brazilian, apparently, and charming), and her services were no longer domestically required. It stung less than she'd feared. As director of intelligence, it was better not to have a place that mattered more than another. Better not to have anything to hold on to.

She couldn't actually enjoy herself at Tivoli either, of course—she was a widow for a while, and there was a period of mourning to observe. But so far the only times she and Leili had been photographed together were on the IA stage and at Ethan's funeral, back in some United States desert. That image was useful, but it had to change, slowly, before the public decided she was too busy mourning to be doing her job. At Tivoli, she could smile as Leili enjoyed herself, and stand in flattering light looking like the battle-hardened guardian of the next generation, and it would work just as well for what they needed it to do. Letting go of grief and becoming unknowable, one photo op at a time.

(Daniel had been cremated, after the HERO BYSTANDER MURDERED BY BLOODTHIRSTY DICTATOR headlines had calmed down and no one would care what happened to him. Suyana had thought of putting his ashes in the courtyard of her building, but it seemed presumptive. She'd given all but a lipstick-case's worth to Bo. He told her he and Kate and Li Zhao had scattered most of them in the Seine; she didn't ask about the rest. Her lipstick-case's worth had been buried under a loose cobblestone of an alley next to a little hotel no one thought of very much.)

"I suspect Leili will be asking for a change of handlers soon," Magnus said, satisfied with his deductions. He'd resigned from the UARC diplomatic office to assist her in her new position. He hadn't told her until it was over; she'd accepted his offer without asking him why.

"How?"

"She'll stage some girlish whim that will cast this whole lot out and give her a chance to hire some people who are slightly better at keeping their Face alive."

Suyana's throat had gone dry. It happened a lot, these days, when she thought about Ethan or Daniel, or Kipa, or Chordata, or all the altars people made for themselves to sacrifice on.

"Magnus." He looked up. "I never thanked you for your help, with—that day we built the vote."

His expression was tinged with something softer these days than just circumspection—not quite fondness, but close. "I know you aren't likely to believe it, but it was my pleasure."

Their new flat (they had moved up in the world again) opened onto a view of the quiet green courtyard below, trees and birds and all, and Suyana looked out at it until her vision blurred and she'd built up the courage to hear the worst.

"Who appointed you?"

He set down his tablet and sat back in his chair, and she watched him and prepared to spot the lie when he said he'd been approached by the Staffing Committee by chance, or whatever other lie Margot had told him to say.

He said, "Hakan."

There had been a time she'd have hit him for that. Even now she felt slightly like a traitor just for sitting still. But when she stared at him, he only shrugged.

"That's a cruel thing to say." She felt so old, and it was a hard name to hear.

"But it's true." He watched her, steady and earnest and with that knack he had for seeming somehow beleaguered in the midst of peace and plenty. "He called me a month or so before…he disappeared. He'd known me when I washed out of IA training and knew I was looking for a way in on the handling side. He was afraid something was going to happen to him, he said, and afraid Margot would put someone of her choice in his office. He wanted someone who seemed amenable to suggestion and made Margot comfortable, so she wouldn't feel the need to replace whoever followed him with someone else she chose."

As if from underwater, she said, "But he had no pull over the Staffing Committee."

"I'm a little insulted you think I don't know how to rig interviews in my favor."

She cleared her throat. "Did he—did he ever say—"

"He never told me anything, if he knew. I have some guesses—don't look at me that way, Suyana, I'm not asking any questions—but he kept his own counsel."

She was nodding; she couldn't stop nodding. "You never said."

"If I had told you, before all of this, 'Don't worry, you can trust me, Hakan knew you could,' what would you have done?"

The silence answered him, and the edges of his mouth thinned even as he raised his eyebrows and dropped them again, putting himself silently in his place. "It was bad enough to demonstrate loyalty before the assassination attempt; you wouldn't hear it. After that it was hopeless. I was very nearly grateful to Margot when she came after you again, honestly. I never thought you'd trust me enough to ask for help."

The room had closed in on her, and it was too small and filled with his voice and his calm reasoning and all the things they would never say. She opened her mouth to breathe, made a noise like she'd been punched in the stomach, turned as much as she could to shield her face. This wasn't for Magnus; this wasn't his fault or his payment; she just couldn't breathe, that was all, it got so hard to breathe sometimes.

The front door closed so quietly she barely heard it beside the drum of her pulse, but when she was alone, she sobbed her throat raw. Eventually there was nothing left but the sound of it and her trembling shoulders, and a little behind her were the phantom footsteps she'd know from anywhere as Hakan's, whenever he was passing her open office door while she was at work, looking in on her to make sure she was all right.

Bo was waiting for her outside. "Blackout," he said, as soon as she was in hearing. Suyana didn't trust it—just because Li Zhao had told Bo he was off-line didn't mean she wasn't gathering evidence as fast as she could—but that was a problem that could be negotiated later (exclusives could always be reassigned to another agency), and in the meantime you could convince a snap to be loyal to you, same as anyone.

She nodded. "Good to see you." She said it every time,

felt slightly like a fool every time. But he was an asset, and she'd say it until it wasn't true.

He fell in beside her, moving half a step ahead to help her cut through the crowd, and steering her away from any streets that didn't have escape routes. They didn't talk much; she suspected he wasn't naturally chatty any more than she was, even if Daniel's ghost wasn't hanging in the empty space between them. Bo had talked about him once or twice, and Suyana had tried to smile, to encourage him, but then Bo stopped mentioning him and there had been nothing since.

Fair enough. If it hurt, she wouldn't make him; if it was her turn to talk about Daniel, she couldn't. She could operate in silences as well as any snap.

Bo left her at the edge of the perfume department, so stoically pained by the olfactory overload that Suyana spared him a smile. "I don't know how long I'll be."

"I'll find you." From him it never sounded like the threat it would be from anyone else.

The old steadies that ringed the wall of the perfume section were comforting, even if it made her feel silly to notice them—it had been a year, not ten. The new scents were scattered among overwrought displays that featured pristinely white models and Elysian scenery and die-cut tendrils to demonstrate just how much of spring could be yours if you wore Lily Soleil.

Suyana had never much been interested in spring. She sniffed two that smelled like citrus, which was better, and one that smelled like a fired gun that she set down too quickly.

She was trying to decide on one that smelled like a forest floor and reminded her of graves when a voice at her elbow said, "Morbid, but I understand."

Zenaida was somehow shorter than Suyana remembered, but her eye was keener, and she looked Suyana up and down with an assessment so frank Suyana had to resist the urge to reach up and see if the makeup had dropped off her under-eye circles. (Zenaida noticed the ring—her eye lingered on it two seconds too long—but she said nothing.) Suyana steeled herself and waited for the judgment, or the joking smile.

But none came. Zenaida shook her head slowly, and then at last she said, "My girl, when Onca said you'd asked for me, I didn't—it's so very good to see you."

It was a technique: designed to make Suyana miss her, to build trust again, to force Suyana into the first overtures of affection so she would remember why she'd belonged to them once and maybe even come back to the fold; so she wouldn't betray Chordata to the Committee and do to them what she was capable of doing. But Suyana didn't care, and when they embraced, Zenaida hugged Suyana back hard enough that her knife wound stung.

She let it go on as long as she dared. Then she collected

herself and smoothed her coat. (She was on camera eight hours a day now, minimum—wrinkles were something she couldn't afford.)

"I hope you have some information for me. I'd like for us to be on good terms, but I have a new position, and you owe me."

"Yes, Lachesis." Zenaida's smile was polite, with something else beneath it. "I've been told."

It's Aurelia now, Suyana almost said; I swallowed the cruelty, and now I'm invisible and hide a hundred stings. But there was so much comfort in the old name from a voice she thought she'd never hear again.

She only said, "And they're unhappy?"

"I've been told."

Suyana thought about being the sort of person who got sought out, who let people think you were loyal because it suited them. She half smiled, like it was an accident. "I see."

Zenaida's smile only got bigger, and she picked up the glass bottle and let the scent of the forest floor mist around them. "You should get this," she said. "Heaven knows you have the money, and it must be useful to smell like you've been burying enemies."

Suyana picked up the box and followed Zenaida to the next display like a trail of smoke. The smile was still on her face. It barely hurt.

"So," said Zenaida, peering at a perfume that looked like a wedding in a bottle, "I have a list of things I'm allowed to tell you, but I think we can agree that it's easier to just be honest, between ourselves. What would you like to know?"

Everything, Suyana thought, and began.

ACKNOWLEDGMENTS

This book is, as books tend to be, the product of more people's love than just the author's. Thanks to Navah, whose enthusiasm for *Persona* and its characters made this book possible. Thanks to Joe and Saga Press for championing it. Thanks to my agent, Barry, for his advocacy and advice. And deepest thanks to Stephanie, Elizabeth, Kelly, Libby, Sonia, and Nora, who were selfless in contributing their time and thoughts to *Persona* and *Icon*; it means more than I can say.